THE
SECRET
CURSE

THE SECRET CURSE
Copyright © 2022 by Bethany Atazadeh

All rights reserved. Printed in the United States of America. No part of this book may be used or reproduced in any manner whatsoever without written permission except in the case of brief quotations embodied in critical articles or reviews. This book is a work of fiction. Names, characters, businesses, organizations, places, events and incidents either are the product of the author's imagination or are used fictitiously. Any resemblance to actual persons, living or dead, events, or locales is entirely coincidental.

For information contact : **https://www.bethanyatazadeh.com**

Cover design by Stone Ridge Books
Formatting Template : Derek Murphy

First Edition: January 2023
10 9 8 7 6 5 4 3 2 1

THE SECRET CURSE

BETHANY ATAZADEH

 GRACE HOUSE PRESS

Copyright © 2022 by Bethany Atazadeh

1

I WORE A DELICATE white-gold crown that signified my engagement to Prince Shem. This morning, I'd specifically chosen a white dress, and not just because it matched the crown. Embroidered gold leaves lined the neckline and hem. Shem's fingers wove through mine, another not-so-subtle reminder of my status to the crowd around us.

I might as well have been invisible.

Smoothing my face, I refused to let them see how much it bothered me.

Shem nodded politely to another group of Jinn. They flashed him smiles that sparkled as brightly as the jewels in their ears, hair, and clothing, managing to make small talk without hardly a word to me before moving on.

We stood at the edge of the Tel Sheba Conservatory, which was an indoor garden named after the same floating island it'd been built on.

THE SECRET CURSE

"It's an honor having you here with us," Judge Baruk, the city judge of Tel Sheba, said to Shem. He took Shem's elbow as he spoke, swiveling almost imperceptibly, until I stood on the outside of their little circle.

When Shem tried to turn back to me, the judge added, "Perhaps, if you have a moment, we could speak privately?"

"Anything you'd like to discuss with me, you can share in front of Jezebel," Shem said in a gracious, but firm tone, drawing me back into the circle and looping my hand over his elbow.

I blew out a soft breath of relief at finally being acknowledged.

His crown looked like white fire in his black hair, somehow giving him an air of authority I couldn't replicate, no matter how hard I tried.

The judge bowed slightly, still not making eye contact with me. "It's nothing. Truly. I won't bother you with it now, when it's almost time for your speech. Come, let's make our way to the front."

Under my fingers, Shem's muscles tensed in response, but he was too aware of Jinni politics to call attention to the slight, as I'd learned over time.

It was like this on every one of the floating Jinni islands we'd visited so far on our engagement tour, which had been scheduled to span the last three months leading up to our wedding.

The wedding that was meant to happen today.

I lifted my arms, wishing I hadn't chosen this particular dress, which clung to my skin. It was far too heavy for the humid space. The sun baked us through the glass ceiling and windows, though no one else seemed affected. Sweat dripped down my back. Even the air was damp.

We'd been here almost an hour, and while the line of attendees at the entrance was finally dwindling, we had at least another hour of mingling with the hundreds of Jinn present, as well as Shem's speech.

If only I could travel briefly outside for a breath of fresh air. But the conservatory walls were spelled with a boundary against travel, making it impossible to pass through them using the Gift, like most other buildings in Jinn. The only escape was the tall doors at the opposite end of the rectangular room—too far away to slip out unnoticed.

"This conservatory was just completed a few days ago when they filled the spring with water," Judge Baruk said to Shem as we walked, pausing by the stream that trickled down the center of the gathering, It ended in a quiet pool full of water lilies. Pointing it out gave him an excuse to fully turn his back on me.

Under different circumstances, I might've admired the space.

Today, I could've sworn the tropical plants sucked all the cool air out of the room—or maybe that was the company.

THE SECRET CURSE

"It's breathtaking, wouldn't you agree, Jezebel?" Shem replied, which forced the judge to turn and reluctantly acknowledge me.

I gave the judge a pinched smile. "Very beautiful," I agreed, and couldn't resist adding, "It'd make a lovely venue for a wedding."

Though we didn't currently need one.

"Oh, it's not nearly large enough for that," he replied smoothly, then tapped his chin. "Though it'd help a small wedding party seem larger, I suppose."

My cheeks burned. He clearly wasn't referring to the prince's lack of guests.

"Unfortunately, that wouldn't work for us," Shem said, drawing me closer. "Jezebel draws quite a crowd."

"Apologies, I didn't intend offense," the judge lied to our faces as he bowed his head.

These little victories were sweet. Shem could put the judges in their place in a way that I couldn't.

The win was short lived though.

"I feel terrible that your wedding had to be delayed," the judge said in a distinctly *un*apologetic tone that made me wish he was still ignoring me. "I'm sure you worry it might never happen."

All the time.

"I appreciate the condolences," was all I could say as my throat closed.

Ever since Shem had proposed, the king, queen, and their councils—really the entire country—seemed to be against us. Jinn loved their secrets and traditions, and my very existence threatened both. After all, who was I? Just an unknown Jinni girl who'd come from a poor home with no influence to speak of. While they'd happily recognized me for saving the royal family during a dangerous moment, it was quite another thing to say I was good enough for their prince. Especially when so many more eligible Jinni daughters had vied for the position.

They did *not* want me to become queen.

"Judge Baruk," Shem scolded with a smile, though his tone was icy. "You know as well as anyone that it'd be poor taste to hold a wedding while the Khaanevaade attacks continue to increase."

"I didn't mean to suggest—"

Shem continued as if Judge Baruk hadn't said a word. "We don't want to celebrate while our people are wounded. But as soon as we gain their surrender, the wedding will be rescheduled."

I pressed my lips together in a strained smile as Judge Baruk murmured more insincere apologies and I pretended to accept.

Shem squeezed my fingers where I held onto his arm, and with effort, I smiled at him more warmly.

It wasn't his fault the wedding was delayed.

He'd always obeyed his parents, and this instance wasn't any different. Being a prince came before being a husband. I'd never needed him to explain that to me.

And I wouldn't complain either.

The only one who wanted this wedding to take

place—besides me—was Shem. I wouldn't risk alienating him. That might be exactly what King Jubal and Queen Samaria were hoping for.

Instead, I'd become as obedient as the prince.

Even when it chafed.

That's why we were here on our thirty-fourth stop in the courtship tour, despite the painful date.

It was also why I ignored Judge Baruk's insults with a false smile, like I did with every other city judge ruling over the different Jinni islands.

The tension in my shoulders crept up my neck, forming a headache. Light poured in through tall windows on all sides, making me fight the urge to squint.

"Come." Judge Baruk startled me out of my musings. "It's time to begin the formalities." He turned toward the low stage at the front of the room. It'd caught my attention when we'd first arrived because of a beautiful arch taking up the entire front half of the platform. The arch rose halfway to the tall ceiling, perfectly centered on the stage, covered in thick vines with sparkling white flowers.

Staring at the judge as he led us to the stage, I studied his thinning gray hair and his ceremonial robes, trying to picture him treating Queen Samaria this way. Somehow, I couldn't quite imagine it.

As we followed, he slowed again unexpectedly, forcing me to let go of Shem or run into the judge's back. "We timed the grand opening around your visit," he said, taking Shem's arm and continuing without breaking stride. "So that we could dedicate it to the crown today."

The prince's political training took over, and he fell in step with the judge, giving me a rueful glance over his shoulder.

I trailed after them, face burning.

Taking a deep breath, I held onto my calm expression by a thread. My goal on this tour was to demonstrate I'd make a good future queen, despite the people's goal of proving the opposite.

I rubbed my brow subtly, trying to ease the throbbing behind my eyes.

At least Shem found it as frustrating as I did.

A hush fell over the room as Judge Baruk led Shem up the two steps to the low stage. They stepped through the flowering arch, stopping in front of an iron railing.

I faltered.

The space was only wide enough for two people to stand—making it impossible for me to join them.

I'd already climbed the steps, which left me standing awkwardly to the side of the arch with Shem's four assigned Jinni Guard members, one of whom was Captain Uriel himself, as they kept a watchful eye on the crowd.

We were obscured by the thick foliage woven through the arch, only partially in view of this ridiculous conservatory.

As every Jinni face turned toward us, they didn't see the prince with their future princess on his arm, but instead were met with the prince alone with their judge.

Behind them, I went unnoticed.

THE SECRET CURSE

No doubt exactly what Judge Baruk intended.

After a short foreword—which I couldn't hear past the buzzing in my ears—he turned to let the prince speak.

Shem immediately beckoned me forward, forcing Judge Baruk to step back, and introduced me.

I held back tears and faked a smile at the blurry crowd as I stepped up to the railing.

The damage was done.

Back when Shem had proposed, I'd thought I'd finally belong somewhere.

I gripped the railing, knuckles whitening. Each time I met unsmiling Jinni faces in the crowds, that hope faded.

"Jezebel will make a fine queen one day," Shem was saying.

I managed to smile, as he thanked them for "so kindly welcoming" me.

Dozens of narrowed eyes pinned on my face made me want to use my Gift to shift into something as small as they made me feel. Something that could scuttle away and hide, and not have to deal with these constant politics anymore.

Pulling my shoulders back instead, I lifted my chin higher and carefully loosened my grip on the railing.

"The royal family wants to send reassurance over the recent Khaanevaade threat," Shem began his practiced speech. "While there are some unforeseen developments we've been forced to handle, we are not concerned."

Having heard this next part dozens of times by now, I was still impressed at the passion in his voice, as if he was saying it for the first time.

"Though the Khaanevaade people have never intimidated the Jinn in the past, over the last several months they've somehow gained access to restricted Jinni magic that allows them to open *daleths* between the human world and our own."

A typical Jinni understatement.

These Vaade burst through the portals and assaulted everyone within range, then disappeared back into hiding, closing the portals behind them. Worse—though the royal family wouldn't admit it publicly—they seemed to be untraceable, making it impossible to find them. It forced us to defend our islands reactively.

"There's no rhyme or reason to their attacks. At least, none that we can see," Shem continued, letting his gaze touch on individual Jinn around the room. He didn't let any of his frustration over this show, though I knew it bothered him to no end.

Personally, I thought they might be searching for something, or maybe someone. But I'd kept my opinion to myself, not wanting to seem foolish if I was wrong.

"No one knows when or where the next attack will be." Shem's hands clenched at his sides briefly. He caught himself, relaxing his body. "The disruption naturally has many of you feeling anxious."

A better term would be dazed. Like a helpless mouse in a field staring up at a hawk, not knowing what to do. The Jinn were used to being the predators, not the prey.

THE SECRET CURSE

Despite the dangers, their reactions were muted. Either they'd heard this news already, which was likely, or they were practiced at keeping their emotions hidden. Probably both.

Before this engagement tour began, all I'd known about the Vaade were the brief mentions during council meetings that made them sound insignificant. To hear those at the castle talk, one would think they were simply humans with startling eyes who disliked Jinn more than the average human.

During these tour speeches, however, Shem painted a very different picture. "If you have the misfortune of a Vaade crossing your path, you *must* let the Jinni Guard handle them. You'll recognize one instantly if you see it, by their eyes, which have an uncanny resemblance to a dragon's."

As he spoke, he tugged at the ceremonial breastplate he always wore, hands drifting to check the leather buckles and gold braces along his forearms. I'd noticed weeks ago that his tour armor appeared far more functional than the usual trendy pieces he wore in the castle.

The fidgeting was so unlike him. That was what had led me to finally start taking the Vaade seriously.

"They're stronger and faster than any Jinn," he continued. "Challenging us in a way no other race in history ever has, not even the Mere in the oceans below. As one of the only creatures in existence that can threaten the Jinn, it makes them extremely dangerous."

As always, I scoffed inwardly, though my face remained composed. These Vaade didn't frighten me.

"Their senses are enhanced like dragons—besides their distinctly dragon-like eyes, their powerful hearing, and an unparalled sense of smell, their skin is also thick like scales, almost impossible to pierce. And they can leap such great distances that they almost seem to fly."

King Jubal called this part of the speech fearmongering, but Shem felt the people should be prepared. I had to agree.

Behind closed doors before our tour began, Shem had revealed the Vaade race may have originally been created by a powerful Jinni—and that this history had resulted in a centuries-old power struggle between our people.

Wanting to be the strongest creatures—to not have a higher power hovering over them like a threat—was frankly something I could understand better than I wanted to admit.

Once Shem finished his warning, he thanked everyone for supporting our engagement, reminding them that we'd choose a new wedding date the moment the Vaade threat was extinguished.

He made it sound like victory was imminent.

I tried not to get my hopes up.

As soon as Shem's speech ended, conversation picked back up, and Judge Baruk hurried to meet us at base of the stairs, forgetting to maneuver around me in his concern. "We'd heard of these attacks, but I'd assumed the Jinn were being taken by surprise, correct? And you're merely exaggerating the danger for the public?"

Shem hesitated, lowering his voice. "Unfortunately, no. The Vaade raids are moving from the smaller islands to the more heavily populated. Until we can pinpoint where they'll be next, we need every island prepared." He leaned toward the judge, speaking softly so no one nearby would overhear. "Our Gifts don't always seem to affect them."

Judge Baruk's eyes widened. "Have they attacked any islands as large as Tel Sheba?"

When Shem nodded, he murmured a hasty, "Please excuse me," and disappeared within the crowd.

Almost immediately, a nearby group of Jinn called to Shem, drawing him into conversation. We moved from one group to the next, following the paths between the flowers. Colorful Jinni eyes watched my every move, but none of them drew me into conversation beyond a greeting or a passing comment on the weather.

Eyeing the opposite side of the room like a finish line, I held back a groan.

Despite the heat, a sudden shiver traveled down my spine.

If I'd actually been involved in the conversation, I might've missed it…

A crackle of magic filled the air.

2

A SWIRLING CIRCLE OF white light the size of my palm appeared beside the stream flowing down the center of the conservatory. It looked like a hundred bolts of lightning, flashing back and forth, fighting each other, but the light grew steadily stronger—and larger—by the second.

It reminded me of when I'd seen Shem's men close a daleth once.

Except, it almost seemed as if…

A portal was opening.

The sheer brilliance burned my eyes the way sunlight did when a curtain was yanked back in a dark room. I ripped my gaze to the side.

Shem had cut off mid-sentence, shielding his own eyes with his hand.

Backing away from the spot, the nearest Jinn started to recognize it for what it was—a daleth forming.

THE SECRET CURSE

They fled.

Traveling from one side of the room to the other, they burst through the exit, shoving each other out of the way.

It caused mass panic.

Chaos descended over the room as they crashed into each other, piling up in front of the exit.

Captain Uriel and his three guards—Noam, Tirzah, and Boaz—surrounded Shem and I, aiming their crystal spears at the daleth as it grew rapidly.

"Your Highness," the captain yelled over the din. "This same manifestation occurred on the island of Zipporah, and the Khaanevaade—"

"I know what it is." Shem cut him off.

My heart was racing.

We all knew what it was.

Shem wrapped an arm around me, tugging me closer.

"We must get you out of the building immediately." Captain Uriel's voice rose over the crowd. He used his body to shield the prince. The other three guards held a protective configuration around us. "It's not safe to stay any longer."

My jaw dropped at the sheer panic in the captain's eyes. I'd never in my entire life witnessed a member of the Jinni Guard afraid of anything.

I tensed. They wanted us to travel? The only way out of the conservatory were the doors on the far side of the room, blocked by dozens of overly-dressed Jinn fighting their way through.

"To the exit." The captain gestured for the other guards to join hands with us. "Now!"

"No!" Shem stopped them. "I'm tired of this game the Vaade are playing. Every attack ends before we have a chance to fight back. This time there are four of you. You can take the Vaade by surprise."

Captain Uriel finally tore his gaze from the nearly man-sized portal to give the prince a harsh look. "Your parents would have my head if anything happened to you. My first responsibility is your safety."

"Jezebel and I will hide." Shem gestured to the flowering arch on the stage where we'd stood not long ago. "We'll be perfectly safe."

When the captain began to protest, Shem interrupted, with iron in his voice. "Go now, all of you. That's an order."

"You first." Captain Uriel stood stubborn and unmoving.

With his arm still around me, Shem traveled both of us across the room to the stage, landing directly under the arch. The décor of flowers and leaves was thick but not wide enough to conceal two people on the same side. "Hide here," Shem murmured, pointing to one side of the arch. "Stay out of sight." Meeting my gaze, he added with a careful choice of words, "Whatever it takes."

Use your Gifts if you have to, I heard the unspoken request.

My brows rose. It would only take one single Jinni

THE SECRET CURSE

witnessing my Gift and exposing it to lead to a severance. If he thought it was worth the risk, he was more worried than he was letting on.

As soon as I nodded, he darted across the stage to the other side, hiding behind the opposite column.

Peeking out, we had a perfect view of the entire scene. Captain Uriel gave us a curt nod before turning to face the daleth with the other guards.

Across the room, Judge Baruk's face was turning violet screaming for an orderly evacuation.

No one listened.

When a figure leapt through the portal in a blur, I forgot the chokepoint at the door completely. He launched over the guards' heads, landing in an empty space a dozen paces away.

Shouting orders, Captain Uriel led the attack. But before the Vaade had even fully landed, he leapt again, flying through the air toward the exit.

He was going after the fleeing citizens.

All four guards gave chase.

Though Captain Uriel threw fire at the Vaade with his Gift, it fell on empty space. Noam tried to throw a wall of air at him next, but the Vaade moved too fast. The strange man was a blur of motion. He slammed into a screaming Jinni, knocking her to the ground. Before I could blink, he'd done the same to three more Jinn.

Boaz and Tirzah joined in the fray. All four guards were completely oblivious to the flash that came from the open portal behind them.

Shem and I gasped as another Vaade stepped through.

He was enormous.

While his friend distracted the guards, he stopped to scan the room, unknowingly giving us a chance to size him up as well.

His bronze skin was a few shades lighter than his brown hair that hung in rope-like tangles past his shoulders. His bare arms displayed rippling muscles as he tensed, searching for something.

I ducked further back behind the arch, peering through the leaves.

Unfortunately, I couldn't see him now either.

My view of the room was restricted to one side.

The other Vaade stepped into my line of vision, chasing a small Jinni woman.

She traveled, but he was too fast.

He caught her foot as she vanished, taking him along with her.

The two of them reappeared beside the wall—the enchantment had blocked her from leaving.

The Vaade man fell to the ground clutching his head. He shook it a little, almost as if disoriented by the travel?

It didn't last long though.

He pulled himself up, widening his stance to fight, and grabbed her wrists.

As she tensed, I could've sworn she tried to travel again, but this time, neither of them moved.

THE SECRET CURSE

Her face paled.

She screamed as he threw her against the wall. The glass shattered. She scrambled to her feet on the dirt and grass outside, covered in bleeding scratches. Before he could follow, she disappeared.

Multiple Jinn at the back of the crowd recognized this as a new escape route. Seconds later, a dozen more jagged holes broke the glass walls.

The first Vaade was already turning back to the crowd. Jinn didn't like physical combat, preferring to use Gifts against any attackers, but they might need both to face him.

I tore my gaze away as the second Vaade quietly prowled along a garden path into my line of sight.

With a gasp, I ducked back again. *Had he seen me?*

Shem held a finger to his lips.

I nodded.

But as the seconds passed, screams across the room drew me until I couldn't help risking another look.

The second Vaade faced the first now, allowing me a soft breath of relief.

He tilted his head up, sniffing the air—what was he searching for? He slowly turned until I could see his profile.

For the first time since their arrival, he was close enough to see defining details. He wore some type of leather hide vest and pants. Buckles in a dozen places held knives and other weapons I didn't recognize. There were no sleeves on those large arms. Anxiously I compared his and the other Vaade's muscles to the Jinn—without Gifts, it didn't seem like a fair fight.

Though a few hundred Jinn had fled the building already, a small number of citizens had turned to stand their ground and fight. They formed a line behind Shem's guards, prepared to reveal their personal Gifts if they had to.

Tirzah was currently engaging the first Vaade, leading him away from the remaining citizens, while the other three guards flanked him, trying to cut him off from the people as well.

The muscled man lunged for her unexpectedly.

She dodged—barely evading him—by floating high off the ground toward the glass ceiling.

But that didn't deter him at all.

The big Vaade launched himself into the air, capable of nearly the same heights as she, grasping for her ankles.

I squeaked.

Clapping a hand over my mouth, I yanked back behind the arch again as the second Vaade man swung around.

I held my breath.

Through the little leaves I caught a glimpse of his legs.

They bent, then disappeared as he launched himself into the air.

He landed near the stage, closer to us than ever.

A tiny motion caught my eye from Shem. He held

his palm up, gesturing for me to stay hidden.

I nodded, peering through the leaves of the arch as the closest Vaade sniffed the air again. He followed some unknown path that fortunately took him in the opposite direction.

Risking another glance at the fighting while his back was turned, I found Captain Uriel leading the guards and citizens in creating some semblance of a perimeter, closing in on the Vaade with caution.

The beast of a man knocked Noam's weapon aside, tossing it across the conservatory. It landed uselessly in a rosebush.

Tirzah leapt forward, capturing the Vaade's brawny arm and traveling, taking him with her.

Just like before, this seemed to overwhelm him, forcing him to slow down.

But when she attempted to travel a second time, the Vaade stayed rooted in place.

Only Tirzah disappeared.

In a flash, she reappeared, trying again.

The Vaade didn't budge.

Though Captain Uriel and the others tensed to fight, they couldn't do much without risking Tirzah as well. A few more citizens took the opportunity to slip out the exit.

With a wicked grin, the Vaade flung Tirzah into Noam. The crash of armor echoed loudly through the nearly empty room. The two guards fell to the ground, unconscious.

Why did the traveling stop working?

Captain Uriel and Boaz raised their weapons higher, calling for the citizens to step back and use caution. They didn't advance. Were they using other Gifts that we couldn't see? If so, it didn't seem to affect the Vaade in the slightest as he prowled forward. How could they fight an enemy who seemed oddly resistant to their Gifts?

A soft thud sounded on the hollow stage.

I yanked back out of sight, heart beating frantically.

I'd forgotten the other Vaade.

He was only a few steps away.

Clutching the little vial that hung on a necklace beneath my dress, I steeled myself.

Though Shem had asked me not to join the fight, I might not have a choice…

I was prepared though.

Just a few months ago, my mother had used an enchantment to paralyze me. I'd spent weeks searching for something similar, finally stumbling across a mixture of foxglove and bloodroot that made a potent black paste. To use it, I simply needed to scoop out a bit of paste and place it over a cut. The moment it entered the bloodstream, it took effect.

I gripped the little vial around my neck tighter, pulling out the stopper.

By using the paralytic, I could protect myself without exposing my Gifts.

Soft footsteps crossed the stage.

A few more, and he'd be here.

THE SECRET CURSE

If I subdued the Vaade, the Jinn would revere me. They'd *have* to.

With a low growl, the brute stopped directly in the center of the arch.

Directly in front of *me*.

Gasping, I flinched, glancing across the space at Shem on instinct.

Except, Shem wasn't there.

My racing heart skipped a beat. Had Shem traveled somewhere else within the room and left me here alone?

Shock left me slow to react as the Vaade took a silent step toward me.

When I glanced at his face, I sucked in a breath.

His eyes…

My lips parted. Honestly, I hadn't believed Shem's stories, but I couldn't deny what I saw.

His black pupils were long and thin, pointed at both top and bottom, and the iris was the color of a deep amber like the gold that dragons were always said to hoard. Within the amber were deep orange and yellow flecks, like a burning sunset.

I should've run, but I could only stare back at him, too stunned to move.

Stopping close enough to loom over me, he tilted his head slightly, not taking his eyes from mine as he sniffed the air with a frown.

I still held the open bottle with trembling fingers. But how could I get the paralytic to enter his bloodstream? There wasn't a cut on him.

When he blinked, it shook me from my stupor.

Use the paralytic.

I began to shift my fingers into claws sharp enough to slice his skin.

To distract him, I shifted my eyes at the same time—to match his.

Just one quick slash across his chest, then wipe the paralytic on after.

But the way he watched my every move made my heart sink.

With his speed, I'd only get one chance to surprise him. Once I cut him, he'd knock me out before I ever reached into the vial.

The animalistic shape of my eyes did make him pause, though.

His own eyes narrowed.

Instead of attacking, he spoke, in a deep voice that raised the hair on my arms. "Where's the prince?"

Though I wanted to glance over his shoulder and search for Shem too, I managed to shrug, despite my racing heart. "How should I know where he is?"

Now he *did* growl.

He might have done more than that, if not for the approaching guards. Attempting to trap the first Vaade as he ran toward the open daleth, they flung out a wall of energy in our direction.

It knocked us back against the thick glass and into the smaller shrubs along the wall, which scraped my arms and face.

From the ground, I stared at the Vaade as he launched himself into the air. He landed heavily on top of the arch. A cracking sound came from the wood as it swayed dangerously under his weight.

"There's two of them." Captain Uriel's panicked voice came from somewhere on the other side of the arch as the Vaade leapt off the arch in their direction.

I scrambled to my knees, shifting my hand back to normal before the captain or any of the guards could see. Crawling forward, I peered around the arch.

The Vaade had landed in front of the portal.

I stood, taking a step toward him, though there was nothing I could do.

With one last furious glance in my direction, he stepped through and vanished.

The other Vaade led Boaz and Captain Uriel on a wild chase around the room, landing in one smooth motion in front of the daleth. He disappeared through it as well.

The two guards traveled to the portal seconds later.

But it'd already flashed closed.

The Vaade were gone.

Sudden deafening silence filled the broken conservatory.

"Find the trail." Captain Uriel's command made me flinch.

"I can't sense it," Boaz replied.

Tirzah roused on the other side of the room where a

few citizens stood over her and Noam to protect them. She turned to wake Noam next.

Soon all the guards were yelling back and forth as they actively searched the space for any remaining threat.

So much for my half-formed plans.

I had to admit I was relieved, since the chances it would've worked had been extremely low.

Corking the little vial around my neck with a sigh, I replaced it beneath the collar of my dress.

As I let go, a warm hand touched my back.

I startled.

There was no one behind me.

Heat radiated from the empty space.

Reaching out, a cold, familiar armor hit my fingers, and I let out a relieved breath.

I should've guessed.

My hands ran along unseen leather armbands with a mind of their own toward invisible shoulders. As I splayed my fingers across a strong chest, Prince Shem appeared beneath them.

His own hand, now visible, came up to cover mine.

3

A GIFT OF INVISIBILITY was even more rare than shape-shifting.

And equally powerful.

A twinge of apprehension passed through me. Was this how he'd felt when he'd learned of my Gifts? It was uncomfortable.

Shem tucked a finger under my chin, raising it until I finally met his eyes.

There was a slight line between his brows—was it worry? Did he not trust me? Or was he wondering how I might react? A dozen more questions came to mind, but there were still other Jinni ears nearby that might overhear. I kept silent.

We stood like that, eyes locked, not saying a word,

until Tirzah approached, breathing hard.

I broke first, dropping my gaze to the ground.

"We must leave immediately, Your Highness," she said, clutching her weapon against her chest, eyes darting around as she spoke. Touching her head, she winced.

"What about the citizens?" Shem asked, though there were hardly any remaining.

"We'll send support once you're safe," Captain Uriel replied as he joined us. "I never should've agreed to stay in the first place. Protocol states we return to the capital immediately." There was no room for argument in his tone.

Reluctantly, Shem agreed, though he insisted that he and I stay together.

We traveled to the now-empty exit, crossed the boundary of the enchantment in a hurry, and immediately traveled again.

At first, the island landscape was fairly open with minimal trees and smaller towns, allowing us to cross long distances as far as we could see. Each time we landed in soft grass, whether on a hilltop or in a valley, it put more space between us and our attackers. We flashed across Tel Sheba in a half-dozen leaps. A smaller island floated beside it, so close that even a human could've almost jumped across, and we were able to travel onto it without looking for a bridge.

"Your Highness." Captain Uriel held up a hand for us to pause. "I'm afraid we're going in a direction I

THE SECRET CURSE

haven't come before."

"I've studied all the islands, Captain," Shem reassured him, slowly scanning the landscape. "This is Tel Yevah. It only has one town, but three bridges. Follow me."

Though Shem could've gone straight to the bridge, the unfamiliar island kept the rest of us limited to what was in sight and slowed everyone's travel.

As we appeared and reappeared in the distance, leading the way, Shem and I whispered in the brief moments it took the guards to follow.

"You weren't supposed to engage," Shem murmured in my ear with an anxious frown. "Remember? *Whatever it takes*." He'd wanted me to shift—or, more specifically, to use my ability to hide.

Captain Uriel flashed into sight behind us with Tirzah and Boaz, who carried a limping Noam.

When I glanced down, my fingers were trembling—now that the danger was past, my body finally reacted. The Vaade had been more of a threat than I'd realized.

We traveled again, landing first.

"I was trying to distract him so he wouldn't keep looking for you," I lied, clenching my fists so Shem wouldn't notice the shaking. Telling him that I'd wanted to be a hero was too embarrassing.

The guards reappeared, and we traveled again.

A little town emerged with a smaller version of the acropolis we had back home, white pillars rising to the sky with a majestic statue of one of the past Jinni kings standing prominently in the town square.

We traveled past the town, landing on a small hill on the other side.

"I was going to stop him," Shem replied at the next opportunity. "I was right there, but I couldn't knock him out without risking your safety. You should've run."

Captain Uriel caught his last words, giving us a look, and when the six of us traveled again, we stayed silent.

A quarter-hour of this passed in a blur, hopping from one island to the next, though most of the time we were forced to search for a bridge.

At one point, we paused again to rest. The guards discussed the fastest path home.

"Tel Haifa would take us in for the night," Tirzah suggested.

But Captain Uriel shook his head immediately. "Returning to Resh is our ultimate priority."

I stood in the group but felt like an intruder.

I knew next to nothing about Jinni geography—my discipline years had spent very little time on it.

Noam shaded his eyes, glancing out at the soft white clouds floating by the edge of the island we'd stopped on, as if he could somehow see the vast connections in the distance. "Bir Harim is close. From there, we can stick to the larger islands, which could help us avoid the Vaade's notice, if that's your concern?"

Though Captain Uriel's brow wrinkled at the mention of the Vaade, he nodded, coming to a quick decision. "The strongest travelers should take over and carry the others. We'll take turns if need be."

"I'll stay with Jezebel," Shem replied. "There's no real chance of another attack at this point."

The captain shook his head, leaning forward to grab Shem's armor and giving it a slight shake. "I risked your safety once already today. Don't ask me to do it again." He turned to Boaz. "You'll take the prince."

When Shem pressed his lips together, looking ready to argue, the captain added quietly, "You need to save your strength. Just because another attack isn't likely doesn't mean it's impossible."

"I'll go with Tirzah," I spoke up, trying to make it easier on Shem. Even I knew the captain wasn't going to budge on this one, and I'd only been in the castle for a few months. Protecting the royal family came before all else, and Shem was the only heir. Captain Uriel had risked his entire career following the prince's command earlier.

Shem ran a hand through his hair. "Fine." He turned to me. "As long as you're comfortable with this."

I tucked my hands beneath my arms and nodded.

Tirzah politely held out a hand and we continued on, though her presence wasn't nearly as comforting as the prince's.

None of us spoke.

Each time we reached the edge of an island, we'd stop at the guard station beside the bridge. One look at the captain's insignia—and face—and the guards posted there waved us on.

Not long after this, we were forced to slow again, both because our line of sight became impaired by more trees and cities, but also to conserve energy.

We didn't normally travel at this speed.

The guards were stretched to their limits.

After another argument, Captain Uriel allowed Shem to transport the others as well, to relieve the exhausted guards. Boaz stayed with Shem, while Tirzah and the captain quietly decided to take turns traveling with Noam, who still had a slight limp, leaving me to travel by myself—I could've taken three or maybe even four at once, but no one asked.

After keeping my true Gifts and full strength to myself for so long, I didn't offer.

Though I should've been looking over my shoulder, watching our surroundings like the rest of them, my eyes kept drifting to Shem instead. How many times had he used his Gift around me, without my ever knowing it?

My eyes widened as I remembered odd moments—the way he'd appeared, seemingly out of nowhere, when I'd gone to reveal my Gifts to his parents, despite the closed doors and the guards outside them. Gasping quietly, I remembered the way I could've sworn I'd felt his presence in my wardrobe as I'd traveled to the royal suites that same day.

I ignored the sunny skies and the thundering waterfall just behind the city ahead, as I thought back over the entire time I'd known him. For once, I understood how

THE SECRET CURSE

such a powerful Gift could make someone afraid.

At this pace, we needed only one more break for everyone to rest before we reached the capital city of Resh. The royal family's spring and summer castle stretched proud and tall in the distance beside the enormous River Mem.

By the time we crossed the border at the bridge and set foot in the city itself, we were all so thoroughly exhausted that we walked the final stretch to the castle. Originally, I'd wanted to find a quiet moment with Shem once we arrived. Now, all I wanted was a hot bath and my own bed. I could learn more about his Gift tomorrow.

At the gate, Captain Uriel gave hurried orders to those on guard, and we were unceremoniously dumped in a secure room covered in heavy protection spells deep in the heart of the castle. There were no windows. A small, round table only large enough for a handful of people filled the center.

I looked longingly at the door. Straightening my shoulders, I tried to unobtrusively shake the cobwebs from my head and focus. This could be my opportunity to finally show my value to the royal family. I had, afterall, gotten a good glimpse of the Vaade—and spoken to him! No one else had done that. Pride put a small smile on my face, and I was determined to stay as long as necessary, despite my exhaustion.

The guards who'd been on tour with us took up position along the walls. Shem pulled out a chair for me and we sat, but we didn't speak by silent agreement. Even the guards gossiped sometimes, and every other word from me lately seemed like it was misconstrued. Better to keep quiet and wait until we were alone.

Along the opposite wall, a large map caught my eye. No—I frowned and looked closer—it was actually two maps.

The left one held dozens of floating islands, names written beneath each island as well as each of their major cities, and the number of bridges—or lack thereof—between the islands.

But it was the little red pins placed at seemingly random locations across the islands that drew my attention. Because on the second map, there were an equal number of red pins, almost as if corresponding to the first map, though not always in the same position.

This second map held cities I'd never heard of. At first, I thought it was a much closer look at a specific island, since the map didn't document any airspace. But a massive mountain range stretched across the upper half of the map denoting steep cliffs along one side in particular.

We didn't have many mountains in Jinn, and certainly nothing that expansive.

It wasn't until my eyes caught on a small drawing of a horde of dragons that my mouth dropped open in understanding.

It was the human world.

The corresponding pins suddenly made sense.

They were daleths.

THE SECRET CURSE

Shem would certainly love to use the one by the cliffs where that dragon was pictured. He'd always wanted to see them up close. Squinting, I made a mental note of where the pin was so I could tell Shem about it later. It was hard to tell without knowing the scale of the map—it could be anywhere from a few hours to a day's travel from those cliffs—but it was close.

I was busy trying to find the corresponding pin on the Jinni map, when the king and queen swept in with their own set of guards.

Shem and I both stood.

"What's going on?" the king asked the closest guard, Noam. "I was in the middle of a meeting."

"My apologies, your majesty." Noam bowed low. "There's been another attack."

Queen Samaria put a hand to her chest, and Shem moved to comfort her.

I followed unconsciously, then caught myself, stepping back to stand awkwardly near the wall.

"We chose to bring all of you to one of the secret rooms until we could guarantee your safety," Noam was saying. "I'll let Captain Uriel explain the details of what happened."

Stepping back, he gestured toward the table. Tirzah pulled out the closest chairs for the king and queen with a slight bow.

The king and queen took the offered seats, and Shem joined them.

Captain Uriel took the fourth and final seat in front

of me before I could move and began to brief the king and queen on the incident, starting with the daleth.

Standing in the dim light, I leaned forward a bit, waiting for someone to notice, but no one did.

I tried to ignore the way they were treating me as neither friend nor foe, but simply as someone of no importance at all.

While I might expect this behavior from the king and queen, who seemed to think of me only when it suited their needs, I'd expected more from Shem. He scowled at the table, lost in thought.

I cleared my throat.

When he glanced up, he blinked at me, brows rising, and turned to the guards still standing. "Could someone please bring another chair for Jezebel?"

Noam nodded and left.

With a glance at the prince, Captain Uriel waited for his nod, then continued speaking.

I pressed my shoulders back and stood taller than I felt. Shem had defended me all day—even now he was trying. It probably didn't occur to him to offer up his own seat, but maybe that was to be expected. He was the prince after all.

"We felt it best to leave immediately." Captain Uriel finished explaining our time-consuming escape.

I noticed that he didn't add another red pin to the map. Since the Vaade had closed the daleth behind them, that must mean the red pins only marked open portals.

THE SECRET CURSE

Though I should've been paying attention to the conversation, that preoccupied me briefly. There were far more open daleths than the citizens were aware of.

"Why not wait to discover the city's plans for adding extra protection?" the king snapped. "We'll have to send someone out. It'll be hours before we get word. For all we know, there could be another attack." King Jubal's fickle temper irked me. It was probably *his* orders Captain Uriel had obeyed to prioritize the prince's safety, but he'd either forgotten or put it out of his mind on purpose.

"There won't be another attack," Shem replied, saving the captain from an impossible position. He flattened his palms on the table in a move that seemed calm but also practiced as he met his father's gaze. "They were looking for me."

Queen Samaria sucked in a breath, hands trembling slightly before she tucked them in her lap and out of sight. "How do you know?"

"I heard it from the Vaade himself," Shem said grimly, lips pressed together in a flat line. A heavy pause said more. The queen nodded at whatever was unsaid.

I frowned.

He'd overheard the Vaade say this when he was invisible, but he wasn't saying so, which meant the other guards were unaware of his hidden Gift. The king and queen probably assumed I didn't know either—and likely didn't want me to.

I shrank back farther into the shadows. My back hit the wall, stopping my unconscious retreat. No one noticed the soft thump.

Noam returned quietly, holding a small chair.

There was no room for it at the table.

He placed it against the wall without a word, turning to stand with the other guards, unwilling to interrupt.

I chewed my lip as I considered dragging the chair up to the table somehow, but the king was in the middle of a rant.

"We need to discern how these anomalies are taking place. I've said it before, and I'll say it again: we have to be more prepared the next time a daleth forms unexpectedly. How do the Khaanevaade sense them forming? We must find out as soon as possible, or they'll continue taking advantage of it."

I frowned, distracted from the chair. His portrayal of the Vaade didn't make any sense. There was no way that portal had created itself. The Vaade man had clearly been standing ready to use it, which meant he—or someone else in his tribe—had opened it on the other side. Intentionally.

Swallowing, I tried to find an opening to insert my suspicions into the conversation. This was more important than a chair.

"That's the fourth time this month," the king was saying, as he pounded a fist on the table. "This cannot continue!"

"I understand, Your Majesty," Captain Uriel replied, but the king didn't give him a chance to say more.

THE SECRET CURSE

"We need to train all Guard members in the details of closing a daleth." The king stood to pace.

The moment for me to speak up seemed to have passed. Clenching my hands together, I squeezed my fingers anxiously. Should I tell them my misgivings? Maybe I was wrong...

"The engagement tour is postponed until further notice," the king continued, gesturing in Shem's direction, but ignoring me. Perhaps he didn't realize I was still here. I'd blended into the shadows against the wall. A gloom settled over me at the thought of delaying yet another aspect of our future together. It played on my worst fears that the wedding might never happen.

"You'll be safe on the main island," Queen Samaria told her son, patting his hand with a small smile, though her eyes were creased with worry.

"I don't think that's the case, though," I blurted out.

All eyes turned to me.

"I think—" I hesitated before stepping forward, suddenly doubting myself. "Well, I'm not certain, but it's possible that the Khaanevaade are forming these portals themselves...?" Under the intimidating stares of the royal family, the statement turned into a question.

"Impossible." The king scoffed, waving a hand at the idea as if swatting a fly. "The Vaade are not nearly advanced enough to accomplish something so complex. They're mere beasts masquerading as men."

He acted as if he wasn't even worried.

But I *knew* that wasn't the case. The Vaade had

abilities we didn't understand. Even simple traveling affected them differently.

For three months now, I'd kept quiet around the king and queen, allowing them to view me as unimportant—encouraging it even, if it'd make them see me as less powerful. As the only other Jinn in the realm who knew of my shape-shifting ability, besides their son, my entire goal had been to seem like less of a threat. But now I could see it'd backfired. I opened my mouth to speak—

"You must be exhausted after this ordeal, dear," Queen Samaria cut in, coming around the table to place a hand on my shoulder. She squeezed my arm gently and smiled. "It seems we're all perfectly safe within the castle, so why don't you go get some rest? I'm sure you need some time to recover from this awful turn of events."

I sucked in a breath, too stunned to hide my reaction. But she'd already moved to return to her seat.

I'd been dismissed.

Every muscle in my body tensed. If Queen Samaria had glanced back, she'd have found fury radiating from every inch of me.

I *hated* being ignored.

Glancing at Shem, I expected him to counter their command and ask me if I wanted to stay. Instead, head in hands, brow furrowed, he stared down at the table lost in thought.

Logic overpowered my rage.

With my future wedding dangling by a thread, I

THE SECRET CURSE

couldn't risk cutting it with an outburst. King Jubal or Queen Samaria could use a single word of defiance against me. In a room with this many witnesses, one claim of aggression against the royal family paired with a revelation that I was a shapeshifter, and my entire life would be ruined.

"I'll bid you all goodnight then," I murmured, cheeks burning in humiliation as I strode to the door.

Shem glanced up at my words, brows knitted together, but still he didn't contradict his mother, only nodding distractedly. "Get some rest. We'll speak soon."

Bowing, because I didn't know what else to do, I allowed a guard I didn't recognize to take me by the elbow as we stepped into the hall. Once outside of the enchantment that protected the room, he instantly traveled with me to the hall in front of my own chamber door.

With a brief nod as the barest sign of respect, he vanished.

I attempted to sense the trail back to the room we'd been in, wanting to rebel against the queen's wishes and return to the discussion.

They wouldn't be able to silence me so easily once Shem and I married, would they?

Once I was a future queen, they'd *have* to listen.

My eyes widened as I discovered the trail from the guard's travel was somehow hidden completely. Not even the slightest trace was left behind.

A Gift perhaps? Or maybe an enchantment over the room we'd met in?

It didn't matter.

Either way, I'd been belittled and insulted.

It left a bitter taste in my mouth.

"Hmm. You're back early," a feminine voice hummed.

In the alcove at the end of the hall, a dark shape rose from one of the lounge chairs in the communal space, stepping into the light of the hallway. It was Milcah.

I wanted to kick myself for not noticing her presence. Not only did she know I was supposed to be on my engagement tour, but she'd seen the guard drop me off without a single word. Any Jinn could read embarrassing things into this situation, but Milcah could manage to spread an especially humiliating story if she chose to.

"There was a Vaade attack," I said without further explanation, hoping to distract her from my solo return.

"Oh my." She fluttered a hand to her chest, highlighting the low-cut dress. "What are the king and queen planning to do about it?"

"You'll find out in the next council meeting, I'm sure," I told her, turning toward my door.

"Ah, I see," she said softly, making me tense. "You don't know."

Hand on the doorknob, I searched for a response that would fool her. My mind was blank.

The long pause was enough to confirm the truth.

"You know, Jezebel," Milcah said as she strolled over to me. "If you want to take control of your life, you

THE SECRET CURSE

have to take it." Her tone was mocking. She'd made it her personal mission to paint me as weak. Probably half the rumors circulating the castle came from her.

Gritting my teeth, I twisted the knob, opening my door. As I entered my room, I gave her a cool look. "Shem knows my value. I don't have to force myself on him the way *some* people do." Before she could come up with some other response to further rub salt in my wounds, I added, "It's been a long day with the attack and all. I'm afraid I'll have to say goodnight."

I let the door slam shut in her face.

With the curtains closed, my room was dark and had a stale smell that meant no one had bothered to clean it for me while I'd been gone. It was empty. I tried to imagine it filled with a welcoming party or even a small group of friends, but I couldn't picture a single face.

Unstrapping my sandals, I flung them at the wall where they made an unsatisfying clack before falling to the ground. I sat on the bed, wishing that it—or anything in this room—felt like coming home. Like I belonged here.

Instead, I turned, only to come face to face with my beautiful white lace wedding dress.

It hung on the side of my wardrobe, waiting for the wedding that was meant to happen today.

When Shem had first suggested we postpone, he'd said, "It'll be brief. Only another month or two. We'll use the time to schedule more courtship tours, to let everyone get to know and love you."

"Of course," I'd agreed, hiding the fact that I hated it. One month had turned into two, and then three.

As of now, our original wedding day had officially passed without any sign of setting a new date.

The one time I'd mentioned it to Shem after the first month had passed, he'd wrapped his arms around me in comfort. "I know," he'd said. "But we have to put our people above everything else, even our wedding. That's the price of joining the royal family." Pulling back, he'd gazed into my eyes. "I hope it won't be too much for you?"

I'd shaken my head. "Not at all." And that was the last time we'd discussed it.

Pinching my eyes shut, I avoided the nagging feeling that no one would mind if the wedding never happened.

Just like no one missed me back at that table.

I ground my teeth together.

I should've made them listen, or at least tried harder to explain my theories.

There was nothing to stop the Vaade from forming a portal here in Resh.

The very first attacks had happened on the far islands, while today's had been much closer to home—to the prince. I had no doubt they'd figure out how to hit their target eventually.

Once they did, they'd come after Shem, as they so clearly wanted to.

My body itched to leap up from the bed and return to

THE SECRET CURSE

that meeting room. I reminded myself that even if my presence was allowed, I didn't know where it was.

It doesn't matter, I repeated yet again.

Not the location, or whether they'd accept me, or even if I was right about the Vaade planning to attack here in Resh—maybe even in the castle.

My opinion wasn't necessary or wanted.

I was merely an accessory for the prince to pull out during times of peace. Not someone with a seat at the table. Not someone with any real power.

I clenched my fists until the nails broke my skin and drew boiling, furious blood.

A year ago, I'd been no one. I'd accepted a life without power, without much at all really.

But how could I go back to that now that I'd had a taste? I was *someone* here. Or at least, I'd thought so, when I'd accepted a seat on the prince's council, and especially once Prince Shem proposed. That should *mean* something. I rubbed my eyes and groaned.

The rest of the night was spent stewing, waiting for Shem to come find me, only growing more upset and confused when he did no such thing.

4

I WOKE DETERMINED NOT to wait for Shem another second. Dressing carefully, I chose an off-shoulder red dress that made me feel powerful, even if all evidence spoke to the contrary. The top layer of the dress was a deep red fabric and nearly transparent, exposing the soft white material underneath. Crystals decorated the red layer where it cinched in to form a tight waist, before fading into a pure white toward the bottom where it swirled prettily around my legs as I walked.

Holding my head high, I strode through the halls toward the garden.

When Shem found me strolling there some time later, he gallantly held out an arm as if nothing were wrong.

Pretending not to see it, I brushed past him with a curt, "Good morning. Did the king and queen agree on a good solution for the Khaanevaade problem?"

THE SECRET CURSE

"We think so," Shem replied easily, falling into step beside me, waving at some of the ladies approaching us from the other end of the path. "I know you're frustrated with my parents after they delayed the wedding. I can try not to discuss them or the Vaade attacks, if that would help you feel better?"

"Good," I said in a flat tone. "That will solve everything."

"Do I sense that you're upset with me?" he murmured, after the small group had passed us and moved out of earshot.

I snorted. Jinni men thought they were so intelligent, but they missed the most obvious things. He'd think I was being childish if I complained about his mother, but after spending months in the castle I'd learned how to bring a problem up indirectly. "I feel certain that the Khaanevaade could attack here in Resh as easily as any other island, and yet, when I made my opinions known, I was dismissed from the conversation completely."

Shem lifted his hands in a helpless gesture, making a sympathetic face that only irked me further. "I know my parents can be abrupt and set in their ways. It's difficult for them to hear outside counsel—"

"From me, you mean," I cut him off. "It's difficult for them to respect and listen to *me*. They had no problem listening to the guards. Ever since our engagement, they've made it clear they don't trust me—they don't think I'm good enough for you."

"Well..." Shem faltered. "They don't know you as

well as I do. And what they do know..." he trailed off, reminding me of my confession just a few short months ago.

I'd planned to tell the king and queen *all* my Gifts, but we'd been interrupted part way through. They didn't know I could persuade them to do almost anything—even now I tensed at the thought of telling them, grateful I hadn't gotten the chance. They *did* however know about my shape-shifting abilities.

So far, they hadn't asked me to use them on their behalf. I'd assumed it was because of our engagement—that they no longer felt right about making their future daughter-in-law spy for them. But Shem seemed to be subtly hinting that it was something else: trust.

"They need... time," he was saying. "It's a lot to ask someone to trust another's Gift, but especially to ask it of the king and queen. Surely you can understand that?"

"I can," I said in a soft voice, turning to begin walking again so I didn't have to look at him. "That's why I'd hoped you might stand up for me." And though I didn't want to think ill of him, I couldn't help wondering if his guilt was the reason he hadn't come to see me last night.

"I apologize," he said from behind, taking long strides to catch up. "I was thinking about other things, but that's no excuse. I should've joined forces with you and convinced my father to listen. Truly." He put a hand on my arm, urging me to slow down and listen.

"What other things?" I demanded, more heated than I usually let myself speak to him, spinning to face him. "What's more important than worrying about where they might attack next? They're looking for you. Who's to say they won't come here?"

"I don't disagree with you." He held up his hands, palms out. "But I was contemplating how we might've reopened their portal and followed their trail." His hands fell back to his sides when I didn't interrupt. He ran a hand through his dark hair. "If we wait for them to come to us, we're at a disadvantage. The only way we have a real chance of stopping the Vaade is if we go on the offensive. But we can't."

"Why not?"

"Because we still don't know where they're located. They're nomadic. And the only sites we've found so far were already abandoned."

We started walking again, more slowly this time, as I processed his words. Our wedding depended on stopping the Vaade, and he was saying that was impossible.

My heart sank.

I couldn't speak past the lump in my throat.

Only when I could manage to sound calm, did I reply, "I still think you should be more prepared for another attack here."

"We discussed where the Vaade might attack last night as well," he assured me. "In fact, that was the reason we finished so late, or I would've stopped by to check on you. I've been worrying over how you fared since the assault."

Pressing my lips together, I stared at him.

His brows nearly met in the middle as he stared back.

Softening, I took his arm when he offered it this time, slowing to walk beside him beneath a trellis covered in red roses. "I've been well enough."

Sneaking a glance at him, I plucked one of the pretty roses in full bloom. The vivid red was the same color as the top of my dress. As I sniffed it, I dared to add, "Well enough to wonder about your sudden disappearance during the attack…"

He sucked in a breath. "Yes. I—Thank you for reminding me. We should discuss it." Clearing his throat, he fiddled nervously with my fingers where they lay on his arm. "I hope… I'm afraid I must ask if you'll keep the details to yourself?"

"I swear on all of Jinn, I wouldn't tell a soul."

We began walking again, and when the path forked, we turned away from the castle toward the apple orchard. For a long moment, I thought he wasn't going to trust me.

"There aren't many details," he said finally. "But I'll show you what there is to know." Tugging me toward the orchard with a smile, Shem waited until we were hidden by the trees before he pulled me off the path. With one last glance around to check that no one was looking, he vanished in front of me, still holding my hand.

It felt like my mind was playing tricks—he could've

just traveled away. It could be that my fingers only continued feeling him because they wanted to.

But then, he squeezed gently.

I grinned.

"Incredible," I whispered.

He let go of my hand, and a moment later his soft voice came from behind me with a smile in it. "You think so?"

I whirled around to face him, laughing. *Invisibility. What a Gift!* It was as powerful as my own, maybe even more so in some circumstances…

"This is why I'm not worried anyone will catch me." His laughing voice came from further away now.

Before I could say anything else, a roar came from the other direction.

Something—or someone—crashed into me.

The massive weight knocked me down, crushing me.

I couldn't breathe.

Dirt covered one side of my face, my shoulder ached where it'd taken the brunt of the fall, and my heart thumped wildly.

Coughing, I turned to the face hovering over me. It came into focus.

My heartbeat kicked up.

A Khaanevaade.

"Where is your prince?" a deep voice growled. "He was just with you!"

"He's not here," I said loudly, hoping Shem would hear me and stay invisible. His Gift would allow him to take this Vaade by surprise. He would fight for me... *wouldn't he?* My body trembled, giving away my fear to the big man pinning me to the ground. My arms were trapped.

The Vaade spat a curse. "Jinn and their traveling!"

I chanced another look at him, only to find his terrifying, dragon eyes studying me like a predator when hunting prey. I flinched. Shutting my eyes, I waited for him to strike. Those eyes burned themselves into my memory—like a sunset, but with a black, oval sun in the center.

When I risked another glance, he grinned wickedly, dropping his head lower until his tangled dark hair framed our faces, forcing me to truly look at him. It was impossible not to notice the strange white paint drawn across those fiery orange eyes, like two fingers scraped from forehead to cheek. The white streaks continued in strange designs across his chest where he pressed against me. "I remember you."

Trying to see past the paint, I took in his strong nose, full lips, and the way his thick strands of dark brown hair tickled my bare arms.

It was the same Vaade from the engagement tour.

I sucked in a deep breath, remembering how he hadn't hurt me then. Maybe he'd liked my courage. Despite the way my heart thundered in my chest, I cleared my throat and pretended to be unaffected. "Are you sure we've met?" I asked calmly, as if we were at a tea party instead of pressed up against each other. I dragged my eyes down his body to where the paint disappeared, noting an enormous tooth dangling from a string of hide around his neck, before returning his gaze. "I don't recognize you."

As soon as I said the words, I regretted them. I shouldn't have antagonized him.

He grunted, eyes narrowing.

Shem only had seconds to attack if he was going to rescue me before—

Unexpectedly, the Vaade smirked. "You wouldn't be so calm if you were alone." He lifted his head, sniffing the air. "Is your prince around here? Are you hoping he'll come rescue you?"

Though I didn't like the way the Vaade sounded so excited for the prospect, I certainly hoped so. Or, if Shem had left, I hoped it was to rally the Guard and return immediately.

The way the Vaade stared to one side, nostrils flaring, made me nervous.

If Shem *was* drawing close to attack, then I needed to distract the brute.

Pretending a bravado I didn't feel, I gave the empty orchard a mocking glance. "Do *you* see him?"

His hands curled tighter around my arms, as he focused on me, murmuring, "You were close to him before as well." The way his voice rumbled from his chest into my own was unsettling. "You wore a crown."

Paling, I searched for an explanation. "Lots of Jinn

wear crowns." That was a poor lie, but I said it with a straight face and a partial shrug, as much as I could while pinned to the ground.

The Vaade's lips slowly curled into a smile, and with a sinking feeling, I knew I hadn't fooled him in the slightest. "No. They don't."

"How would you know?" I challenged him, stalling. "I doubt you spend a lot of time in Jinni circles."

Instead of answering, he sniffed the air again, eyes scanning the same trees to one side. My heart raced faster. Shem was trying to get close.

Though I didn't want to compare him to the Vaade, the thick arms pinning me down were twice the size of Shem's and likely making him hesitate. Knowing his preference for strategy, he'd be waiting for the right moment. But if he didn't hurry up, there might not *be* a right moment. Trying and failing to take a full breath under the weight of the big man, I sucked in shallow breaths instead, with rising speed.

If Shem didn't act soon, I would.

"I was hoping to finally catch the prince," the Vaade murmured without taking his eyes off the empty space. "But we've run out of time, so you'll have to do."

Eyes widening, I was about to shift into something—anything—with claws, no longer caring if another Jinni saw my secret Gift anymore, when his weight suddenly lifted.

I could breathe again.

THE SECRET CURSE

The Vaade had disappeared completely.

Whipping my head around, I leapt to my feet, trying to watch every part of the orchard at once.

Was that Shem? Had he traveled with the Vaade?

There!

A few dozen paces away, the Vaade reappeared, stumbling into a tree. Just like in the first attack, they hadn't gotten far before he seemed to drop out of traveling like an anchor. "You!" he roared, pointing at me. "What did you do to me?"

I tensed to travel.

With a leap, he crossed the distance between us faster than I expected, crushing me in his grip and hauling me over his shoulder.

My head whipped back painfully.

I had only a split second to search for Shem as the Vaade flung us through the open portal.

There.

His horrified face appeared in the same place the Vaade had materialized.

After that, it all happened in a single heartbeat.

My whole world shimmered and shifted around me.

The cheerful orchard with its carefully groomed walking paths turned into a dark forest full of thick undergrowth that swallowed us up.

Thin pine trees shot up all around us, so tall that I couldn't even see the top through the branches covered in needles.

Even the sun was smaller.

We were in the human world.

From behind me, a new voice called, "Close the daleth!"

5

I WAS SURROUNDED.

Khaanevaade loomed over me on all sides with blank, unreadable faces. At least a dozen men and women, all streaked with white paint, wearing animal furs that blended in with the forest around us.

Light hardly dared to peek through the trees, turning them into dark silhouettes in the dusky green gloom. Leaves and twigs crunched beneath me as I struggled against the Vaade's hard body. A violent tearing sounded as my skirts ripped.

He eased back suddenly.

I lurched forward, but his strong hands held their grip on my arm, tightening when I resisted.

Taking in the fearsome group surrounding me, I tried to think past the panic clawing at my mind. If I shifted now, I'd have to make it count. There were so many of them. And where was Shem? Had he traveled after us?

Had there been enough time?

Even as I searched the surrounding forest for a glimpse of his face, some part of me knew he hadn't followed. He was the sole heir to Jinn. He'd never put himself in that type of danger, not even for me. His father had drilled it into him at a young age.

Still, I dared a glance at my captor, hoping to see him sniff the air for Shem again.

Instead, he lifted me to my feet roughly.

"This is not the prince," one of the other Vaade snapped at him. "Your father said to get the *prince*."

My kidnapper snorted and didn't bother to explain himself, holding me tight. "Make sure they can't reopen the daleth before we go."

My free hand lifted halfway to the little vial around my neck, still hidden underneath my dress. This was my chance to use the paralytic.

Almost a dozen eyes followed the movement.

I changed direction and pulled a twig out of my hair.

There were too many of them.

The vial only held enough for two or three at most.

My mind raced through the other possibilities.

I could shapeshift into a little creature and run, or a large creature and fight, or use my manipulation to make them let me go—though that would only work on one or two.

If all else failed, I could simply travel away, couldn't I?

THE SECRET CURSE

From what I remembered of the last attack on Tel Sheba, the Vaade man had grown disoriented when the Jinni dragged him along. If I traveled enough times, he'd let go, wouldn't he?

Unless he somehow anchored himself again, like he had before…

Around us, the Vaade moved on silent feet where the daleth had been.

When I tried to peer over the shoulder of the big Vaade holding me, he put pressure on my arm to hold me back. With a frustrated glance, I turned away to find a dozen more dragon eyes pinned on me. It gave me the distinct impression of how a wolf might study a helpless sheep.

Though I wasn't completely defenseless, the sheer number of them made me tremble.

I could fight, poison, or outrun one or two Vaade, but over a dozen?

I wasn't sure.

With the Vaade's big hand wrapped around my arm, I was afraid to start something that I might not be able to finish.

As if he could hear my heartbeat pick up, his fingers tightened to a bruising strength, and I could almost sense him growing roots. He expected me to fight back. Maybe he even *wanted* me to attack.

"That hurts!" I hissed at him under my breath.

"Then stop acting like you're about to run," he replied easily, but his fingers loosened a bit.

A small chuckle ran through the Vaade, making me blush.

"Who says I'm planning to run?" My voice quavered slightly. I cursed the way the adrenaline made my fears rise to the surface.

Though I hadn't expected him to answer, his deep, calm voice said, "Your heartbeat sped up and your whole body tensed."

He had an entirely unfair advantage.

If I traveled now, I might accidentally drag him with me. Once I revealed my ability, I'd lose the element of surprise, so I needed to time this carefully.

"You're misreading the situation," I lied. "I'd be foolish to run when I have nowhere to go."

"You speak the truth," he said with a slight grin, as if we shared a friendly exchange.

Something about his words caused another ripple of laughter among the other Vaade, though.

"Then, we're in agreement. You might as well let me walk on my own."

He chuckled as if that was part of the jest. "Not a chance."

Huffing in frustration, I didn't bother to answer. He couldn't hold my arm forever.

Reminding myself to act fearful, like the foolish little Jinni he took me for, I bowed my head and stayed still.

The panic wasn't fully an act.

He seemed pacified, though, turning to study the

Vaade behind him. Careful not to move my arm, I leaned my head forward and managed to catch a glimpse of what they were doing. They'd drawn shapes in the dirt and were now sprinkling ashes across the space where the daleth had been.

"It's sealed," one of the Vaade told my captor. "No one will follow us."

My heart sank.

That meant Shem couldn't reopen them like he'd hoped. If the daleths were sealed, he'd have no way to find my trail.

"Back to camp," the big Vaade said.

Without another word, he began to drag me through the heavily wooded area. There was no sign of a path.

I tensed. My heart leapt into my throat, racing fast enough to make the Vaade tighten his grip.

We don't know where they're located. Shem's words came back to me.

If the Vaade brought me back to their camp, no one would be able to find me.

With every passing second in this vulnerable position, my fear grew. None of the Vaade spoke as they traipsed through the woods, but they held their weapons ready. They'd fight if I tried anything.

I wasn't pretending to be afraid anymore.

I was alone and painfully aware.

Stay calm and focus on gathering information. I'm sure Shem's rallying the Guard right now. Maybe one of the Jinni Guard members would have a Gift for tracking lost Jinn? It was a stretch, but I clung to the idea.

He'll find me, I promised myself. *And if he doesn't...* Swallowing hard, I made myself finish the thought. *If he can't for some reason, I can save myself.*

When the right moment presented itself, that's exactly what I'd do.

I shivered. *Hopefully.*

I'd never attempted to fight so many at once... I could only hope the Vaade would leave me alone at some point.

Distracted by my thoughts, I tripped over the ripped piece of my dress where it dangled crookedly. The fabric tore again. A strip of dirty white fabric fluttered to the ground.

The gruff Vaade yanked me upright, keeping me from slamming face first into the ground.

I pressed my lips together, unwilling to thank him. All he'd done was remind me of his disproportionate strength.

When the time came to fight back, I wouldn't underestimate the Vaade the way the royal family had.

No, I'd wait to use my Gifts until the opportune moment, when they least expected it.

Despite my strategy, my skin tingled feverishly as we wound deeper into the woods until I was thoroughly lost. Every tree looked the same: thick trunks so tall they blocked out most of the sun, with pine needles covering all the branches.

THE SECRET CURSE

It was suffocating.

I nearly risked shifting into a leopard and making a run for it, just to make the panic stop.

The Vaade's fingers curled tighter around my upper arm when my heart rate increased.

I tried to slow my breathing.

Don't give yourself away yet. There's only one chance to surprise them.

I allowed him to shove me on through the endless trees.

An hour passed. Maybe more.

If there weren't a dozen Vaade following us, I might've tried to cut my dress and drop scraps to leave a trail.

Each time I glanced back over my shoulder, however, a dozen dragon-like eyes in varying shades of fire stared back at me from dark faces streaked with white paint.

Many of these Vaade had the same thick tangled hair as my captor, with little gold circlets decorating some of the rope-like strands. They wore animal hides and furs with splashes of color in a necklace here, feathers there, or sometimes red paint streaked across a chest or face. Despite the cool shade, there were a *lot* of bare chests and arms.

Though my heart continued pumping rapidly, the chaos in my mind was clearing with the quiet walk.

They were taking me to their *camp.*

The one location that Shem said our people had been

unable to find.

And they were taking me directly to it.

What if I let them?

If I pretended to be weak and defenseless a bit longer, they'd lead me right to it, finally revealing their home. I could escape with the knowledge of where to attack.

It could change the entire war.

Not to mention, I'd finally get to set another wedding date.

I made my decision.

He'd kidnapped the wrong Jinni.

When the time was right, I'd make them pay.

Despite my decision to stay of my own free will, the instinct to flee refused to fade completely, making me jumpy.

A wiry older man strode forward, pushing through the group. When I saw his bare, muscled thighs and chest, I realized his only covering was a small flap of animal hide over his groin and backside.

My face flooded with color. I whipped around to face forward.

It didn't do me any good.

Seconds later, he fell in step with my captor and I at the lead, giving me an eyeful of his chiseled arms and chest that almost rivaled my captor's own, despite the gray in his hair. "You can't bring it back to the camp," he hissed. "Koda, your father will be furious."

THE SECRET CURSE

If I hadn't been forcibly connected to the Vaade, I wouldn't have noticed the brief hesitation. His face didn't change. His feet didn't slow. But one stride faltered slightly. This "Koda" jutted his chin out. "I don't care."

With a glance at me, the other Vaade shoved himself in front of Koda until he couldn't continue without running the man over. As he swung around, a long bow and a quiver full of arrows on his back became visible.

For a split second, it looked like Koda might keep walking right through the other man. He stopped so close that they breathed the same breath, both scowling. "Ahriman. Move."

Ahriman only stared back at him. His face was hard and unreadable. Like Koda, he had heavy brows and a strong nose, but unlike Koda, his lips were thin and pressed together.

Shoving me roughly behind him, without loosening his grip on my wrist, Koda hissed something else in Ahriman's ear. The exchange was brief and too soft for me to hear. I wanted to make this Koda regret turning his back on me—a foolish mistake—but I also didn't want to give away my strength quite yet, while I was still outnumbered, so I waited impatiently.

When he finally stepped back, my brows shot up at his next words. "We'll use a blindfold." It wasn't spoken to me. He didn't even look at me.

"No, thank you," I replied anyway, but they all acted like they didn't hear.

I considered using my newest Gift of manipulation.

Since I'd yet to learn how to use it without both eye contact and somehow touching my subject, I'd be forced to twist at an awkward angle to look at Koda. *If* he let me. While the other dozen Vaade stood on and watched.

I chewed on my lip. It might ruin the element of surprise if I couldn't manage to control him or if the others stopped me.

Act naturally, I told myself, turning to attempt it without anyone else catching on. Koda clamped a hand on my shoulder, stopping me.

I drew in a deep breath and sighed, pinching my eyes closed, and spoke without my Gift. "I'd rather not have a blindfold."

"It'd *rather not*," another Vaade mocked, and they laughed as a female Vaade stepped forward.

I tensed.

She wore a long deerskin tunic with a wide neck that bared her graceful shoulders. Pulling a wicked looking knife from her belt, she bent to cut a strip of the thin hide from the bottom of the dress.

I frowned as the strip formed.

She stood.

My hands trembled.

It was torture to keep still. I reminded myself of my new plan: *find their camp. Wait until they let their guard down. Then escape with a clear path and valuable information.*

Glancing at me so briefly I almost missed it, Koda

held out a hand to the Vaade woman. "Give it to me."

I matched the Vaade woman's scowl as she stepped forward to hand it over.

Koda turned to face me, blindfold in hand.

Shaking, I imagined shifting my fingers into claws and slashing it into pieces—or wrapping my hand around his wrist and whispering, *You want to let me go.*

With a frustrated breath, I lifted my chin and glared at the Vaade.

While the blindfold wasn't ideal, it didn't affect my plan. Once they brought me to their camp, I'd flee. There'd been over a dozen daleths on that map back in the castle—if I could remember where even one of them was, I could travel there and return to Jinn. I'd alert the Guard immediately and they could follow my trail back to the Vaade camp. We'd finally have the upper hand, thanks to me.

While Koda wrapped it over my eyes, I stayed still, hands clenched at my sides until he finished.

"We should take its clothes," someone sneered. "A naked Jinni is a humble Jinni."

I tried to hide the way I clutched the skirts of my dirty red dress. It'd felt so empowering this morning, but now it felt like my last defense against them.

Absolutely not.

I might be forced to fight after all.

"The Jinni needs a lesson in humility," someone else snapped. When a few of the other Vaade yelled in agreement, I instinctively stepped away from the sound.

And right into Koda's hard, bare chest.

"No," Koda said simply. This time when he pressed me behind him, I didn't mind nearly as much. "We'll blindfold her and no more." Koda didn't raise his voice, but he clearly expected obedience.

I hope he's their leader. It'd seemed like it at first, but when he'd submitted to Ahriman, I'd assumed it must be him instead. Now, though, they *all* complained about my presence loudly as if each had a say.

I shivered, unable to help myself.

They argued as if there were no consequences. In Jinn, *no one* argued with the king and queen. If they did, they'd be silenced immediately.

"At least make sure it can't see anything," a male voice said, and the bitter grumbling sounded like Ahriman.

Koda listened to him and pulled on the cloth, tugging a piece of my hair caught up in it.

I winced. "How far do I have to walk like this?" I dared to ask, trying to appear unfazed.

No one responded.

Without my sight, I felt off-balance. The Vaade were so quiet that if Koda's hand wasn't around my wrist, I'd have thought they'd left.

We began moving again.

Almost immediately, I tripped.

When Koda moved his hand from my wrist to my arm, I flinched.

THE SECRET CURSE

It could be worse, though.

Most of these violent Vaade wouldn't think twice about killing me, but my captor at least seemed to be sane... More than the others, anyway.

Maybe he could even be reasoned with.

"I can work with you, if you'll let me," I tried in a quiet but firm tone. "We could come up with some terms for peace that I could bring back to the royal family?"

"We don't want peace," he growled in my ear, tugging on my arm to keep walking.

I stumbled a bit, mostly because it was unexpected. Once I righted myself, his grip on my arm kept me surprisingly steady. "What *do* you want, then?" I said back without thinking, and accidentally let some of my frustration seep into my tone.

Instead of infuriating him, it made him chuckle. "Many things."

I drew in a deep breath, trying to keep my temper, and replied in an even tone, "Such as?"

"Power," he replied simply.

Frowning made the blindfold shift, and it began to itch. I reached up a hand to rub the spot, but someone on my other side yanked my arm down roughly. I yelped.

There were sounds of a scuffle.

For a brief second, my captor let me go.

I stood still.

A thump sounded, followed by a grunt of pain.

Someone fell to the ground near my feet and I jumped back instinctively. As I did, I tripped over an unseen root. A warm hand caught my waist, keeping me upright, then wrapped around my wrist once more.

What just happened?

My body tensed, not knowing who held me now, until he spoke, "Come." After a slight pause, he added, "And don't touch the blindfold."

I recognized his voice. Relaxing, I let Koda lead me through the woods, finding myself leaning closer to him now.

Behind us, the other Vaade followed silently.

My mind raced as we walked.

If I'd interpreted it correctly, that was twice now he'd kept me safe. I would stay close to him. Not that I'd be with the Vaade much longer. Only long enough to find their camp and have something to report back home.

Koda surprised me by continuing our conversation, though his voice faded as he turned away, almost as if he were talking more to the others than to me. "We want power over the Jinn—not to abuse it, but to be stronger and better so that your kind never take advantage of ours again. And we're prepared to take it."

A few grunts of agreement came from behind us. "More than prepared," one of the men added, and a few others laughed.

That caught my attention. "Take it?" I repeated softly, not liking the sound of that.

"Yes," he replied with another one-word answer, and this time it was clear I wouldn't get any farther.

Unease crawled over my skin.

Was learning the location of their camp really the advantage Shem hoped it'd be, or was an attack from Jinn exactly what they wanted?

6

AFTER WALKING AT LEAST an hour across uneven ground, my ears picked up voices in the distance, growing louder as we approached. We must be nearing their camp. As we stopped weaving around unknown obstacles—trees, I assumed—our path smoothed out as well. A clearing? Or had we left the forest behind altogether?

I tried to control my nervous reaction, to keep my heart from picking up speed. It was almost time.

Koda's grip tightened anyway.

My feet ached and my arm was already sore, so I opened my mouth to complain, but before I could, his deep voice whispered in my ear, "Don't speak. You'll regret it."

Pursing my lips to hold back the torrent of questions, I scowled in his general direction.

He probably didn't even notice.

THE SECRET CURSE

What did he mean? Who would make me regret it? Him? Or was he warning me about someone else?

Only his actions back in the woods convinced me to listen.

For now.

As soon as I confirmed this was their camp, however, I planned to run.

"Dragon." Koda's tone was deferential.

Not a *real* dragon? An involuntary shiver touched my skin. I caught myself and shook my head. It must be a strange title for the Vaade leader… Despite the obvious logic, my fingers itched to rip off the blindfold to confirm.

"The prince continues to evade us," Koda was saying. "But we stole something equally valuable to them."

Some*thing*? I had to bite my tongue to keep from snapping, *I'm not a thing!*

"They only have one son!" a voice even deeper than Koda's rasped. He even sounded like a dragon. I shivered again. "Any other Jinni is worthless! Get rid of it."

Eyes widening behind my blindfold, I could only assume he meant to kill me. The way he spoke sounded like he was used to being obeyed too.

Against Koda's advice, I called out, "I'm not worthless! I can influence the royal family!"

There was a long pause.

A growl so animalistic it made the hair raise on my arms came from the same direction as this "dragon's" voice.

As I flinched back, the blindfold shifted the tiniest bit, allowing me a glimpse of two moccasin-covered feet coming to stand in front of me.

When he answered, that deep voice held a tremble of barely contained fury. "What does it mean?"

It.

He wasn't even addressing me. He was talking to Koda.

"She's important to the prince," Koda replied, fingers squeezing my arm to convey his frustration.

"His betrothed," I corrected.

His fingers dug into my soft skin harder, and I gasped.

Another stretch of silence passed.

"Take it to one of the longhouses."

"I'm not sharing space with *that*," someone yelled, and what sounded like a few dozen other voices echoed the sentiment, startling me. For some reason, I'd imagined the Vaade fighters as a smaller group. How many Vaade were here?

The leader allowed the dissent, just like Koda had. Even more shocking, he *listened*. Raising his voice, he called, "Where would you have me put our prisoner, then?"

"A deep ravine!" someone snarled.

"Below ground," said another.

It took all my willpower not to recoil.

Koda's calm voice spoke up, and while it was

probably meant to be a question, it seemed more like a statement. "The smokehouse."

Chatter quieted.

"Acceptable," the Dragon said, voice fading as if he was already turning away. "It will need to be spelled. Take it to the longhouse until the smokehouse is prepared."

Without further debate, I was dragged forward through a hissing crowd. Holding my head high, I ignored the urge to cower away from sounds, to hide behind Koda's big, bare shoulder. I wouldn't let them see the pure terror snaking through my body.

Unfortunately, my uncontrollable trembling told Koda the truth.

My plans were falling apart. This was the Vaade camp, but with each new Vaade voice I heard around me, fleeing seemed even more impossible. How could I take on so many?

Bright sunlight beaming through the blindfold cut off abruptly, turning my world pitch-black.

I shuffled forward.

"Stop there or you'll hit a wall," Koda's voice rumbled beside me as he tugged my arm.

I sucked in a breath and stumbled slightly when the blindfold was ripped off.

At first, I thought we were in a dark cave. But as my eyes adjusted, the room took shape.

It was truly a long house, like the leader had said, with one big room stretched out, made of thick logs and some kind of sweet-smelling mortar.

We stood at the far end, tucked away in the back, next to a pile of animal skins resting on the dirt floor. Beyond us were sleeping bunks built into the walls that went on and on, though most were empty at this time of day. They hinted at a huge number of people living in this building alone.

One of the longhouses, the Dragon had said. There were more of these? Clearly the royal family underestimated the Vaade numbers.

In the center, a cooking fire was surrounded by dozens of tree stumps, which Vaade were using as seats. Men, women, and even children moved around the fire, shooting curious glances in our direction. Or, at least, the children were curious. Most of the adults were openly glaring.

Directly above the fire, a single opening in the ceiling allowed wisps of smoke to curl up and out while the Vaade around it cooked and ate. Sunlight lit up the cozy circle, but couldn't quite touch us this far back.

It was oddly communal.

Koda let go of my wrist.

I'd grown so used to the pressure that I felt almost weightless. *Free.* I could travel if I wanted to.

Though I tried to hide my reaction from him and the Vaade who'd entered behind him, he caught my expression. "The longhouse is spelled against traveling, and the smokehouse will be very soon as well. Something

THE SECRET CURSE

we learned from *your* people."

Just like the castle. Hearing this and knowing it to be true were two different things, however. *What if he's only saying that to prevent my escape?* Now that we were here, I couldn't stand to wait anymore.

I attempted to travel outside the longhouse.

A barrier stopped me at the wall, flinging me back.

Oof.

I fell on the hard-packed dirt.

My chest ached. The enchantment had knocked the breath out of me. Coughing as my lungs spasmed, I blinked, trying to clear my head.

I hadn't tested a boundary spell since I was little. I'd forgotten how much they hurt. But my pride hurt more. Cheeks burning, I ignored Koda and the others looming over me.

Though he kept a straight face, the others chuckled.

"They never listen," one said.

Another agreed. "They always think they know better than us."

Mutters of "fool Jinni" and "the Dragon should never have allowed this" followed that statement, and some of the onlookers opened the door to leave.

I pulled myself to my feet, trying to ignore them and the pain in my backside that rose with my fury.

If they thought they wouldn't have tried too, they were lying to themselves.

Though I fully intended to feign indifference, my eyes still flew to the door as it closed, marking the loss of my only escape route.

"Two guards at all times," Koda was saying as he moved through the group. "Bull and Kele to start."

I panicked slightly as two of the Vaade swung around to face me with hands on their unsophisticated weapons—mostly knives in a variety of sizes, though all of them were large enough to slice off an arm. One of them also carried a bow and arrows. "You're not staying?"

Koda didn't look back at me. He barely even hesitated at the door, but it was long enough for the other Vaade to begin jeering, "Koda and the Jinni? Who would've thought—the Dragon's son has a soft spot for one of the lying snakes."

That confirmed my suspicion that he was the leader's son.

He didn't answer the taunts, or me, shoving through the door and slamming it behind him.

That left me with the two guards and a handful of other Vaade staring at me like a prized horse. "Did you see how it talked to Koda? How strange..." One of the women spoke to a friend loud enough for me to hear.

With a huff, I turned my back on them and dropped down to sit on the pile of furs. My vibrant red and white dress looked especially out of place against the dirt floor. Next to their simple deerskin tunics and colorful woven skirts, my crystal covered gown stood out, and not in a good way.

THE SECRET CURSE

Though it was difficult to ignore dozens of eyes on me, I pretended not to notice, tentatively leaning back against the wall. Instead of being rough and scratchy, as I'd expected, it was rubbed smooth. I was surprisingly comfortable. Or, at least, I would've been, if I hadn't had an audience. I felt like a captured Lacklore put on display for entertainment.

I wished I hadn't waited to run. I should've pulled free back in the forest. All I would've needed was a moment of surprise, but I'd hesitated too long.

Closing my eyes, I drew my hand slowly over the soft pelt beneath me, over and over, calming myself with the motion. It worked briefly. Until my troublesome mind pointed out that I was petting a dead animal, specifically one that the Vaade had killed.

Heartbeat in my ears, I stilled through sheer willpower, pretending to fall asleep.

Stuck here without a plan, I finally faced the questions I'd been avoiding—why did they take me prisoner? What were they planning for me? And more importantly, how would Shem find me if they'd never been able to find the Vaade camp before?

I needed to get out of this longhouse and travel back to Jinn—or rather, to the nearest daleth.

Peeking out beneath my dark lashes, I confirmed that the dozens of eyes in the room were all still aimed in my direction.

If I shifted into a flea, odds were good they'd step on me before I could crawl out through a crack in the wall.

Even if I shifted into a large animal to attack these two ridiculous guards, and somehow fought past all the others, I didn't know if there was a portal nearby. During the Vaade's last attack, they'd traveled a good distance from camp before opening a daleth.

If they were opening and closing the portals as needed, that likely meant we were a good distance from any nature-made daleth.

Keeping my eyes closed, I tried to envision the map of all the daleths in the human world—why hadn't I studied it closer? Though I had a rough sense of the landscape, I couldn't picture the names of any of the nearby human cities.

Maybe it'd only take a day or two to find a daleth, but it could just as easily take weeks. Especially if there was nothing marking the portal's presence.

I nearly groaned out loud. I hadn't thought of that before.

My earlier plans to travel straight home from the Vaade camp felt foolish now.

A traveling trail faded in a few days at most.

If it took longer than that to find a daleth, any trail I might leave behind would be long gone.

Even if I somehow marked the trail physically or remembered landmarks that could lead me back, that plan still depended on the assumption that the Vaade wouldn't pick up and move.

The seemingly simple task I'd created for myself

THE SECRET CURSE

now seemed impossible.

My shoulders sagged.

Hot tears pricked my eyes unexpectedly.

I'm in over my head, I finally admitted.

If the only way to prove myself to the royal family was through dying here in the Vaade camp, I'd prefer to remain insignificant and live.

Blowing out a breath, I returned to my original plan: I'd cut my losses and look for the next chance to run.

The opportunity would present itself if I could be patient. Perhaps when they transferred me to this "smokehouse."

The number of Vaade increased as they gathered around the small cookfire at the other end of the room for the noon meal.

Everyone left to join them except my guards.

I sat up expectantly.

My mouth watered at the smells of bread and meat cooking, but no one offered me anything.

As the afternoon passed, the sunlight pouring in through the opening in the roof grew dimmer much sooner than I expected, hinting at either a storm approaching or some other enormous form blocking the sun. A mountain perhaps? That could help me find my bearings once I got away.

I will *escape,* I assured myself again as my stomach growled, trying to keep my spirits up.

Wrapping my arms tightly around myself, I glared at the onlookers who'd returned to ogle me. They discussed me with each other like a fancy pet.

"It's bad-tempered," a nearby Vaade woman whispered.

I rolled my eyes. "*She* can hear you."

The woman spat at my feet. "You are not to speak." Turning to the two Vaade that Koda had set to guard me, she snapped, "Punish it."

The one with his knife out at the ready leaned forward on the balls of his feet, as if tempted, but something held him back. "Not worth it." I probably had Koda's reaction back in the forest to thank for that.

With a huff, the Vaade woman turned on her bare heel, storming out of the longhouse. A few others followed. As the hours passed, and I ceased to do anything else of interest, the group of onlookers slowly dwindled again. After the evening meal, only the two guards were left.

This might be my best chance. Maybe even my *only* chance.

"What am I to do for personal needs?" I asked as delicately as I could, slowly standing, pretending not to notice the way they tensed. When their faces remained blank, I sighed, shifting on my feet as if my need was urgent. "Is there a bathing room, or somewhere I can go for privacy?"

This time, the blank faces had to be intentional. I clenched my fists. "I'd like to hope that your people don't usually soil the floor in their own home," I said, gesturing to the space around me, as I moved toward them. "So I'll be going outside to—"

They stepped in front of me, blocking my path.

"Go get Koda," I tried next. "Explain to him that even a Jinni has needs…"

They refused to respond.

Fine. I'd take my chances.

Narrowing my eyes at them, I moved my hands behind my back and began to shift. "If you insist on treating me like an animal," I said softly in a dangerous tone. "Then maybe I'll act like one."

Without warning, I finished the shift. Looming over them with the height of a bear and the claws to match, I lunged.

I landed on empty space.

Where the two Vaade guards had stood, now there was only hard packed dirt beneath me.

Roaring my fury, I spun around.

Something sharp plunged into my shoulder. With a yelp, I flung the attacker off.

He slammed into the wall behind me.

Before I could react, the other Vaade was on my back, pushing that knife in my shoulder deeper. Pain streaked through my body.

Swinging around, I raked my sharp claws across the Vaade, grabbing him by the shoulder and slamming him to the ground, unconscious. Instead of long, deep gouges along his body where my claws landed, there were only light scratches.

There was no time to process that.

The far door burst open, crashing into the wall, and Koda strode through it.

He was the only one who'd treated me even remotely decent. I didn't want to hurt him… but I would if I had to.

Snapping my sharp teeth in warning, I darted away from him toward the door at my back.

Once again, the Vaade strength and speed caught me off guard. He crossed the room in one big leap. A heavy weight crashed into me before I could squeeze through the exit, forcing me to retreat.

I eyed him for only a moment, then lumbered as fast as I could in bear form across the longhouse, aiming for the door on the opposite side.

He landed in front of it while I was still a dozen paces away.

Digging in my heels, I stopped in the middle of the room.

We stared at each other.

He was effectively blocking all the exits, unafraid of me. And why should he be? These Vaade were more powerful than I'd been willing to believe. Shem's claim that they were true rivals of the Jinn might actually be true.

I couldn't win this way.

So, I did the one thing he wouldn't expect.

Backing up slowly, I stepped beneath the circle of light from the smoke hole in the ceiling.

THE SECRET CURSE

I leapt into the air, shifting at the same time.

Koda's eyes widened.

With one powerful push off the ground, he soared through the air in my direction.

My bear form had taken me over halfway to the ceiling as I shrunk smaller and smaller, until I was a tiny fly—a form I'd shifted into often enough to know it would come quickly.

I flapped my clear, membranous wings the last few beats to the opening.

I still underestimated Koda.

His eyesight had to be incredible.

Though I made it through the opening, wings pumping, his huge hand shoved through after me, nearly snatching me out of the air.

His fingers closing in a fist below me caused an air current so strong I was flung forward, spinning end over end, flying wildly until I could right myself.

A second later, his hand disappeared back inside the longhouse.

He'd be outside and on me before I knew it.

The fly form wasn't good enough.

With no time to waste, I shifted into an eagle with a generous wingspan, pushing myself to make the change faster than I ever had before.

I flew straight toward the sun, where it was making its way across the sky. *How high can the Vaade jump?* I didn't know the answer, and I couldn't risk misjudging again, so I soared past the tall trees and then higher still, until the air grew thin.

Like I'd guessed from inside the longhouse, a mountain range trailed along one side of the Vaade camp.

Despite the throbbing pain, hope rose.

There.

In the distance, the mountains formed steep cliff walls—just like the map of the human world back at the castle.

Though I didn't see any dragons from this distance, it *had* to be the same one. After all, how many massive mountain ranges in the human world could have a sheer set of cliffs like that?

Circling, letting the air currents carry me along, I searched for a nearby human town.

Nothing.

Doubt dragged me down, but I pushed through it, turning back to the mountains. I'd paid careful attention to that daleth so I could describe its location to Shem. The one defining detail I remembered was the town close by. If it wasn't here, then it must be on the other side of the mountains.

Looked like I'd be crossing them.

I risked a glance back.

The Vaade camp was already far behind me. Koda would be a tiny speck, but in my eagle form I might still be able to spot him.

Other Vaade milled about their camp—a few hundred, maybe more, including women and children, which was far more than I'd expected from the voices I'd heard—but Koda was nowhere to be seen.

It didn't matter.

I knew where to go now. All I had to do was make it to the other side of the mountains.

I pushed myself on, aiming for the summit of the nearest cliffs.

As I flew, the shock and panic wore off, and my wing began to burn where the knife had struck.

Ignoring it, I glided on. But as time passed, it became harder to overlook.

I tried to move the wing less and less. That caused me to sink lower in the sky, dropping toward the forest.

The searing ache steadily grew, turning intense. I couldn't go much further. Floating in a slow circle, I would've frowned if this form was capable. I could hardly keep the wing extended, much less reach that peak in the distance.

Perhaps I should land briefly to rest and catch my breath.

The cliff heights I'd originally aimed for were still so far away.

Too far.

But the wound in my shoulder threatened to give out.

If I didn't land soon, my body might force me into a dangerous descent.

Since the Vaade camp was no longer visible behind me, I gave in to the urge.

Flapping the damaged wing as little as possible, I

glided down into the woods and landed on an open branch near the top of a tree.

For a long minute, I just perched there, trembling.

My body hurt too much to shift.

So, I simply sat.

The shaking continued as I waited for my strength to return, but it didn't. After not eating all day and shifting so many times, I would've been exhausted anyway, but with this wound, I could hardly see straight.

I didn't know how much time was passing but I also didn't care.

The Vaade threat was over.

My concern now was this wound. If it was as bad as it felt, I didn't know if I could continue flying or if I should settle in for the night.

Finally, I twisted my neck to look at the damage. Fresh blood still leaked from the deep wound, dripping down to the forest floor. The sight made me dizzy. I nearly fell from the branch and had to flap my wings to catch my balance. The movement shot agonizing pain throughout my whole body all over again.

My wound was worse than I'd wanted to admit. If I didn't get back to Jinn soon, I might die out here.

I needed to find that daleth.

Racking my brain for a sense of where I was, based on those nearby cliffs, I tried to decide if I should shift so I could travel or remain in this form and attempt to fly again.

THE SECRET CURSE

My energy was draining fast. Maybe I should shift while I was still capable.

But traveling would be restricted in the trees. With the density of the woods, I could only see a short distance, which meant it'd hardly be any faster than walking.

Flying was the obvious decision—but when I tested my wing, trying to lift it, black spots filled my vision.

I breathed shallowly through the pain.

No. Flying wasn't an option.

Something tickled the back of my neck, an animal instinct of sorts, making me look down just in time to see a Vaade form launch himself off the forest floor and up through the trees toward me.

Squawking, I flew without thinking, barely making it out of his grasp. A sharp yank on my tail feathers made me screech again.

Circling away, out of range, I let out another angry caw at the sight of two of my tail feathers in the Vaade's fist.

It was Koda.

7

THOUGH MY INJURED WING ached so badly my eyesight blurred, I strained toward the cliffs once more. I'd fly higher. Ride the air currents. Push past the all-consuming fire in my wing.

Somehow, I'd get to that daleth.

The sun was setting where it peeked between the mountains, casting the tops of the trees in a golden light.

"I only want to talk," Koda called after me, before I could fly out of earshot. "I have a deal to offer you."

When I ignored him, he yelled louder, "I tracked you here. I can find you again!"

I hesitated, letting myself sail on an air current for a moment, resting my throbbing wing.

"Even if I couldn't smell your blood, your magic is a trail, plain as day!"

My hopes sank.

It didn't matter if I flew for the portal or not. He'd

capture and kill me before I ever had the chance to find it.

I'd never get home.

"Come speak with me," he yelled, though his voice was growing faint in the distance. "I mean you no harm."

Lies! I wanted to shout back. But perhaps he might pretend a truce long enough for me to recover?

After another long beat, I finally circled back. *I'm listening,* I thought, as I hovered on an air current, wishing he could hear my response. Flapping my wings only when I absolutely had to, I stayed in the air. He'd have to take the hint because I didn't dare land. He could make all the promises he'd like, but that didn't mean I trusted them. Trusted *him*.

"I want to make a deal," he repeated, head flung back, waving an impatient arm for me to land.

My only response was to look away toward the cliffs. *Talk fast,* I thought now, struggling to stay airborne. I couldn't do this much longer, and there was no way I'd come any closer.

Were other Vaade hiding somewhere nearby? I couldn't see them anywhere, but that didn't mean much. I hadn't seen Koda coming either. Even if I landed far away from him, they could easily ambush me.

"I came alone," Koda called now, as if he'd guessed my fears. "Not all Vaade would be so lenient. Come. Hear me out."

I don't believe that for a second. I spun away on the wind again.

A few more seconds, and then I had to leave, whether

he'd said his piece or not. *Hurry up,* I tried to urge him mentally.

As the air current disappeared and I was forced to flap my wings again, pain speared my shoulder so intensely I nearly blacked out, spiraling out of control, heading for the forest floor at breakneck speed. I pulled up with extreme effort, wanting to weep at the pain, but I could barely control my descent as I came hurtling through the trees.

I hit the ground in a bone crunching landing.

Koda crashed through the woods toward me, not bothering to hide his advance now.

He'd be on me in moments.

I screamed as I shifted faster than I'd ever done in my life, shuddering through the pain, forcing myself to take on the shape of the most dangerous creature I could think of: the Lacklore. Part bear, part ox, with talons as long and sharp as a dragon, and wicked teeth and horns to match.

It was less agile than the bear I'd chosen earlier, but far more deadly. I only hoped it might be enough.

That last push strained my energy to the point that I could barely stand. If I tried to shift into any other form besides my own right now, I'd fail. Even my own form would be difficult, draining the last of my energy reserves. I hid my unsteadiness by leaning subtly against a tree as Koda came into view.

He slowed, eyeing my new form. His nostrils flared

as he openly sniffed the air, then he nodded to himself. "This is a fascinating Gift you have," he said without a trace of fear, stopping only a few paces away, as if the fact that I could skewer him with one swing didn't bother him at all.

If anything, he seemed intrigued.

I couldn't help but be impressed by his reaction—both to the Lacklore form and my Gift.

A Jinni would've run in the other direction.

Instead, he continued as if there was nothing unusual about it.

"My father wants the prince of Jinn to make a covenant with the Khaanevaade," he began without preamble. "We've spent years crafting this enchantment to mutually benefit our people."

An enchantment? I wanted to ask, but of course I couldn't. It was an intriguing idea, but it could be a bluff. More likely they wanted to kill Shem and end the royal family lineage. Jinn had long lifetimes, but rarely had more than one or two children, if that. Did the Vaade not know that new rulers were chosen once every fifty years? Shem wasn't guaranteed to rule—though, of course, he would. He was loved by the people. Still, if they somehow took his life, another would take his place.

Keeping one eye on Koda, I tried to also watch the forest, flicking my ears back, listening for any surprise visitors. This Lacklore body might've been a mistake. It was better suited to offense than defense, with terrifying fangs and razor-sharp claws. Hopefully the massive body would at least deter any unknown attackers—and Koda.

His sharp eyes took in my response, and he crossed his thick, muscled arms, leaning against a tree as well. "My father believes we can only deal with the prince. But we haven't been able to speak to him. Now that you're here, we might finally get his attention."

Get his attention—for negotiations? Swinging back to face him fully, I considered his words. *Or use me as bait in a trap?*

"I'm the only one who wants to help you," he continued reasoning, though I found that hard to believe. The question wasn't whether or not he had ulterior motives; it was what exactly were they? "The others would happily let you die out here in the forest," he added, making it sound inevitable.

A little voice whispered that maybe he was right. I hadn't even crossed the cliffs yet. Once I did, what if I couldn't find the daleth on the other side? What if I bled out while looking?

Noticing the direction of my gaze, he turned to glance over his shoulder, where the cliffs rose above the trees. "If you go that way, you'll die even sooner," he said with a shrug, crossing his arms as he turned back to me again. "The dragons live in those cliffs. They don't always listen to the Vaade anymore, especially during hatching season. I can't guarantee I'd be able to stop them from eating you."

Trembling overtook my legs. I leaned harder into the

tree. *Dragons.* I didn't want to believe him, but my weary mind chose that exact moment to remember the map back in Jinn. *The drawing of dragons.* That little detail was exactly why I'd remembered the location of the daleth in the first place, when I'd wanted to show Shem.

I squeezed my eyes closed briefly.

"If you come with me"—Koda's voice drew closer—"we can discuss terms with your prince that will allow you to return home."

My eyes flew open. I glared at him until he slowed to a stop, hands up.

Though I hardly understood what he was offering, I was tempted to agree. The burning wound in my shoulder had yet to stop bleeding. Exhaustion threatened me.

Not taking his deal was becoming more of a risk than taking it.

As I deliberated tossing my desperate plans to the wind and accepting the dangerous offer, Koda slowly crouched, glittering eyes on me. "I can see you're spent," he said in a low voice that held a promise of something. "You couldn't beat me in a fight anyway."

I snarled at him.

When he leapt, I expected it this time.

Hurtling my huge body at him, we slammed into each other, but my extra weight took him down.

We hit the ground hard.

Just like the other Vaade, Koda's skin seemed nearly impenetrable—my talons left only shallow scratches along his shoulders and stomach, and he laughed in my face.

I roared my fury and pounded the ground next to his head.

Without warning, his thick arm pulled free and he hit my shoulder, right where the knife had gone in.

Mid-roar I shifted to a scream, snapping back into my Jinni form without thinking, a protective reflex to return to myself before I physically couldn't anymore.

He immediately rolled on top of me, looming much larger now that I'd shrunk to my normal size. Those huge, muscled arms trapped me in on both sides, and his body pressed tightly to mine, making me acutely aware of him. It pressed my wound into the hard ground, setting my entire shoulder on fire.

"Not. Fair." I gasped.

His face was so close that his warm breath brushed my face.

For a long second, I thought he'd kill me after all.

Then he grinned. "Fair doesn't win fights." Slowly, he peeled himself off me, clearly enjoying the way I grew flustered. He crouched next to me, leaning back on his heels, but made no move to capture my wrist or arm.

He probably knew it wasn't necessary.

Breathing hard, I held in a groan.

"Can I trust you to stay?" he murmured as my breathing slowed.

I nodded, wincing when I moved to sit up and it set my shoulder on fire once more. Instead of taking the hand he held out, I sank back to the ground and closed my eyes. I'd reached my limits.

"I knew it," he said on a laugh. "I *knew* you were pretending to be fine."

That annoyed me enough that I cracked open my eyes to glare at him, but I didn't waste any energy on speaking. The woods around us were starting to spin and grow dark at the edges. Or was that my vision playing tricks on me?

"Stay with me," Koda's voice murmured somewhere to my left, but I didn't hear anything more as I lost consciousness.

8

THE SMELL OF SOMETHING spicy and sweet cooking woke me. Opening my eyes was an effort.

Sure enough, to one side, a little more than an arm's reach away, was a cozy fire with a makeshift spit hanging over it, cooking a small, bird-shaped animal. Koda's glowing eyes met mine from the other side of the fire as he turned the meat.

It was dusk now. Stars had yet to come out, but it'd be fully dark soon.

The reflection of the embers gave him a predatory look and yet when I shifted to sit, I discovered a clean bandage wrapped around my shoulder, smelling of an unknown herb that seemed to be doing wonders for my pain.

I crossed my legs awkwardly beneath my long dress, copying Koda's relaxed posture across from me, ignoring the way the white fabric at the bottom of the dress was now a dirty brown.

Pulling the food away from the fire, he finally spoke. "You shouldn't push yourself so hard next time you try to escape."

I coughed. "Next time?"

His lips curved in a wolfish smile.

"Is that—" I tried to find a polite way to ask about the food, but when his grin grew wider, I frowned and got to the point. "Can I have some?"

Nodding, he stood and passed the steaming meat across the fire to me on a stick, returning to a crouch.

I took the stick gingerly. No silverware or plates out here in the forest, but after not eating since the previous morning, I was too hungry to care. Burning my fingers as I held the stick, I ripped meat from the bone with my teeth and gulped it down.

Koda watched me eat in silence, not saying a word when I ate the entire small bird—or was it another animal? I didn't know, and I didn't care. All that mattered to me right now was food and rest. I couldn't shift in my current condition and that left me more vulnerable than I wanted to admit.

When I handed him the stick with only the bones remaining, he tossed it in the fire without taking his eyes from mine. From his pack, he pulled out some yellow bread, pulling a hunk of it off and handing it to me.

"So, you'll come back to camp?" he asked finally, once I'd finished and was unashamedly licking my fingers.

It took me a minute to remember what he was referring to. Negotiations. Convincing Shem to listen, though the details were a little too vague for my comfort. I couldn't remember much else. Maybe he hadn't said. Either way, I didn't really have a choice, did I?

I pursed my lips. "I will if you get rid of the guards."

"Not possible," he replied without missing a beat.

I chewed on my lip, knowing he was right. They'd never allow it. "*You* guard me then."

For the first time since he'd tracked me down, he shifted uncomfortably. "That might raise questions."

"That you might actually *care* for a Jinni?" I asked sarcastically, remembering the way they'd mocked him back at the longhouse. "I doubt anyone will truly believe it."

The silence stretched as he considered. "If you're with me, you won't be able to stay comfortably out of sight."

I snorted at that. "You must not have seen all my visitors."

"We were preparing the smokehouse to hold you," he said, scowling. "They didn't like sharing their space either."

He unbent from where he crouched across the fire, straightening to his full height, towering over me. "I may have conversations where you're not allowed to listen. You will agree to let my sister guard you at these times."

It made sense. They'd never let a Jinni hear

important plans. I couldn't think of an argument for this.

Though I kept my face smooth, my hopes rose. This arrangement might suit me perfectly. I could recover my strength while with Koda and test my Gift of manipulation on them when the opportunity presented itself. It might be too good to be true… But once I was in better condition, perhaps I could manipulate him into leading me directly to a daleth.

If he could be believed, this was a much safer way to get home.

Sighing, I nodded. "Deal."

"Good." He took two steps around the fire to where I sat, leaned down, and offered me his hand.

Hesitantly, I took it. His skin was warm from the fire, and though he could easily crush my fingers, he kept his grip gentle as we shook on it.

I swallowed at the gravity of our deal.

Shaking on it made his shoulders relax, as if he truly believed I'd keep my word. I nearly frowned. I couldn't put my finger on why his trust bothered me, but I wished he wouldn't.

"We should leave," he said, letting go. I almost missed his warmth. "It's a long walk back."

I waved a weary hand in dismissal. "Give me a little more time, and I can use my Gift to travel."

"Absolutely not," he said in a flat tone.

My eyes, which had fallen to the fire, swung up to meet his. "What? Why not? Walking would take the entire night."

"No traveling," he snapped, moving around the fire restlessly. He picked up his pack and went through the contents, almost as if for an excuse not to look at me.

I waited.

If he wanted me to press for answers, he'd be disappointed. I didn't care.

Studying him, I frowned slightly. Okay, fine. I wanted to know a little, but it was purely curiosity. "Why?"

Throwing the pack down roughly after a few more moments, he crouched in front of the fire with a scowl and met my gaze through the thick strands of tangled hair that hung in his face. "Traveling feels akin to riding a dragon hurtling directly down the side of a mountain at breakneck speed."

Raising my brows, I leaned back against a nearby tree. "Do you know what riding a dragon feels like from experience?"

He smirked as he looked up. "Yes."

That left me speechless.

As he returned to his pack, I tried to hold in a groan at the thought of walking. Back when Koda had attacked our engagement tour stop, I'd seen the Jinni travel with him, and it'd clearly left him disoriented. On top of that, it *did* require a certain level of trust. Clearly, I'd misread him. He didn't trust me any more than the other Vaade.

Still. Walking when I felt like this sounded not only miserable, but impossible.

"If we take much longer to return, your father will likely send others out looking for you—and for me," I dared to argue. "And then you won't have your heroic return." *They also might not let you keep your end of our deal,* I added silently.

Yanking the pack closed without pulling anything out of it, he crossed his arms and studied me. "If you're not up to walking, just say so."

"I'm *not* up to walking," I said immediately.

He nodded to himself, calmly setting the bag down. "Then we'll stay here until you are."

I drew in a deep breath and blew it out, confused. Apparently, I'd guessed wrong, and no one else would come looking for us. Or maybe they would, but he didn't care? "Why did you come alone?" I asked finally.

"Because I don't need help to track a lone Jinni and bring her back," he said with a smug expression that grated on my nerves.

"You would if I wanted you to," I muttered to myself, tipping my head back against the tree to look up at the first few stars peeking through the branches. When had it gotten so dark? I'd spent hardly any time in the human world at night, and had forgotten how dim the moonlight was here compared to back home.

"No," he said with that irritating confidence, reminding me the Vaade's hearing was better than most. "I wouldn't." Dropping down to lay by the fire, he closed his eyes, shutting me out.

The arrogance made me want to shift into something

with claws and teach him a lesson.

Maybe I would.

My eyes burned, and I struggled to keep them open.

Maybe in the morning, after a good night's rest and more food. Then I'd show him who he was dealing with. He wouldn't be so quick to underestimate me then.

* * *

Despite the hard ground, I didn't wake until something touched my arm. I lashed out blindly only to yelp at the sudden agonizing pain of moving my injured shoulder.

Blinking away tears, I found a blurry Koda crouching just out of reach, shaking his head at me.

"Typical Jinni," he said with a scowl. "Attacking the hand that feeds it."

At the possibility of more food, I bit my tongue and sat up, keeping my retort to myself. "Breakfast?"

"More like a late noon meal." He handed me some more of that yellow bread he'd kept in his pack, letting me have most of the loaf.

I'd slept through the morning?

As I sat up, another sharp twinge in my shoulder made me flinch.

While I was still rubbing my watery eyes, Koda reached out to unwind the wrapping on my shoulder without asking.

I recoiled slightly before controlling my reaction.

He slowly tugged the bandage around and around.

THE SECRET CURSE

The pressure from his hands was surprisingly light. "Do you foresee the prince coming after you himself?"

Pausing mid-chew, I lowered the yellow bread, insulted that he'd even ask. I wanted to yell at him that Shem cared for me more than any Vaade was capable of understanding. But something held my tongue. Would Shem send help? I hoped so. Would he come for me himself? As much as I'd like to say yes, I couldn't imagine his parents or the council allowing it. "You're fishing for information?" I said instead. "Is that why you're helping me?"

"One of the reasons," he said simply.

Words escaped me. I searched for an underlying meaning—some sort of subtext beneath the simple words like every conversation in Jinn—but failed. "What's that supposed to mean?" I finally snapped.

He hesitated. "Some in our tribe don't feel as strongly about the Jinn as the elders and my father."

I tried to read between the lines. Was one of his reasons... to protect me?

"Some," I repeated. "You being one of them?"

He didn't answer.

"Would admitting it mean crossing a line of some sort?" I said, almost teasing, surprised to find the big, scary Vaade struggling with anything.

Instead of answering, he tugged the last of the bandage from my shoulder. When I glanced down at the exposed wound, I winced. It didn't hurt that badly—it was mostly numb thanks to whatever he'd given me—but seeing the mangled flesh caused a fresh burst of pain.

He took a wooden bowl and a sickly yellow plant from his pack, using a nearby rock to mash the herb until it turned into a thick yellowish paste. "Yellowroot," he said simply, before scooping it out with two fingers and gently spreading it over my wound.

Though he didn't press hard, I still gasped at the sharp pain, tensing. But it faded almost immediately as the paste soaked in and began to work.

He finally met my gaze, and a hint of a smirk crossed his lips. "You point out my pride while ignoring your own. I'll admit to whatever you'd like, if *you* admit that you could never outrun me in your condition."

I scoffed. "I could've gone on for days."

One brow twitched up and back down, so fast I might've missed it if his face weren't inches from mine. He couldn't hide his grin for long though. "Is that a challenge?"

For some reason, my face flushed, and my arm tingled where his fingers brushed the bare skin. "Maybe another time," I said finally, trying not to sound breathless. "When I'm not wounded."

That irritating smirk didn't change, but he didn't remind me that only moments ago I'd claimed that I could outrun him *even* when I was wounded.

"Tell you what," he said, using the edges of the stained bandage to wipe his hands before taking a large hunting knife to the edge of his long deerskin tunic. I frowned at the sound of the hide tearing. "We have a long walk ahead of us. Half a day at least, maybe longer if you're slow. And we also need to hunt."

I noticed he didn't ask if I could walk this time. Apparently, it wasn't optional anymore. Drawing a deep breath, I was surprised to find I felt up to it.

He twisted to continue cutting the long strip from the bottom of his tunic. "Let's just say if you choose to make our walk interesting and try to relocate, I'm not worried."

Relocate? As in travel?

Now I raised a brow. "You're so sure of yourself?"

He grinned. "Absolutely."

Ice slid over my skin, though I kept my face expressionless. Could he really keep up with me if I traveled? Glancing around at the thick forest, my heart sank. With the density of the trees, I couldn't see more than maybe a few dozen paces—and without familiarity of the forest, I could only travel as far as I could see.

Having seen Koda's speed up close, and the way he could leap so far it looked like flying, reality slammed into me with unfortunate clarity.

He wasn't bluffing.

Not only could he keep up with me in these conditions, but he might even be faster.

If Koda heard my heartbeat speed up, he didn't give any indication.

When he took the fresh strip of soft deerhide that he'd cut from his tunic and began to wind it around my arm and shoulder, I swallowed hard.

For an enemy, he didn't seem so terrible.

"I'm not really in the mood to go exploring on my own right now," I said after watching him wrap my wound more carefully than I probably deserved. "I'll keep the invitation in mind for another time, though."

To keep myself from staring at him too closely, I stood as soon as he finished tying the hide tight.

"Though I have no doubt you can take care of yourself," the Vaade's deep, rumbling voice came from behind me in a murmur. "I'd suggest you stick close to me, just to be safe."

Safe from what? Animals? Or other Vaade out looking for me?

When glanced back at him, my eyes caught on the rippling muscles in his arms as he lifted his pack and straightened, and I forgot whatever I'd planned to say. Instead, I nodded at him like a fool, before turning away to hide my burning face.

As his nearly silent footsteps took him away from the fire through the trees, I followed. A twig snapped under my foot. Then another.

Koda sighed and sheathed his knife. "Have you never gone hunting before, Jinni girl?"

I scowled. "My name is Jezebel."

He just looked away.

"And no. Why would I?"

Another long-suffering sigh and he moved forward without another word.

THE SECRET CURSE

Though he acted nonchalant, if I stepped too far off the path he made through the trees, I always found his eyes on me.

Small twinges of pain pulsed rhythmically in my shoulder as we walked, making me move slowly. I tried to listen to the forest but couldn't hear whatever prey Koda was tracking, if any.

"You walk like a buffalo after eating mushrooms," he complained for the hundredth time. "You're scaring all the animals away."

I stifled a laugh. He was accidentally teaching me quite a few things about the animals in this forest.

As the afternoon passed, he taught me how to walk without disturbing all the twigs and leaves until I could manage a nearly soundless approach—at least for Jinni ears. Whenever my stomach growled, Koda pulled out dried meat or flat bread or berries, letting me eat to my heart's content without judgment.

If I ignored the way my shoulder ached and the fact that I'd had to pee behind a bush earlier, this was almost pleasant.

Koda had taken to circling a bit further out from my "stomping footsteps," so when he strode past on silent feet, I didn't flinch.

Without a word, he stilled and put a finger to his lips, staring at the foliage as he pulled a knife from his belt.

He threw it.

The leaves shook with a little tremor, then grew still.

Frowning, I crossed my arms. "Well done," I said

dryly. "You killed a bush."

He chuckled.

Part of me wished he'd be more annoyed by my attitude so I could continue to hate him. It was all too easy to forget he was the enemy when his company was better than almost everyone back home.

Striding toward where the weapon fell, he stooped down, pulling what looked like a dead pheasant from the ground.

My brows rose.

I hadn't even seen it there.

"We should get it cooked for dinner," he said as he gathered nearby sticks for a fire.

My stomach growled.

How had it gotten so late? The entire day had passed, and I'd only thought about escaping a handful of times.

Even now, all I could think about was food.

Without waiting to be asked, I started gathering firewood too, watching him discreetly for a sense of what kind of sticks to gather.

"That should be good." His words pulled me out of my relaxed state of gathering to find he'd already built the beginnings of a flame and was plucking the feathers while he watched the fire grow.

He cooked the bird, and we ate without speaking.

"We should've gotten back to camp by now," he finally said, as the sun dipped below the mountains for the second time, painting everything around us a golden orange and pink. His words seemed overly loud after so much quiet. "We took longer than I expected."

"Is anyone out looking for us?" I wondered out loud.

No answer.

"Or maybe they don't really expect you to bring me back," I taunted, trying to get a reaction. Frustration seeped into my tone when he didn't even glance up. "Well, in that case, we wouldn't want to keep them waiting, would we?"

He turned his back on me.

I shook my head, crossing my arms. Just when I'd almost forgotten our places, he reminded me. I couldn't stand being ignored.

It occurred to me with growing satisfaction that, unlike the engagement tour, I didn't have to accept it this time. "I realize the Vaade are uncultured, but you should know it's rude to ignore someone when they ask a question."

He snorted. "I haven't decided yet if you deserve an answer."

That did it. My calm mask snapped. "If you can't decide whether we're friends or enemies, then let me make it simple for you. *I'm* not the one who kidnapped someone, wounded them, and is holding them hostage."

Those intense fire-colored eyes of his lifted slowly to meet mine. "You weren't the one we wanted." It seemed like he might say more, but then he pressed his lips together. Turning away from me again, he packed up his bag and hoisted it over his shoulder.

The message was clear. *We're done talking.*

I scowled at him. *Enemies it is.*

As the sky continued to darken, he kicked dirt on the fire. Apparently, we weren't staying here. How he thought we could keep going in the dark, I didn't know, but I wasn't about to ask. Maybe his Vaade senses compensated for the lack of light.

Leaving the now smoky pit behind with a creeping sense of anxiety, I trailed after him through the shadowy trees.

His words left a strange sting behind. Obviously the Vaade didn't want me. I'd already known that. He didn't need to explain for me to understand that the prince had value, and I did not. I was no one and nothing, just like I'd always been. Powerless once more.

Darkness slowly settled over us.

The stiff branches and pine needles irritated my skin as I started to brush up against the nearby trees by accident.

The Vaade's big, muscled body, strong nose, and dark hair all became one solid lump ahead of me. An outline that could be mistaken for a small tree or a bush when he was still.

Opening my mouth, I snapped it shut multiple times, before finally blurting out. "I can't see anything."

"That's your problem." His deep voice floated over to me lazily.

In spite of his sluggish tone, I was clearly slowing

him down.

I let a layer of condescension fill my voice, as if talking to a child. "Any chance you've gotten over your ridiculous fear of traveling?"

A growl came from his silhouette ahead, and I allowed myself a small smirk in the darkness.

"My shoulder hurts," I whined next, though the ache was surprisingly minimal. If he didn't slow down, I was going to run face first into a tree. As if to prove my point, in my hurry to catch up to him, I tripped over a tree root.

Koda's voice startled me, closer than expected. "If you're waiting for me to carry you, you'll be waiting a long time."

"It's dark!" I snapped, taking a tentative step forward, then another. My hand caught the bark of a tree right before I would've walked into it.

"Is it?" he asked in a shocked tone. "I hadn't noticed."

Snorting, I stopped walking and crossed my arms.

"Do all Jinn throw childish tantrums? Or just you?" he taunted.

I ignored him, trying to focus.

Carefully, I shifted my eyesight to imitate an owl. Shifting only one body part was always tricky. It needed to still speak to the other body parts and fit seamlessly, despite being at complete odds with the rest of my body. Not to mention the energy it forced me to expend as I shifted. Though we'd eaten an enormous amount a few hours prior, my stomach gurgled softly.

I ignored that too.

Opening my eyes, I blinked a few times to adjust to the new vision. Everything was grayscale, but the trees were darker and Koda's outline a few steps ahead was now clearly visible. Though I couldn't read the details of his expression, I thought his brows seemed to rise when I turned and stared directly at him. Could he see the change even in the dark? That alone made the shift worth it.

Striding past him, I walked with confidence now, able to see the roots trying to trip me and stepping over them.

"You're going in the wrong direction."

Halting, I clenched my fists and turned. "Well, maybe if you'd walk faster, I wouldn't have to guess."

He lifted his arm and pointed to his right.

Refusing to give him the satisfaction of showing my embarrassment, I simply turned in the direction he pointed and began walking once more.

"Are you always this antagonistic?" he asked as he fell into step beside me.

I huffed a laugh in disbelief. "Me? Once again, I ask you: who's the prisoner here and who's the captor?"

He chuckled. Softly, but I still caught it.

Slowing, I allowed him to pass me and take the lead, but instead he kept even with me, walking side by side.

For a few minutes, silence reigned.

"Are the rumors true?" Koda's voice broke the hush unexpectedly.

THE SECRET CURSE

"What rumors?" I took the bait without thinking.

Out of the corner of my eye, his dragon-like eyes were pinned on me. "They say you enchanted the prince."

"Who says that?" I snapped, whirling toward him. Were they using that particular word for dramatic flair, or was someone actually suspicious of my Gift?

He held his hands up, palms toward me. "I have sources."

"Sources?" I repeated, barely noticing that we'd stopped walking as my mind spun with the new information. I didn't know what to focus on first. "That would mean a Jinni willingly shared information with a Vaade. *False* information, by the way."

I started walking again, pushing a branch roughly out of my way as he followed, letting it fling back in his direction. A soft *oof* rewarded me. I started to relax as I finished my thought. "Since I know that's not possible, that means you made up this so-called rumor yourself."

He laughed audibly now. "While I'd love to take credit, I'm afraid I can't."

My mood soured. If he was telling the truth—a big *if*—then I couldn't honestly say I was surprised. Though no one would say something so disloyal to my face, I didn't doubt some were thinking it.

We didn't have time to walk all night. I needed to get back to the Vaade camp, glean as much helpful information as possible, and return to Shem before this insufferable Vaade managed to ruin all my plans for the future.

I'd had enough of this charade.

The sooner this was all over, the better.

While my familiarity with the forest was limiting my traveling to what I could see, there was one place in the human world I'd already seen well enough to travel there.

Reaching out without a word, I gripped Koda's big, muscled arm.

And traveled us back to their camp.

9

WE LANDED DIRECTLY IN front of the longhouse where they'd kept me the first time, since that's all I remembered clearly from my rushed escape.

This time, however, it was dark. Through the woods, I made out three more longhouses, visible only because of the soft glow off their fires inside. Smoke curled out through a hole in each round roof and into the starry night sky.

The line of buildings was slightly uneven as they curved around one side of a large bonfire, where a small number of Vaade huddled.

With a growl, Koda ripped his arm away from me and hurled himself out of reach. Though he caught himself, he nearly tripped as his balance was thrown off. "I told you, *no traveling*!"

I tried unsuccessfully to hide a smirk. "Your way was too slow."

Grudgingly, he returned to my side as nearby Vaade turned to look at us. Some of them stood from the fire and moved in our direction.

Averting my owl-like eyes, I shifted them quickly back to normal.

It was pure instinct.

After so many years of hiding my Gift, it didn't occur to me until I'd finished that it was a waste of energy. Multiple Vaade had seen me shift just the day before.

For the first time in my life, it wasn't a secret.

I shivered, feeling exposed.

Koda stepped closer to add under his breath, "Don't *ever* use your Gifts on me again."

I barely heard him, but his words caused some of the approaching Vaade to titter. He glared at them in return. Their remarkable hearing never ceased to surprise me.

"Where did it go?" one of the women asked Koda, eyeing the bandage on my shoulder.

Half my mind wondered what she was referring to, while the other half slowly registered she meant me.

My mouth soured.

Refusing to react and give her the satisfaction, I instead turned my focus to studying the camp. If I squinted, I could make out some smaller buildings along the far side. A small fire illuminated a structure large enough to house one or two people. Another partial building stood near the big bonfire with only a roof and one wall to shelter a huge pile of stacked wood. And on

THE SECRET CURSE

our side, there was another, even tinier shack. It wasn't nearly large enough to live in. I frowned, wondering what it was for.

When the girl turned her violet dragon-like eyes on me, I ducked behind his big body.

Koda ignored the girl, walking toward that smallest building.

I hesitated.

He'd promised I'd get home.

Though I didn't know if he could be trusted, I could hardly make a second escape this exact moment.

Rest. Eat and drink. Pay attention to anything that could help Shem. Despite my promises to Koda, I'd still run if I had to. But if his way was easier, I'd give it a chance. Shivering at the thought of the dragon cliffs, I tried to shake off the image of dying in the forest that he'd planted in my mind.

I could make it if I had to.

I just hoped I wouldn't have to.

Though it was a war camp, the sounds of children giggling floated on the air, making me wonder if they brought their whole tribe with them each time they moved—or if maybe this settlement was more permanent? The longhouses looked time consuming to build, but then again, what did I know about their construction? Perhaps they built them quickly and then moved on just as fast.

Tilting my head at all the noises coming from within the big building, I couldn't fathom why anyone would want to live in those, without any semblance of privacy. Then again, with their ridiculous sense of hearing, smell, and sight, maybe privacy didn't really exist for the Vaade.

I shrugged, tucking away the information to share with Shem when I returned. I didn't have to understand the Vaade; I only needed to keep my eyes open.

One of Koda's friends elbowed him in the ribs for "letting the weak little Jinni get so far away." Another chimed in, "Took you long enough."

I bit my lip, trying not to smile at the deepening frown on Koda's face and tried to look appropriately subdued. *Maybe I'd been more difficult to apprehend than he let on.*

Behind the longhouse, a small group of Vaade stepped out and strode past. The firelight flickered across their painted faces, arms, and chests.

Koda noticed them at the same time I did. "Where are the warriors going?"

Warriors?

I took a second glance. It looked like the war paint the group had worn when they'd captured me. The hairs on the back of my neck rose at the implication.

The same friend tilted his head meaningfully in my direction, answering Koda, "You know we can't tell you in front of one of them."

Koda blinked away whatever thought flitted across his face, too fast for me to catch it, taking hold of me again—I noticed he chose my uninjured arm, whether by

THE SECRET CURSE

choice or by accident, I couldn't say. He turned and tugged me toward the longhouse. "You'll *stay here* this time. I'll come back shortly."

"No!" I dug in my heels, not caring anymore how it looked. "You promised!"

Ahead of me, inside the longhouse, multiple pairs of dragon-like eyes glowed in the dark shadows. Possibly the same Vaade that I'd left behind last time. My heartbeat kicked up, and I gave Koda a pleading look that I fully expected him to ignore.

His eyes returned to the warriors, where they'd disappeared into the woods. Arguing with me would waste time that he seemed anxious not to lose. "Fine," he snapped, grabbing a torch from one of the Vaade nearby, though they muttered it was a bad idea. He pulled me forward so suddenly I nearly stumbled. "Let's go."

I tried to keep up with his long strides, thankful for the light of the torch. Though he didn't *seem* to be slowing down for me, we somehow couldn't catch up to the others.

Almost as if… were we trailing behind intentionally?

I would've assumed we'd lost them once the trees hid them from sight, but Koda sniffed the air, following his nose, and continued on. I waited until we were—hopefully—out of earshot of both the camp and the so-called warriors, before I whispered, "What does the paint mean?"

I was terrified I already knew the answer, but wanted desperately to be wrong.

"We wear it for significant events," he replied.

"Different lines mean different things."

That told me nothing.

I rolled my eyes. "Yes, but what does *this* design mean?"

He didn't answer.

Irritation prickled my skin, but I refused to make myself look weak by asking again, so we walked on in silence.

Far ahead, a flickering light shone through the trees—glowing, like flames from torches, but also the cooler, ghostly glow of magic—answering my question without him needing to.

A daleth.

"You're still attacking the Jinni islands?" I hissed.

He didn't reply, but the orange torchlight flickered across his face, revealing an uncertain frown.

"Why aren't you with them?"

He growled—actually growled—and kept walking.

Oh right… That was my fault.

Tripping over yet another tree root and wishing I'd kept my night vision, I had to jog a little to keep up. "Your father doesn't trust you to lead the attacks anymore? You'd think he'd wait for you." I probably should've kept my mouth shut.

He whirled to face me, stopping so suddenly I slammed into his chest and nearly bounced off him, grabbing his soft deerskin tunic to keep my balance. My palms flattened across his chest, feeling the muscles tense underneath. While he still held the torch, his free hand had caught me at the small of my back and remained there, warm and steadying. He seemed as surprised as I was, neither of us moving.

Until I cleared my throat and pulled back.

Koda's face flickered with an unreadable emotion, but when he spoke, he was calmer. "I don't know if it's an attack. I don't know where they went tonight. I don't know why they went without me. I've been pursuing *you*, remember?"

My traitorous face blushed. I wasn't going to apologize for that, but I fought not to take another step back, lifting my chin defiantly instead.

"My father may still believe he can capture the prince," Koda said, offering more than I'd expected. "I, however, believe there's a hidden reason we've not been able to locate him so far. A certain Gift…"

I tried not to react.

He studied my face, staring down at me, unblinking.

I swallowed, and it was audible in the quiet forest. The pressure built. If I denied it, that'd only make him more suspicious, but I refused to betray Shem's trust either. So I said nothing at all.

Koda dipped his chin in the barest nod, as if my silence confirmed something. "That's what I thought," he said simply, turning to walk again, though at a slower pace as we drew closer to the daleth.

Now I wanted to kick him. His straightforward conversation had tricked me into letting my guard down, revealing more than I'd meant to. It wouldn't happen again.

I clamped my mouth shut and didn't try to talk anymore.

The portal came into view ahead, flashing with the same white light as the previous one, which I was starting to realize probably meant it was temporary—or somehow still in the process of forming? As if it was not yet stabilized like the nearly invisible daleth I'd seen in the past.

The Vaade warriors were nowhere to be seen.

"They all went through?" I whispered, briefly forgetting my vow to stop speaking to Koda. "And left the daleth unguarded?

"Who would we guard it from on our side?" Koda countered.

Good point.

Still, was it my imagination, or did Koda approach with caution?

"Are we not supposed to be here?" I spoke louder this time, just to annoy him.

He didn't flinch—probably because our obvious torch light was already a dead giveaway we were here—swiveling to pin me with a look. "No," he said slowly, as if speaking to a child. "*You're* not supposed to be here."

Oh.

That made me glance around for any hidden Vaade as we stopped in front of the portal.

THE SECRET CURSE

I shifted on my feet uneasily. There could be an attack happening on the other side right now.

Frustration creased Koda's face.

He wanted to go, but clearly wasn't going to bring me.

Attack or not, though, this was a portal to Jinn.

My first real chance to get home.

Despite my deal with Koda, there was no way I was going to pass this up.

Before he could stop me, I dove for the daleth.

As I crossed through, a rough hand wrapped around my wrist.

Koda followed through on my heels.

The air changed, growing thinner with the elevation. Glancing up, I confirmed my suspicions when the moon appeared twice as large.

We were in Jinn.

On what island, I had no idea. I didn't recognize the surroundings, though there wasn't much to see beyond the trees lit by Koda's torch. It looked exactly like the forest we'd just left, though perhaps the trees weren't quite as large or tall here.

Listening closely, all I could make out was the wind in the trees and the soft song of crickets.

No voices, no lights, no sign of a city or buildings of any kind. Even the warriors we'd been following were nowhere to be seen.

"So much for our agreement," Koda growled, gripping my wrist tighter.

"You clearly wanted to come," I reasoned with him, still studying our surroundings for some clue of why the portal was here. "And I'm still with you, aren't I?"

Koda didn't argue, and that alone told me how badly he wanted to be here.

A slight frown flitted across his face.

It smoothed out so quickly, I almost thought I'd imagined it.

"Is this normal for an attack?" I pressed, knowing full well it wasn't.

Koda's fire-colored eyes fixed on my face. "It's not an attack." He'd lowered his voice to a soft rumble.

Without warning, he turned the torch upside down and slammed it into the dirt. It killed the fire immediately, turning the woods around us into pure darkness.

"The negotiations have begun."

10

SHEM WAS NEGOTIATING FOR *me*.

A hopeful breath filled my lungs, and for a brief moment, I didn't even notice the throbbing in my shoulder. If Koda was right, maybe I'd make it home tonight after all. Unless negotiations went poorly, and the Vaade were merely using it as an excuse to capture the prince, in which case…

My breath hitched. Suddenly I hoped very much it *wasn't* Shem they were meeting. Would he risk being involved?

I turned to beg Koda to let me listen in on the negotiations, but he was already moving, tugging my wrist to pull me after him. "Not a single word once we see them, do you understand?" he murmured in my ear.

I nodded eagerly.

My foot crunched on a stick.

With a hiss, Koda scooped me up and slung me over

his shoulder.

I bit back a gasp as the blood rushed to my face, gripping the back of his tunic in my fists. In any other circumstances, I'd kick and scream until he put me down. It was utterly humiliating.

Though he didn't change his grip on my thighs, all my senses narrowed on the warmth from his hands.

As we crested a ridge a long minute later, he lowered me to the ground.

My entire body was tense.

He wasn't even out of breath.

I tried to yank out of reach, but he kept a solid grip on my arm, ignoring my glare. *Koda, the anchor,* I thought irritably.

Calmly, he tipped his head toward the valley below, where the trees cleared and moonlight shone down to reveal the warriors.

Over two dozen of them in all, both men and women, stood on one side of the clearing, all holding torches, lighting up the empty space, waiting.

While Koda and I were hidden in the foliage, and the portal was on lower ground, blocked from view by the hill, the Vaade below us seemed oddly... exposed. Though they stood tall, the open space clearly made them uncomfortable. Their eyes darted in different directions, shoulders tense, and some of them shuffled their feet.

"What—" I began to question Koda, but he waved a hand and cut me off.

THE SECRET CURSE

"Shh," he whispered directly in my ear. His hot breath tickled the sensitive shell, making me shiver. "My father will hear you."

I frowned, grabbing his tunic and tugging at him until he caved and bent down, allowing me to whisper back, "You can hear across this distance?"

Warmth gusted over my ear again, as he hissed, "Only if I have *silence*."

I rolled my eyes. Fine. Why beg him to explain when, with a little effort, I could match his hearing? It took a few precious moments, but I carefully shifted to the hearing of a majestic eagle, known to hear their prey squealing underground from high in the air. Now, if things went south during these negotiations, I would know. Maybe I could even prove my value to Shem and his parents by joining the fray and thwarting the Vaade's plans.

Though it was frustrating to leave my vision normal, I chose not to risk the owl eyes a second time when the Jinn would be here soon and might see. It made the faces below hard to read in the dim torchlight.

The thought made my heart skip a beat.

What if that was the point of meeting so late? The Vaade had the advantage with their ability to see in the dark... If they doused their torches—

Koda's fingers tightened on my arm in response to my rapidly beating heart, probably worried I planned to run again.

But I hardly noticed.

I couldn't seem to catch my breath.

What if Shem showed up to this meeting and it was a trap?

A small retinue of Jinn flashed into existence in the clearing. From here, I registered their heavy armor first. It wasn't decorative the way it was usually worn in the castle. And instead of primitive torches like the Vaade, they'd enchanted their breastplates to have a white orb in the center, glowing white.

Most were members of the Jinni Guard.

After scanning the group for another long second, as well as the Vaade reactions, I blew out a breath, both relieved and disappointed.

Shem wasn't with them.

Of course he wasn't.

King Jubal and Queen Samaria would never risk their only son on negotiations when his council could do the job.

Sure enough, the guards surrounded three equally armored Jinn from Shem's council in the middle. I would've recognized Milcah by her extravagant peacock feathers anywhere. Beside her on each side stood Jerusha and Laban.

"We're here on behalf of the royal family of Jinn," Milcah declared so loudly I probably would've heard it even without my advanced hearing.

I itched to step forward and reveal myself to them, to yell, "Take me home!" But I didn't want to ruin the

THE SECRET CURSE

negotiations by causing a fight to break out—Koda would drag me back through the daleth in a heartbeat and the Jinn were more outmatched by these Vaade below than they realized.

I forced myself to wait until they asked for me.

Though I tried not to get my hopes up, I couldn't quite help myself. *I'm going home!*

Up until now, the royal family had refused to meet with the Vaade, so Shem had likely had to fight for this meeting.

I wished there was a way to let them know I was here without alerting the warriors.

Maybe they'd attempt to bargain first, or maybe they'd decide to fight...

Either way, I'd be ready.

From the front line of the Vaade, an older man with long white hair and a wrinkled face took a few menacing steps toward them.

"The leader of the Vaade, the Dragon," Koda murmured in my ear, and after a slight hesitation, he added, "My father."

I bit my lip.

Something about him set me on edge.

Milcah lifted her chin at his approach, making those ridiculous feathers flare, but she didn't flinch.

The Jinni guards, on the other hand, quickly raised their weapons higher.

A tense silence filled the woods.

The whistling of the wind through the trees was the

only sound that reached us. Not even the crickets were chirping now.

Beside me, Koda leaned forward, as if he was preparing to forget about hiding and leap into the clearing.

But the Dragon surprised me—and the council as well, judging by their startled expressions—by smiling and spreading his hands wide. "We welcome you to this meeting of good faith," he finally replied. "Despite your prince not bothering to show."

My eyes narrowed.

Was he mocking the council? Were they about to die? Though I couldn't think of anyone I liked less in the castle, without them I'd remain a hostage. I desperately hoped they'd ignore the slight.

Milcah's lips curved in a matching smile, and though I couldn't tell for sure from the distance, I could almost guarantee it didn't reach her eyes. "We should be the ones welcoming *you*, since you're on *our* land."

I nearly groaned, running a hand across my brow.

Koda snorted softly beside me.

His fingers had noticeably loosened on my arm. I was tempted to try pulling away again. Unconsciously, I tensed, which immediately made him tighten his grip.

I sighed softly. *Patience.*

Milcah continued before the Dragon could react, voice laced with thinly-veiled annoyance. "We understand you've taken a hostage. We would like to negotiate her return along with a truce to cease all future attacks."

Finally.

The first thing I'd do when I got home was take a long, hot bath, followed by a proper meal at a table with silverware and napkins. Nothing like the messy meals over a tiny fire with Koda. My mouth watered.

"You understand correctly," the Dragon replied, managing to sound like he was speaking to a child. It made me wish I could see Milcah's face more clearly. I allowed myself a tiny smile. "Tell your prince that in exchange for the female, I would like to use a Jinni enchantment to form a binding covenant between our people."

My ears caught on the word *covenant* and the fact that he'd said it was a *Jinni* enchantment. It seemed significant.

Even from here, I caught the way Milcah shifted to glance at the others, but she spoke calmly. "This is a term we are unfamiliar with. Before we bring this message to him, would you care to elaborate?"

Though her tone would've raised the hair on my neck, the Dragon merely laughed. "I wouldn't expect *you* to know it."

I shook my head, holding in a soft laugh of my own. Milcah had met her match!

Turning, the Dragon waved a young Vaade woman in the group forward.

Koda tensed.

"What?" I hissed. "What is it? Are they going to

attack?"

"No," Koda snapped, forgetting to be quiet, though the murmurs below hid his voice. His orange and yellow eyes glowed with fury.

The Dragon placed his hands on the woman's shoulders, drawing her forward, toward the Jinn. From here, I couldn't see the details in her face, but she looked young and pretty, with long dark hair split into two thick braids and a colorful patterned shawl over her shoulders. She stared at the ground between the Vaade and the Jinn.

"Then what?" I asked louder when Koda didn't answer.

Lips pressed together in a silent snarl, he didn't take his eyes off the clearing, but finally he muttered, "That's my sister."

That didn't clear anything up for me.

"A covenant between our people would mean an end to the fighting between us," the Dragon declared, cutting off my questions. His word choice made me want to scoff. The only ones attacking were the Vaade. "We would not only agree to terms of peace, but if this covenant is put into place, both our people would be magically bound by it." His words struck me as funny as I remembered Koda's words the day I'd met him. *We don't want peace.*

"For this to be possible," the Dragon was saying, "the covenant will be completed in physical form through the unity of my daughter, Tehya, and your prince." He paused, and enunciated clearly as he clarified, "In marriage."

Cold shock flushed through my whole body.

The council members gaped at him.

His daughter's arms were crossed tight as she glared at the Jinn, and her sleeveless deerskin dress revealed tensed muscles almost as large as Koda's.

The Dragon raised a hand to grip his daughter's shoulder, holding it for a long moment until she dropped her gaze. Her chest rose and fell rapidly in heavy breaths.

Tell them, I mentally urged Milcah, the council, or even the Jinni guards—someone—to speak up. *She can't marry him because the prince is* already engaged.

But they didn't.

"This is your bargain?" Laban spoke up for the first time instead, studying the tall girl standing beside the Vaade leader. "Would you perhaps consider—"

"I will consider *nothing* else," the Dragon said with a note of finality.

Laban drew a long breath, looking to the women. When they nodded, he turned back. "We will bring your request to the royal family. Wait here."

He, Milcah, and Jerusha disappeared.

How far they had to travel to reach the prince, I didn't know, but a long minute passed, then another, and the Vaade stood tense and silent across from the Jinni Guard. Both groups glared at each other. Tehya yanked her multi-colored shawl back over her shoulders. The Dragon gave her a quelling look.

I barely noticed any of it.

My heart pounded so loudly in my ears, I doubted I would've heard them if they had spoken. Slowly, I registered the fact that Koda *was* speaking. It seemed almost under his breath.

"What?" I tried to snap, but it came out as a whisper. I couldn't focus on him. My eyes drifted back to the clearing, waiting for the council to return and say, *Absolutely not. The prince refuses your request.*

Shem *would* refuse.

But if he did, the Vaade would have no more reason to keep me alive...

I shivered, blinking rapidly, trying to clear my head.

"Breathe." Koda's voice finally reached me.

I sucked in a deep breath. Then another. My hands trembled. Wrapping my free arm around my ribs, I gripped the layers of my ragged dress hard to hide the weakness. But with Koda holding my other arm, he no doubt felt it.

I slowly became aware of the way his other fist clenched and unclenched, as if around someone's throat.

"It won't happen," he assured me without sparing a glance in my direction. Louder, he added, "My father is a fool."

The Dragon's head slowly swiveled to face us.

I paled.

Koda didn't flinch under his father's stern gaze, but he also didn't say anything further.

When Milcah, Jerusha, and Laban reappeared, the

THE SECRET CURSE

Dragon turned back to face them as if no time had passed. He waited patiently.

"We will need to see the hostage to verify her safety before we can give you our answer," Milcah said.

The Dragon didn't hesitate. "Not possible."

I whipped my gaze to Koda's. He knew we were here! He'd *seen* us.

Koda never took his eyes off the group below.

"Well then, perhaps we can meet again tomorrow, and you can bring her—"

"No."

Milcah paused, speechless for once, then tried again. "I'm afraid that—"

"You brought someone with the Gift of truth, did you not?" the Dragon interrupted in a bored tone.

My eyes widened. How did he know the Jinni Guard always used a Jinni with that Gift in negotiations? He seemed to have quite a bit more information on the Jinn than King Jubal realized.

"We happen to have someone here with that Gift," Milcah gritted out the words.

"Then you'll know I tell the truth when I say our hostage is alive and unharmed. And I will give you no opportunity to steal our bargaining piece." The Dragon crossed his arms, face unchanging as he added, "Either the prince accepts the covenant, or the Jinni girl dies."

Though it was hard to judge Milcah's expression from here, she seemed to pale. Subtly she glanced at Laban, who hid his responding nod by stepping forward to speak, placing his hands on Milcah and Jerusha's arms. "We'll confer with the prince."

They vanished again without another word.

It was time to make a move.

As soon as they returned, I'd travel directly behind Milcah and yell, "Run!" It'd have to be timed perfectly.

I drew a deep breath, tensing.

Koda responded immediately, shifting on his feet, almost as if planting himself.

He's worried I'm going to travel with him again. I held back a snort. As if I'd take him with me.

Taking slow, steady breaths, I did my best to seem calm as I prepared for the Jinn to return.

The second Milcah's face appeared, I tried to travel.

Nothing happened.

I felt the blood drain from my face.

Tugging on my arm, I strained my Gift to its limits, struggling to get away from Koda both physically and magically.

He wrapped his arms around me, holding me firmly in place.

I opened my mouth to scream.

Heavy fingers clamped down over my mouth and nose, muffling my shrieks. Multiple Vaade from the group glanced toward us, all quickly returning their gaze to the Jinn as soon as they saw me and Koda.

The Jinn, thanks to their pathetic, *normal* hearing, were too far away to hear a thing.

THE SECRET CURSE

"Be still," Koda snarled in my ear. "My father would happily kill you in an instant along with all your friends. You'll only give him the opportunity."

I slowly lost the fight in me as I absorbed his words. But it was the way the Dragon tilted his head in our direction, while at the same time letting his hand casually land on the wicked long sword at his waist, that finally stopped me.

I sagged back against Koda.

He didn't remove his hand.

In a strange way, I was thankful he took away my choice, since part of me still wanted to risk it.

"The prince..." Jerusha was saying below, pausing to clear her throat, "has decided to consider your request. He asks for a fortnight to negotiate the details of this covenant with you and gain a better understanding of the full enchantment. If all is as it appears—and as long as your hostage remains unharmed—he will accept your offer. We'll meet again tomorrow to begin discussions."

Without another word, the entire Jinni party vanished.

I barely noticed the way Tehya cried out in frustration or Koda's hiss of breath beside me.

Instead, I replayed Jerusha's words over and over, piecing them together, searching for a hidden meaning. Shem had *decided to consider their request*.

Shem couldn't possibly want this.

He was equally trapped.

Wasn't he?

If he said no, he couldn't guarantee my safety. So he'd made my wellbeing a requirement for his participation. Logically it made sense, but… he'd still agreed.

I mentally curled inward, allowing Koda to pull me along by the elbow back toward the daleth, stumbling frequently, uncaring.

Focusing on my breathing, I tried to make it even out.

Hurt weighed down my bones, making me sluggish.

Shem didn't have a choice.

I imagined him struggling with this decision—how he'd pace the length of his council room, staring at the bookshelves, as if they held answers to yet another impossible dilemma. His options were to let me go—which he'd never do—or refuse, knowing the Vaade would go on attacking our people, after killing me. But maybe he'd seen a third option…

He asks for a fortnight to negotiate the details, Jerusha had said.

Two weeks was a long time. Negotiations could easily go sideways. I read between the lines, hope rising. Shem had said they must *gain a better understanding of the full enchantment.* I sucked in my first deep breath since the meeting took place. He was going to look beneath the surface of the enchantment for a loophole. *That's his plan.*

Drawing a deep breath, I nodded to myself. He'd find a reason to back out, but he'd *had* to say yes for now to keep me safe. His agreement was only a way to stall and search for a weakness while he came up with a plan. He always put his people first. He was doing this for them.

He didn't *want* to abandon me. He just couldn't help it.

Either way, though, he wasn't here. Even as his betrothed, I was powerless.

Alone.

When I pulled my attention back to the present, the Dragon, Tehya, and his warriors, all holding torches high, were approaching fast.

Up close, rage contorted the girl's face, but even then, I could tell she was gorgeous. Glossy brown hair framed her perfect, heart-shaped face with honey-colored skin, full lips, and thick brows. Her cheeks were flushed dark red. Shem would probably think she was beautiful.

Her feelings clearly didn't matter. If the Dragon continued to lead the negotiations, then this covenant—this *marriage*—would happen.

I winced.

There were still Jerusha's final words to consider: *if all is as it appears*—meaning if Shem couldn't prove the Vaade had some ulterior motives for this truce—*he will accept your condition*.

"The filthy Jinn aren't worthy of marriage!" Tehya protested as we approached.

No answer.

"I want to marry Akeena!" she yelled next, though it continued to land on deaf ears.

The Dragon's voice interrupted my examination of her. "What is it doing here?"

My eyes snapped back to him and widened.

In our last encounter, I'd been unable to see him through the blindfold. Now I took in his long white hair and wrinkled face in the torchlight—the way his mouth turned down made him almost seem to have jowls. His fierce, dark eyes with flecks of fire reminded me of his son's. Unlike Koda, though, his eyes were deeper set, almost buried in the folds that came with age, but if possible, they were even more piercing. Though he wasn't taller than the other Vaade, he somehow loomed over us. His glare made me shiver.

"You were supposed to leave it in the smokehouse."

I tensed.

"No time," Koda lied. "And good thing, too, since you were able to use it against their truthsayer. If we hadn't been here, negotiations would've failed."

He was a quick thinker.

The Dragon's face didn't change. I couldn't tell if he was pleased with Koda or furious. Without a single glance in my direction or his daughter's, he waved everyone toward the glowing daleth a short distance ahead.

In my anguish, I hadn't been thinking logically. I should've shifted and fought Koda one-on-one while I had the chance.

Now, not only did Koda's firm grip somehow anchor me, but we were also surrounded by over two-dozen burly

THE SECRET CURSE

Vaade warriors. Beneath the white paint streaked across their faces, they were all scowling, itching for a fight. If I became a Lacklore, two dozen swords would run me through. If I became a tiny flea, they'd smell me out and crush me. No matter how many possibilities I considered, there wasn't a single scenario where I could win.

I glanced longingly over my shoulder for any Jinn who might've remained behind on Shem's orders, but the forest around us was empty.

Of course it was. I sighed. They hadn't known I was here.

When we reached the daleth, I reluctantly allowed Koda to lead me through.

11

"HOW DARE YOU GIVE me away like a prize horse?" Tehya's voice rang out through the otherwise quiet forest as she and her father stepped through the portal a minute later, followed by the remaining Vaade warriors.

Her father's only response was to turn to the last two coming through the daleth. "Close and seal it." With a dark look in Koda's direction, he added to them, "Wait until we're gone. I don't want it"—he gestured in my direction—"to see."

They nodded.

The Dragon then extinguished his torch and gestured for the others to do the same. He probably didn't want me to see the way back to camp either. As if I cared.

I could easily shift my vision back to spite him, if I was willing to waste the energy.

Licking my lips, I imagined shifting into an actual

dragon and attacking him from behind. He was the reason all of this was happening.

As my muscles tensed, Koda's fingers tightened on my arm in response.

I tried to think, but I was distracted by the way the Dragon's daughter continued to berate her father so freely in front of his men. And also by the warm, muscled arm that brushed against mine as Koda led me through the forest.

When Tehya ran out of steam, the Dragon finally replied in a calm but firm tone, "We'll speak later." She took another breath, and he spoke over whatever she planned to say, adding sharply, "In private."

After that, she fell silent.

Gratefully, I let my gaze fall to my feet and tried to think.

I had two weeks.

Two weeks to find an excuse not to go through with the Vaade covenant.

Shem would be doing everything he could, but the answers were here. In the Vaade world.

Barely holding back a groan, I swallowed the sour lump in my throat.

I had to stay and learn more about this covenant—and how to stop it.

Nothing else mattered.

Not even escape.

A nagging thought came to me, and once it was there, it refused to be ignored: if I returned home now, was I still engaged to Shem? Did I even have a place in the castle if the covenant moved forward? If I didn't end these negotiations, there might be nothing to go back to.

Lifting my chin, decision made, I almost tripped at the sight of everyone waiting for us in their camp. The small group of Vaade returning merged with dozens more, until we were surrounded, despite the late hour.

I fought the growing feeling I'd just missed my last opportunity to get home.

There was no "home" until we stopped the covenant.

Pressing my lips together, I breathed slowly, inhaling through my nose, then a long exhale.

I would find answers.

If I was forced to stay here, I'd learn everything I could about these people—especially their weaknesses. The thought made my breath hitch. I hoped they *had* a weakness. For Shem's sake, and my own.

Because as much as I wanted Shem to come save me, the truth was King Jubal and Queen Samaria would never willingly send their son into danger, even if they did know where the Vaade camped.

Though Shem would do everything in his power to rescue me, I feared, after witnessing the Vaade up close, it might not be enough.

I had to save myself.

Bitter disappointment flooded through me. Nothing ever really changed.

The Dragon headed toward one of the longhouses,

THE SECRET CURSE

calling over his shoulder, "Lock it up, Koda."

Cold snaked down my skin as the surrounding Vaade eyes all swung to me. The group slowly began to break up. "I was hoping for more of a fight," one of them mumbled, and another thumped him on the back. "I'll give you a fight." That group moved toward the forest, while others followed the Dragon into the longhouse or headed for the bonfire in the center of the camp.

Tehya huffed, throwing up her arms, and turned on Koda unexpectedly. "You have to talk to him."

Nodding, he lifted my arm toward her, as if it was a rope to hold onto. "Stay with her."

"I'm in no mood to babysit a Jinni." She glared at him. "Get someone else to watch her."

At least she hadn't called me an "it" like the rest of them.

Fist clenching as he lowered our arms, Koda watched her stalk off into the forest alone.

When Koda glanced at the fire, I thought for sure he was about to break our bargain. "Please," I whispered, not knowing how to plead my case but knowing I should.

He couldn't drag me along to talk to the Dragon. Even *I* knew how that would go. But he couldn't help his sister if he stayed with me either.

Tension built in his shoulders.

I clenched my fists, struggling not to say more.

With a growl, he spun on his heel toward the forest in the opposite direction of his sister, tugging at my hand for me to follow. "Come."

Pure gratefulness flooded my body like soothing cool water. I hadn't been sure he'd honor our agreement.

Blowing out a heavy breath, I hurried to keep up with him. We crossed through camp, passing all four longhouses and the bonfire to the side, heading for a smaller building nestled between two trees on the edge of the clearing. It was barely larger than my bed back at the castle. This must be the smokehouse they'd mentioned.

He pointed behind the building. "If you need to relieve yourself before you sleep, go now. This is your only opportunity until morning." Before I had a chance to get flustered, he added, "You have one minute, and then I'm coming to get you." The implications were clear—whether I was still peeing or trying to flee again, I wouldn't get far.

I only hesitated a moment before quickly hurrying into the dark to take care of business, tripping over roots as I went.

With heat reaching all the way to the tips of my ears, I returned. As someone raised in an extremely private culture, every aspect of the Vaade's world left me completely unbalanced.

When he opened the wooden door and gestured to the pitch-black space inside the smokehouse, I took one look at his brooding face and obediently entered.

It would be spelled against travel at this point, unfortunately, just like the longhouse. But escape was a secondary goal now—first I needed to gather all the

THE SECRET CURSE

information I could on this covenant.

Two weeks, I reminded myself yet again. *That's all.* I only needed to endure for two weeks and be ready for any opportunity that arose to gather information or escape.

That didn't stop me from imagining shifting into a little flea the moment Koda closed the door and slipping out into the night. Though I had no plans to follow through, I bit my lip. Could Koda smell my magic even if I shifted to that size? An image of him finding me in that form and using one of his big hands to crush me made me flinch.

Don't cause trouble. The Vaade had promised to keep me alive. I'd be a fool to test how much they meant it.

I took a few steps further into the smokehouse.

There were no windows.

The light from the bonfire was too far away to illuminate much without shifting my eyes again. I nearly ran into the opposite wall, which was only a few steps in.

The door banged shut behind me.

Yet again, my hopes plummeted. How was I supposed to gather information alone in a locked room?

A hot breath tickled my neck.

I jumped and spun around.

Koda's shadowy outline blocked the faint line of the fire shining through the cracks in the door. He loomed over me.

"What're you doing?" I blurted.

"Did you change your mind?" I couldn't see his expression, but his tone was bored. "I'd be happy to leave someone else to guard you."

"No...?" I didn't understand how that answered my question.

"Then my options are either to stand outside or inside, and I don't trust you out of my sight, even if it is a warm night."

He's sleeping in here. I processed his words, swallowing nervously. Somehow, though I'd slept across the fire from him once already, this little room felt far more intimate.

"Sit," he said when I didn't immediately move.

Eyes still adjusting, I moved toward a lump in one corner, hoping it was a chair. Feeling carefully, I found a small stool with a large pile of furs laid over it. Not wanting to upset Koda further, I sat.

A few cracks in the wooden walls allowed a bit of moonlight in. Not enough to make out much of anything, though.

A flame flickered to life between Koda's hands as he lit a candle. He placed it in a holder by the door that I hadn't seen.

I took in the small space again. There was no bed. No other furniture. In fact, the room was so small I didn't know if someone Koda's height could lie down without knocking their head or feet into the walls.

Soft candlelight danced over his scowling face. I

couldn't tell if he was upset with his father's plans or with me—probably both.

When he turned to lean against the door, arms crossed, I looked away quickly, not wanting to upset him more.

On the other side of the tiny room, what I'd mistaken for a wall when we'd first entered was actually a second door. "What's behind that?" I asked without thinking.

"Not your concern," Koda muttered.

My shoulders tensed at his tone. It reminded me too much of my father growing up. I chose to stay quiet after that. I wasn't usually curious, but if it was another way out, it'd be good to know. I had limited time to figure out the details of this so-called covenant and then find a way to nullify it.

Carefully avoiding Koda's gaze, I bit my lip, considering. From the way he'd reacted to the negotiations back in Jinn, there was a good chance we wanted the same thing. I just didn't know how to broach the subject when he was like this.

"It's where the meat is kept," Koda said on a sigh out of nowhere.

I blinked. It took a long moment to realize he was answering my question from earlier, as if the last few minutes hadn't passed in silence.

When I didn't respond, he growled softly, grabbing the second door without leaving his post, swinging it open with a rough gesture. "The meat. Smoking. This is the smokehouse."

Sure enough, venison and other meat hung above a vent that poured out heat and smoke into the room, slowly cooking and preserving the meat. I blushed at how obvious it was in retrospect, especially as my nose finally registered the smell.

The smoke started to fill our room as well and Koda was quick to shut the door, though he didn't slam it this time. "This side is for storage. *And* detaining annoying Jinn."

I stared at him, lips parted. Was he making a joke?

"You wanted to know," he mumbled when I still didn't speak. He crossed his arms, returning to scowling at the wall.

I slowly released a breath, unsure what to say. "Thank you...?"

In response, he lowered to a crouch and sat against the door, getting comfortable.

I sighed at the idea of sleeping here, but doubted I had a choice. It couldn't be worse than a forest floor. Standing, I took a bunch of the furs from the stool and began to spread them out across the floor, layering them until they made a surprisingly comfortable bed.

Koda watched without a word, but when I started making a second line of furs for him, trying to get in his good graces, he snapped, "What are you doing?"

I froze, cringing back instinctively. Some things I'd learned growing up with my father would take a lifetime to unlearn. "I assumed we were spending the night. Do you prefer the hard floor?"

"I won't be sleeping." His tone was less annoyed now, more carefully flat.

I frowned. "You barely slept last night either." *Or at all?* I'd been unconscious so I couldn't be sure.

"I'll be fine."

I drew a breath to argue, then let it go. Why did I care? *I don't,* I told myself. *I just need him to trust me.* Keeping that focus in mind, I rebuilt my nerve and turned back to the furs, dragging the remaining ones off and building the second makeshift bed around him, while saying, "Fine. Don't sleep. But you can at least be comfortable."

When he narrowed his eyes at me, I pretended to be far more confident than I felt and tossed the last two furs in his direction. "It's not like I'll be able to get out, if you're blocking the door."

He still didn't respond.

Or move.

My logic was sound, and I frowned, not understanding, until it dawned on me. *He thinks I want to escape while he's sleeping.*

I crossed my arms, unreasonably irritated. It was a smart move on his part. After all, I *was* planning to escape eventually, when the time was right, and I'd learned everything I could. I could've shifted to attack him in his sleep. Or used the paste that still hung in a jar around my neck to paralyze him, roll him away from the door, and run. But the frustrating part was that hadn't been my intention at all.

I laid down with my back to him, pretending to get comfortable, determined not to say another word all night.

Candlelight wavered across the rough wood wall in front of me. The furs prickled a little, but were surprisingly thick and soft. I'd thought I'd need at least one as a blanket, but with the warmth of the smokehouse right next door, I found myself pleasantly warm.

If not for the soft breaths coming from behind me—and, I admitted to myself, the slight throbbing in my shoulder—I could've fallen asleep in a few moments. I didn't want to use my small store of energy on shifting my ears back to normal—I might need the extra-sensitive hearing again tomorrow—but between the lit candle and Koda's obnoxious breathing, sleep evaded me.

It had to be nearly midnight. Maybe later.

Exhaustion turned the soft lighting and gentle breaths into torture.

I gave in and shifted back to normal, throwing an arm over my eyes for good measure.

Drawing in a deep breath, I blew it out, and tried to ignore Koda's presence.

It didn't work.

I could *feel* him an arm's length away, even if I didn't hear him anymore.

If I couldn't sleep and he refused to, I might as well try to gather some information.

Taking another fortifying gulp of air, I rolled over,

THE SECRET CURSE

sitting up. His fiery eyes pinned me to the wall, unreadable. For a long moment, we only stared at each other, before I got the courage to whisper, "You don't want this covenant to happen either."

It wasn't a question, really. But I still wanted to hear his answer.

His frown returned. Pulling up his knees, he rested his thick arms across them, staring aimlessly at the wall behind me. "Not with my sister," he said after a long pause, just when I was beginning to think the conversation had ended before it'd begun.

"What does that mean?" I asked without thinking.

Koda pressed his lips together.

"Who am I going to tell?" I asked, gesturing to the four walls around us. "I'm clearly not going anywhere."

"It was supposed to be a hostage situation," Koda snapped, almost before I'd finished speaking, as if he'd desperately needed to say this to someone. "Not a marriage. My father was going to force the prince to complete the covenant with us, swearing peace between our people, and shifting the balance of power to—" he cut off. "It doesn't matter. That's no longer how it will work."

No, I agreed mentally. King Jubal and Queen Samaria would've never allowed that. *But will they actually consider a marriage between our people?* I honestly didn't know if the negotiations were a front, or if the royal family was truly contemplating it...

It only served to remind me how much this covenant could *not* happen.

Maybe this barbarian might even be willing to help me stop it…

"I don't want Shem to marry your sister any more than you do," I said, nearly choking on bitterness toward the council. They hadn't even *tried* to argue that Shem was already engaged. "Believe me. If there is *anyone* who hates this plan more than you, it's me."

Some of the tension in the air around him seemed to melt away as he stared at me in the soft candlelight. I met his gaze, unsure what else I could say to prove it. Whatever he saw seemed to make him believe me, and he shook his head ruefully. "My sister would disagree with you." Rubbing a hand across his face, he sighed. "If you think Tehya wants to be bound to a Jinni, you'd be a fool."

"Shem's not so bad," I murmured, struggling to console him when I wanted to shout that she didn't deserve him.

I had so much more to lose.

If Shem married another, not only was I no longer engaged to a prince, with a future as queen, but I likely would lose my place on Shem's council. I doubted his new wife would want him spending time with a former betrothed. If I wasn't on the council, then I wouldn't have a place in the castle anymore, either.

I squeezed my eyes shut, trying to stop the tears before Koda saw them.

Glancing at him once I'd regained control, I could tell he thought I was mourning the loss of the prince. He respectfully kept his silence and averted his eyes.

But the truth was, I was mourning more than losing Shem, my place on the council, and my current home. If this Vaade revealed my shape-shifting Gift to anyone else, I could never return to Jinn at all. The Dragon could choose to reveal my secret during negotiations, or worse, he could be planning to kill me once the negotiations were over. Or, at least, to try. Quietly to myself, I admitted there was an even greater chance that there was nothing I could do about that.

After all, Koda had captured me.

I hadn't gone easy on him, no matter what I'd pretended. The Vaade were more powerful than I'd imagined, and I was no longer certain my Gifts gave me much of an edge.

One thing was certain, if this covenant wasn't stopped, I'd be back to who I was before I'd met Shem: a nobody with no future.

I gritted my teeth.

It was time to try using my newest Gift of manipulation again.

We were alone. No one besides Koda would notice if I reached out to touch him.

For the thousandth time I wished that part of my Gift wasn't necessary, but the ability was still new to me. I had yet to manipulate others without that extra support.

Koda sat just out of reach.

In other circumstances, I'd say he was too close, but for my purposes, he might as well be as far away as a Jinni island.

I needed to be subtle.

I cleared my throat, which made him meet my eyes, brows raised.

Though I'd learned to be delicate in many things, this wasn't one of them.

The silence between us grew thin. If I didn't speak soon, any action on my part would seem suspicious.

"What is this—" I reached for the large tooth that hung on a string of hide around his neck, intending to brush his skin and use my Gift as I held it.

Instead, he caught my hand mid-air.

12

HIS GRIP WAS FIRM, unyielding.

My mouth was suddenly dry.

I cleared my throat. "I was going to ask about the necklace," I whispered, oddly afraid to meet his gaze, even in the dim light of the lone candle. It felt like he could see through me. Forcing myself to look up, I pasted a smile on my face and added, "Are you scared of a little Jinni girl?"

His lips twitched. "Ask whatever you'd like."

When he let go, my sense returned, making me want to groan. I should've used his defensive reaction as an opportunity. I could've manipulated him while he held my hand.

I cleared my throat again, trying and failing to think of a clever way to try again when my focus had never really been on the necklace. He waited impatiently, so in the end, I asked the obvious: "What animal is it from?"

"Dragon."

Eyes widening, I gave the tooth a closer look. It was about the length of his palm. "I thought dragons were bigger than that?"

"It was a hatchling," he said calmly, not seeming offended, but also never taking his eyes off me. When he saw my furrowed brow at the idea of hurting a baby, he added dryly, "It tried to take a bite from my leg. Believe me, it could've gone much worse for the beast."

Taking a tooth from a dragon and evading certain death seemed pretty fearsome to me. I tried not to show my awe.

If possible, that made me even more nervous to touch him.

Two weeks, I repeated to myself, trying to see it as a positive though it was beginning to feel like a nightmare.

I should try again… It's not like I had anything better to do.

"Koda," I began, trying to prepare him for my movement this time, inching forward until I could reach his knee and set my hand down. It looked anything but casual. His eyes fell to my hand, making me want to pull it back. I forced myself to wait until he looked back up. Making sure his eyes locked with mine, I put all my energy into my Gift as I said, "Tell me about the covenant."

He didn't look away.

My shoulders relaxed as a small smile touched my

lips.

Finally, things were going according to plan.

A long pause followed.

He must be fighting my Gift.

No matter, it would win.

It always did.

Koda's eyes drifted across my face, lingering on my lips, before falling back down to where my hand rested on his knee. He tilted his head thoughtfully. When his gaze returned to mine the strangeness finally registered: his eyes were clear. Bright, intelligent, and devoid of the typical indifference usually brought on by my manipulation.

In fact, he was smirking.

"Did you just try to use a Gift on me?"

I flinched and yanked my hand back. In hindsight, it was the worst possible reaction.

I should've feigned innocence. He couldn't prove anything.

Except, now I'd given myself away.

Though my mouth opened, I couldn't come up with a single explanation.

Koda's smirk turned into a full-blown grin, and he shook his head. "You Jinn and your secrets. This is what the Vaade have never understood. You try to control and drive a conversation instead of being willing to simply ask a question. This constant attempt to conceal things from everyone, including your own kind, is what will allow us to win in the end."

Crossing my arms, I scowled at him.

It only made him grin wider. "For example, here is a secret that your kind clearly kept from you: the Vaade are immune to Jinni Gifts."

My jaw dropped, and I breathed, "Impossible."

He only shrugged and gestured toward my hands, where they were tucked tight against my body. "The evidence is before you. Our minds are too strong to be twisted by your wickedness."

Snorting, I looked away. But I turned over his words. That wasn't exactly immunity, was it? There was a loophole in there somewhere... Their *minds* were too strong, he'd said...

It hit me.

"I *traveled* with you!" I sat up straighter, eyes widening as another memory came to me. "And during the other attack, one of the Guard members traveled with you too! Until you—" I cut off, remembering how he'd suddenly become rooted to the earth, like an anchor held him in place.

He shifted uncomfortably, avoiding my eyes. "That was a moment of weakness."

Their minds weren't always strong...

But something told me it was more than that.

He hadn't seen Shem either, and he'd certainly been trying his hardest. And what about when I'd shifted? The Vaade's immunity seemed more defensive than anything, almost like their thick skin made magic bounce off them, but did nothing to stop Gifts used on someone else.

Contemplating what this might mean, I jumped when he leaned toward me. When I met his gaze, he spoke slow and clear, "It won't happen again." *Traveling,* I reminded myself, trying to calm my frantic heart. *He's talking about traveling, not using my other Gifts.*

He waited for me to nod understanding before relaxing back against the door.

We were quiet for a minute.

When I risked a glance in his direction, curiosity shone in his colorful eyes. "Have you considered I might answer your question without your useless Gift?"

I lifted my chin, pinning him with my gaze, and said in a flat voice, "Fine. Tell me about the covenant."

Tilting his head thoughtfully, he paused, and for a long moment I was sure he'd been taunting me, but then he said, "Tell me about the Gift you tried to use on me, and I'll tell you about the covenant."

Absolutely not.

He was a Vaade, so he didn't know what he asked, but it still made me flush with anger.

I turned away from him and lay back down.

This conversation was over.

I thought he felt the same, but then I heard shuffling behind me. I peeked over my shoulder to find him laying the last two pelts across the floor and stretching out across them beside me. It was oddly intimate. Was that his way of saying he was trusting me?

He lifted his muscled arms and flexed, placing his

hands under his head to stare up at the wood ceiling.

I was mesmerized.

Calmly, as if long minutes hadn't passed without talking, he continued to stare at the ceiling as he asked, "What do you have to lose?"

I blinked at him. What a ridiculous question.

Back home, I'd have *everything* to lose.

Breathing slowly, I took in his handsome face, only a few breaths away from mine, allowing myself a chance to stare for once. Who would have thought I'd be considering what a Vaade said?

But he was right…

Here, everything was already lost. Now there was only gain.

He rolled onto his side to face me, waiting less patiently now.

"I—" Heat flooded my face before I even began. Everything in me resisted telling him, after keeping it hidden for so long. "I don't completely understand the Gift myself yet. It's still new…" It felt traitorous to tell him even that, but I made myself continue, in the hopes that by sharing, he might choose to share with me as well. "…It seems to make people believe what I say and"—I had to clear my throat before I could finish—"want what I want."

He burst out laughing.

Startled, I froze, unsure what to do.

"That *would* be convenient," he said on a chuckle,

relaxing onto his back again, shoulders shaking with mirth. "I can see why you'd try it."

Scowling at him, I rolled onto my back as well and crossed my arms. "It certainly would be useful right now," I agreed.

When he started laughing all over again, I glared at him. "Not everyone finds it so funny, you know. Back home, they'd sooner sever my abilities than trust me with them."

His laughter cut off, and I tried not to miss it. I didn't know why I'd told him that.

"And the Jinn think *we're* barbaric," he muttered, shaking his head.

"You're saying you wouldn't do the same thing, if you had the opportunity?" I challenged, meeting his piercing stare.

"Never."

He hadn't hesitated for a second.

I didn't want to believe him, but... I did. Skirting away from the personal, I came back to the point. "You promised you'd tell me about the covenant in return."

"Why do you want to know about it?" he asked in a soft tone.

"That wasn't the deal," I argued, sitting up again. "I don't have to tell you that."

"How could I forget," he said, and without moving a muscle, the cold distance returned between us. "You Jinn and your secrets." He snorted. "Why share something unless you absolutely *have* to?"

I was tempted to brush him off again and demand answers, but his earlier words came back to me. *What do I have to lose?*

"It's not really a secret." I leaned back against the wall, wincing when I accidentally bumped my sore shoulder. "I would've thought you'd already guessed—I want to stop it."

Koda didn't react.

Had I lost all the progress we'd made by saying that? I'd thought he wanted to stop it too...

He continued to stare at the ceiling.

I squinted at him. It seemed almost as if he'd forgotten I was there.

Finally, he blew out a breath. "I don't want Tehya forced to marry your prince."

"Then we're in agreement. Let's find a way to end it."

"There's only one other way." He slowly met my eyes with a fiery intensity, as if he knew what I'd say. "We take your prince as our hostage instead."

Never.

My sense of self-preservation kept me from speaking right away. I pretended to think. "Obviously that's not possible or you would've done it already. And the covenant isn't an option either. What else would you do?"

"There is no alternative," he muttered darkly.

"There has to be another way," I said, though I wasn't sure I believed it myself at the moment.

THE SECRET CURSE

A pause hung over us as he sulked and I tried to think.

"Tell me more details about how the covenant works," I said finally, unsure if he would listen. "How does it benefit your people—or mine? And why does your father want it so badly he'd give up his own daughter for it?"

When he still didn't answer, I added, "You can trust me. In this, we're on the same side."

13

"THE SAME SIDE?" KODA'S stillness had lulled me into such a peaceful state, I startled when he leapt up to pace. In a space this size, he could only take a step and a half before turning, which gave the impression of bouncing off the walls. He seemed to come to the same conclusion, stopping to crouch in front of me instead. "I was raised to believe the Vaade and the Jinn are *never* on the same side."

His breath tickled my nose, an odd thing to notice. My own breath was faster than I'd like, but that was only because he'd scared me. *Wasn't it?*

Hesitating, I licked my lips, noticing that this drew his gaze. "I understand. The Jinn are taught that *no one* is on their side. And yet…" I cleared my throat. "We want the same things. Which means we *are* on the same side, whether we like it or not."

He leaned back abruptly.

I would've moved back too, but there was nowhere

THE SECRET CURSE

to go.

Koda settled against the opposite wall, studying me before giving in. "At first glance, the covenant is a marriage ceremony—but the Jinni enchantment built into the vows forms a magical truce."

"What kind of truce?"

"Neither side can harm the other. They become incapable of it."

When he didn't continue right away, I frowned. "A marriage is between two people. This truce would only affect Shem and your sister."

He shook his head. "Using blood, rings, and an ancient spell, the enchantment imbues the rings with the power to speak for the entire race."

I was sure he could hear my heart skip a beat. My mouth was dry. "If anyone can do this covenant, why wouldn't someone have tried to form this truce before?"

"Not everyone can." Koda stared up at the ceiling as he spoke. "Only a royal can imbue a ring with that power."

I tilted my head at that. "You mean, it'd have to be done by King Jubal or Queen Samaria."

Koda cleared his throat. "Or your prince."

That's why they'd tried to capture him.

"And once this covenant is complete, it prevents both sides from harming the other," I repeated.

Fidgeting with the dragon tooth around his neck, Koda didn't answer. His words when I'd first met him came back to me: *we don't want peace.* That must've changed.

"It sounds too good to be true." I scoffed. "How does the enchantment work?"

He paused longer than seemed necessary, making me wonder what this supposedly straightforward Vaade might be hiding.

"The most important requirement, according to the spell, are the 'sacrificial' rings," he said slowly. "That's what my father and your prince are currently negotiating right now. Both sides must imbue the rings with the power to speak for their people through their blood. We believe the rings will then draw out our abilities once the covenant begins—that's the sacrificial part."

"Draw out…" I repeated, not understanding.

"Like a weakening," he explained. "Both the Jinn and the Vaade will slowly lose all our unique strengths and abilities until we become like the humans."

My pulse picked up, though I kept my face neutral. "That doesn't sound good."

He smiled at me wryly, letting me know that I hadn't hidden my reaction from him at all. "It's only temporary. And a required part of the sacrifice—we must willingly give up a part of ourselves."

"That's… unusual." An understatement. It must be an old spell to have so much emotion written into it. Jinn these days avoided doing spells so based in passion. Or in most cases, any spell that needed a second person. It required too much trust. Who would risk it?

THE SECRET CURSE

"It's meant to be a true marriage covenant based on love." Koda unwittingly answered my unspoken question. "But we've been led to believe that the magic also works with a real trust."

I snorted at that. "Trust is for fools. Which is what someone would have to be to willingly submit to that."

"That's the whole point of the sacrifice," he snapped. "To have the benefits, they must risk everything."

I had to bite my lip to keep from smiling. He was a secret romantic, it seemed. "I still can't imagine it. I'd never *choose* to weaken myself for someone else."

"It's not permanent!" He threw up his hands, exasperated. "Unless the covenant is left incomplete, it's just a symbolic gesture."

"Of what?"

"Of *trust*," he said, shaking his head at me as if it was obvious. "Something you clearly know nothing about."

No, I thought darkly, *I know all about it and how impossible it truly is.*

"It doesn't matter anyway," he added, bringing my attention back to his smirking face. "No one's asking *you* to complete a covenant."

Once again, he'd managed to wound me.

I glared at him. "You Vaade can keep your covenant and your *trust*," I retorted, crossing my arms, hating how he made me react when normally I could keep a calm mask. Taking a careful breath in and out to control my temper, I added in a detached tone, "As far as I'm concerned, you all have a strange obsession with weakness."

Koda didn't seem offended or entertained by that. If anything, he grew more serious. "Yes. We do."

I blinked at him, not knowing what to say in the face of such honesty. After spending so many months in the castle, my mind was trained to search every phrase for subtext. But with this Vaade man, it felt like looking for the answer to a riddle I wasn't even sure was there. It was draining.

I rubbed my forehead. This whole day had been overwhelming. The thought of sharing anything further of myself with Koda frankly scared me. Turning my back on him, I lay down, mumbling like a coward, "We should get some sleep."

From the lack of sound behind me, I knew he stayed upright. But I wasn't his caretaker. If he wanted to be exhausted tomorrow, that was his problem.

My mind, however, refused to rest. Wrapping my arms around myself to keep from tossing and turning, I couldn't stop thinking about this covenant and all the details he'd shared. I tested them from different angles, trying to find a weakness or catch.

Instead, I kept coming back to the same question: *Would Shem really agree to this? Or is he stalling?*

From the sound of it, the magical truce would stop all Vaade attacks forever. If he thought of his people alone, he might say yes.

But he would also consider me and what this

THE SECRET CURSE

covenant would mean for us, wouldn't he?

I hated that I didn't know for sure.

Biting my lip until it hurt, I tried to distract myself from the salty tears filling my eyes, but they fell anyway, crossing my cheeks and slowly soaking the fur beneath my head. I hoped Koda couldn't somehow smell them.

It's not final, I reminded myself yet again. I still had two weeks to find a way out of the covenant for Shem. Tomorrow, I'd win Koda over with false kindness and convince him to tell me more about it. He'd obviously been holding something back. If I continued to remind him that we wanted the same thing, I could persuade him to help me. It was a flimsy plan, which didn't provide much comfort, but at least it was something.

At some point, Koda's soft breathing seemed to even out, and after listening to it for a while, so did mine, until I drifted to sleep.

"Wake up, Jinni girl." Koda's voice startled me out of a nightmare. Shem had been apologizing to me while holding Tehya's hand, calling her his *new wife*. It left a sour taste in my mouth and put me in a foul mood.

Rubbing my eyes, I winced at the headache forming. Forgetting my plans to be charming, I snapped, "I have a name, you know."

Unfazed, he swung open the door. "I'm sure you do."

Though the sun was peeking over the horizon, leaving the air misty and softly lit, the sudden change in lighting still hurt my eyes. I shaded a hand over them, squinting at Koda's outline.

"It's Jezebel," I reminded him in a more neutral tone. I attempted a smile as I stepped out of the smokehouse, but it probably looked like a grimace. "Where are we going?"

He nodded toward the longhouse and strode off, clearly expecting me to join him. Gut twisting at the thought of interacting with the other Vaade here, I sighed and followed. "Can you at least tell me more about the covenant if—"

My question was cut off when he whirled to grab me by the arms, glancing around to make sure we were still alone. "Do *not* mention the covenant."

When he didn't explain further, I frowned, trying to pull away, but stopped at the way it made my shoulder hurt. "Why not?"

His grip was firm, and he held my gaze. "My father would be… upset with me for sharing the details with you."

Having met his father, upset was probably putting it nicely.

I nodded. "Understood."

Finally, he let go, heading for the longhouse again. Thinking of the Dragon being nearby, I stayed on Koda's heels.

Over his shoulder, he said, "It might be best if you don't talk much around the others in general. At least until they get used to you. A lot of them have strong feelings about the Jinn."

I snorted. "I hadn't noticed."

That earned me a slight smile, which I only glimpsed because I'd caught up to him, standing beside him as he reached for the door to the longhouse.

"Wait!" I didn't realize I'd grabbed his arm to stop him until he glanced down at my hand. I pulled back, forcing myself to meet his piercing gaze. "Before we go in, will you keep my last Gift a secret?"

His forehead wrinkled. "Why?"

Taken aback, I could only blink at him at first. "Because of the consequences. If they knew what I could do…" Each reason made me stumble when it suddenly didn't seem valid here. In Jinn, my Gifts might be severed, but the Vaade didn't know how to do that. And if the Vaade were truly as immune to Gifts as Koda had led me to believe, they wouldn't care about my abilities anyway. "I just—I would feel more comfortable if they didn't know," I finished lamely.

Considering me, his frown deepened. "I don't want to keep secrets from my people."

My shoulders sagged. I nodded at his feet, understanding. Why would he keep an enemy's secret? I shouldn't expect anything less.

"If it doesn't come up, I won't bring it up."

Sucking in a breath, relief flooded through me. I opened my mouth to thank him, but he'd already opened the door and started through it.

This far side was quiet, full of empty bunks. A small group of Vaade sat talking and eating around the fire in the center of the longhouse, a few dozen paces away. Smoke drifted up through the hole in the ceiling that allowed light throughout the rest of the longhouse, though it was much darker on the ends where we were.

I'd only just closed the door, eyes still adjusting to the gloom, when Tehya stepped out of the shadows to one side, blocking our path. Close up, her deep-brown eyes made the dragon-like irises even more startling. She wore a chunky blue necklace over her pale deerskin dress. "What Gift?"

I gaped at her.

When I didn't answer, she turned to Koda, hands on her hips, long braids swinging over her shoulders as she turned. "She has more?"

I faced him too, silently pleading with him not to tell her.

He spread his hands wide and shrugged, as if to say, *It came up.* To Tehya, he said, "She travels, shape-shifts, and apparently can trick the weak-minded into doing what she wants."

"We already knew about the first two," Tehya said, waving them off as if they meant nothing.

My mouth hung open at the way she casually dismissed my abilities.

Without a second glance, she turned away again, moving toward the cookfire at the heart of the longhouse.

THE SECRET CURSE

I glared at Koda. "Good to know you can keep a secret for a whole two seconds."

He shrugged again. "It's not my fault you chose to speak within earshot of a Vaade."

My skin crawled at having all my secrets exposed like this. It only annoyed me further that he was right. Forgetting about their ridiculous hearing was my mistake.

No wonder the Vaade didn't keep many secrets. How could they?

The smell of food wafted toward us, and my stomach growled.

Koda's mouth twitched. "Come." He waved toward the center of the longhouse, adding over his shoulder. "Breakfast."

Tehya was leaning over the group, gesturing toward us as she spoke, and eyes were turning in my direction.

Now, I *did* groan.

Not knowing what else to do, I dragged my feet after Koda toward them.

14

WE'D BARELY REACHED THE small cookfire and the wooden stumps around it where half a dozen Vaade were seated, when Koda put a hand on Tehya's shoulder and said, "Watch the Jinni girl until I get back."

She scowled. "He won't change his mind."

Did she mean the Dragon?

The fact that Koda didn't immediately argue said a lot. "Tehya," he murmured after a long pause, "I have to at least try to talk to him."

The others around the fire kept their eyes on their food, pretending they couldn't hear every word. "If you want my help, watch her."

Tehya gave him a short nod, turning away.

Startled, I opened my mouth to protest too.

Koda cut me off with a sharp look, as if to remind me of our deal. "Stay."

Glaring at his back, I wrapped my arms around

myself, wrinkling my nose at both Koda abandoning me and also a little bit from the way I'd started to smell after living in the same clothes for so long.

Tehya studied my dirty red and white dress with a similar expression. "Come with me," she said on a sigh.

Following her through the bunks, we stopped halfway down the row, stepping between two of them, where Tehya dug through a wooden box until she found whatever she was looking for.

"Here." The cloth hit me in the stomach, and I caught it instinctively.

Standing again, Tehya pulled the blankets from the bunks on each side down, forming a privacy screen. "Change."

"What about a bath?" I countered, wishing I could scrub an entire layer of dirty skin off.

Tehya shrugged. "Only if you want to do it with company."

Glancing back over my shoulder at the other Vaade, I wordlessly shook my head. I'd ask again later and hope for different results.

Unraveling the bundle of clothes, I found a sleeveless deerskin dress with a pretty, blue pattern sewn around the neckline and waist. It was simple compared to my multi-layered, off-the-shoulder gown, but it was clean.

With a glance at Tehya, who simply stared back, I figured she wasn't going anywhere, so I stripped without complaint.

As soon as the stiff red and white fabric hit the ground, I breathed a sigh of relief. The soft deerskin dress felt like wearing a cloud after being so tightly wrapped for the last few days.

Tehya picked up the dress, leading me back to the fire, where the Vaade all blatantly stared at me. A delicious smell wafted through the air that had my mouth watering. They were eating something that looked like yellow-colored bread or cake.

As I watched, Tehya poured a similar yellow liquid over a large flat rock in the center of the fire. It sizzled, starting to cook instantly.

"What is it?" I asked, trying to sound indifferent so they wouldn't know I was drooling over the sweet smells.

"Corn cakes," Tehya replied without looking at me. She made a few more circles of the thick liquid until the rock was full, then sat, still not looking at me.

The tense atmosphere reminded me oddly of the Jinni castle. I scowled, not liking the comparison. Oddly enough, though, the hostility was almost relaxing in its familiarity.

A short log beside her was open. It didn't look like I was going to get an invitation anytime soon, and I didn't want to stand all day. I lowered myself onto it.

No one stopped me, but they didn't acknowledge me either.

My stomach growled. Loudly.

There was no way the Vaade's sharp ears hadn't heard, but they all continued quietly going about the meal without speaking. One woman worked on weaving an intricate basket, one piece of thick dried grass at a time. The man next to her shucked corn, while a third man was deftly skinning a small animal. I averted my eyes, before I lost my appetite.

"Can I?" I asked finally, sounding more sullen than I'd meant to. I gestured to the corn cakes that for all appearances seemed done cooking. The edges were turning a golden brown.

Raising a single brow at me, Tehya shrugged. "Help yourself."

I glanced around for a plate or any other serving tools, finding none, and under Tehya's cold stare, I licked my lips and reached forward to pick up one of the thick corn cakes with my fingers.

"Ah!" I howled, tossing the steaming bread from one hand to the other as it burned my skin. Blowing on it to cool it down, it was still too hot to hold, forcing me to set it on my new dress to avoid forming blisters.

Chuckles came from the Vaade around the cook fire as well as a few more around the room that I hadn't realized were there.

Tehya tried to hide her smirk, but not very hard. Nodding to my lap, she said, "Don't waste that."

I didn't know where Tehya's dress had been. But I was too hungry to argue with her and too humiliated to agree, so I chose to copy their silence, ignoring them completely.

Blowing on my fingers to cool them, I was wishing

for ice, when she calmly reached out and picked up one of the hot cakes.

My mouth fell open.

Steam curled up in a thin smoky wisp above her hand, yet she didn't react. Letting it rest in her hand, she gave me a cheeky grin. If my fingers weren't burning, it might've tempted me to smile back. As it was, I leaned into my irritation instead. I hated being the focus of ridicule.

Bizarre Vaade skin.

I let my eyes skim over her, then lifted my chin and looked away, as if unimpressed.

Only yesterday I'd seen what should have been a fatal injury cause a mere scratch, so I shouldn't be surprised. The lack of plates or serving tools made sense now. Why worry about hot food if the heat didn't bother them?

My own little hot cake had cooled enough to eat, even if it burned my tongue a bit. I swallowed the last bite, but I was still starving. They were so small.

Uncertainty and hunger twisted my stomach, making me less reasonable than usual. It wasn't like me to use my Gifts recklessly, not to mention, in front of anyone else—but they already knew about them.

Koda's words from the night before floated back to me.

What do I have to lose?

I made a split-second decision and shifted.

My fingertips grew long and sharp, thick and pointed

like claws.

Tehya's eyebrows rose, grudgingly impressed. A couple other Vaade nudged each other and studied me. But every face around the fire was curious. None of them held fear.

My shoulders lowered from where they'd unconsciously risen to my ears, and I let out the breath I'd been holding when I'd shifted.

They didn't care.

Using my new claws, I scooped up two more steaming hot cakes, not feeling the heat at all. I couldn't help a self-satisfied smile as they watched.

Tehya waited until I chewed the last bite before speaking up, "We should fight."

I choked, tensing.

"Not like that." She rolled her eyes as I coughed, trying to catch my breath. "For fun."

Fun? I blinked at her, not understanding.

"I've heard all about your shape-shifting and now your mind-tricks. I still think I'll win."

She let the challenge hang in the air.

A fight. For fun. I couldn't wrap my mind around the concept. "I'm injured…"

"It's not that bad," she scoffed, dismissing my shoulder wound in a handful of words.

I glanced over my shoulder, hoping Koda would rescue me from his crazy sister.

"Koda won't like it," one of the Vaade murmured, obviously thinking the same thing.

Tehya shrugged. "Don't care."

I couldn't help but compare her to the Jinn back home. Instead of fearing my Gift, she wanted to test it, to face me head on. Part of me was intrigued. "What kind of fight?"

Jumping to her feet, eyes lighting up, she gestured for me to follow. Instead of answering, she cheerfully called to the rest of the room. "To the clearing."

I hadn't actually agreed to the fight, but curiosity took over. When she took my arm at the door, I didn't protest. This was my opportunity to learn more about the Vaade—their strengths *and* their weaknesses. It could be valuable information to bring home.

Even if none of those things happened, it'd be easier for Shem to rescue me if I was *outside* the longhouse, wouldn't it?

Tehya surprised me by letting go of my arm. I supposed she wasn't worried about an escape when there were so many of them to give pursuit and only one of me.

Every other Vaade in the room trailed after us. The idea of fighting one of them was intimidating on its own, but having an audience nearly made me change my mind.

All of my instincts screamed to run.

Logic took over, reminding me I wouldn't get far in an area like this. I couldn't see past the surrounding trees. With their speed, they could probably run as fast as I could travel. I needed to play along with Tehya's challenge.

As we passed through the camp, other Vaade seemed

to recognize the direction we were headed, joining us until our small group held a few dozen. The majority chattered excitedly, although I heard a few grumbles about how Tehya "shouldn't allow the Jinni brat to wander around camp."

"We allow attacks in most forms," Tehya was saying, and I made myself pay attention. "But no going for the eyes or the throat."

Odd. A shiver of anticipation mixed with dread washed over me. "What if I hurt you?"

Tehya and a few others laughed. "Do your worst," she said. "You won't get past me."

Her reaction was so unexpected that I slowed.

Grabbing my elbow, she dragged me on. "Keep up," she said, but not angrily. It was almost as if the idea of a fight had raised her spirits.

"Do you do this often?"

"Sometimes."

We reached the clearing she'd mentioned, and I knew she'd been playing it off. It looked like it'd been used at least a hundred times before, like they came here often, maybe even daily.

Were the Vaade not as nomadic as the king and queen assumed? I filed away this new information, hoping it might mean something, even if I didn't know what right now.

The dirt was packed down, with a circle in the center created out of logs, with taller tree stumps cut and placed around it as seating around the little arena.

Though the nerves made my skin tingle, the excitement was starting to take over. I'd never had a chance to test my Gifts publicly before. Not only was everyone okay with it, but they wanted to *watch*. I didn't scare them at all. Part of me liked the reaction more than I would've expected.

But when Tehya stepped into the circle and waved for me to join her, I balked. "I've never fought anyone before."

She jutted out a hip and crossed her arms, frowning at me. "You're saying you just let Koda capture you?"

"That's different," I mumbled. And the truth was, I kind of had. I'd never needed to know fighting tactics before. If I ever made it back home, I'd make sure that changed. "How do we know who wins?"

"First person, or Jinni"—she added with a wicked smile—"to step outside the circle loses."

I frowned. "That doesn't seem like a test of our abilities?"

Hiding her thoughts behind an innocent mask, she spread her hands wide and said, "Why not enter and find out?" Almost as an aside, she added, "You can also yell 'defeat' if you find it's too much for you."

Some hecklers who'd joined us shouted insults, while others looked genuinely curious to see how this fight would go. One angry voice yelled, "Give up while you still can!" I recognized Ahriman by his seemingly permanent scowl.

My pride immediately rejected his suggestion. But

this wasn't a simple fight either, and I didn't want to appear foolish. If I stepped into the ring in front of her, she'd use her Vaade strength to shove me out. This seemed like an unfair advantage. It was her strength against my wits.

But if I use my Gifts... There was something thrilling about the idea of using my Gifts so openly. It was just a fight. The worst that could happen would be if Tehya humiliated me, and that couldn't be much worse than what I'd endured here already.

I grinned.

15

STROLLING AROUND THE CIRCLE to the other side, I kept my eyes on Tehya. She smiled at me and allowed it.

Trying to catch her off balance, I leapt into the circle without warning, running toward the center, where I planned to hold my ground, shifting into a Lacklore as I ran.

Even after multiple encounters with the Vaade, I still managed to underestimate how fast they were.

With one leap, Tehya crossed the circle.

On all fours, claws partially formed, my body was still growing to the full Lacklore height, when she slammed into my side. A half-scream and half-roar ripped out of me as I forced the rest of my shift. Baring my teeth, I bit her arm and flung her toward the boundary lines.

She flew through the air in a graceful arc, landing on her feet like a cat, eyes flickering as she glanced down at the shallow puncture marks on her arm.

THE SECRET CURSE

I hadn't held back.

Drawing in a frustrated breath, I realized breaking her skin would never be an effective way to win. I needed a different method.

At least she approached more warily now, though she circled me with the determination of a wolf hunting its prey.

She pounced and managed to wrestle me to the ground until I rolled, crushing her with my weight briefly before a well-aimed kick at my shoulder made me retreat with a yelp. We landed on opposite sides of the circle, panting.

I moved on instinct as she continued to attack without giving me a chance to recover. Snarling, I extended my claws, swiping wildly to fend her off. She dodged near and away, not giving me a chance to think.

She caught me by surprise, tossing me across the ring. I dragged my claws, barely catching myself before I slid out of the circle.

Cheers disrupted my focus. This was Tehya's element. Maybe I should let her win and get this over with.

"What's the matter?" she mocked when I remained on the other side of the circle instead of charging her like before. Looking me over, she tsked. "If you're the best Jinn has, we should skip the covenant and just invade."

Cheers sounded from the onlookers, along with a few more choice insults about the Jinn. For some reason, though, those didn't sound as light-hearted as Tehya's had.

Pride smarting, I shook my head and hauled myself to my feet, teeth bared. A memory of Koda fighting the first time I'd seen him came to me. I'd have to time it right...

She prowled toward me, which was her first mistake.

It gave me time to shift.

Pushing my body, I changed as fast as I had when Koda pursued me.

I returned to my true form.

A split second later, I traveled, landing behind her.

Wrapping my arms around her waist, I caught her off-guard, traveling again immediately.

It worked!

She wasn't mentally prepared, and I was able to take her with me, just like the guards had taken Koda. I could've traveled outside the circle, but then I'd lose too, and I wanted to *win*.

So I dropped her at the edge of the circle, as close as I dared, and gave her a push.

She wasn't nearly as confused as Koda had been, though. It was almost as if she'd prepared for this—she caught me by the arms, twisting and using my weight to pull herself back, nearly making me fall on top of her.

I traveled again in a panic.

It worked, but she held onto me so firmly that I couldn't shake her when we reappeared.

I traveled again, and again. A fifth time, a sixth. She was like a leech. It was almost as if she was letting me

THE SECRET CURSE

travel with her...

It was wearing me out, but if I stopped for too long, she'd defeat me, so I kept going, flashing from one side of the circle to the next. I tried landing closer and closer to the edge. If I could put her across the line, I could still win.

Suddenly she wasn't moveable anymore. She slipped from my arms as I traveled, ripped away from me like an anchor from a current.

I reappeared alone on the other side of the circle, whirling around, confused.

What'd changed? Had *she* done that?

I didn't have a chance to think it through, as she sprang at me with a snarl.

I traveled out of the way.

She landed awkwardly as she wrapped her arms around thin air.

On the defensive now, I stood right next to the edge, hoping she'd jump too far, but she was too smart to fall for that. She stalked toward me with careful steps.

When she neared the center of the arena, I traveled behind her, attempting to use the full force of my Gift of manipulation as I commanded, "Stop!"

Instead, she flung me backward across the circle.

I landed on my injured arm and gasped.

The pain blinded me for a moment.

Dragging myself to my feet, I wiped the sweat out of my eyes with my good arm, trying not to cradle my injured arm too obviously even though it throbbed to the point I could hardly think straight.

Tehya didn't press her advantage, which a quiet voice in the back of my head whispered was odd.

She kept near the edge instead, stalking me.

I moved in the opposite direction, keeping my distance.

The Vaade around us were hooting and calling out encouragement to her, but she only circled cautiously.

I tuned them out.

I couldn't afford a distraction right now.

She *had* to have felt me trembling during those last few attacks. Why didn't she attack?

Keeping one eye on her, I took in our surroundings, searching for something I'd missed—was Koda here? Was she somehow injured too and hiding it? Nothing made sense, but as I listened to the Vaade around us jeer at me, one of them yelled, "Stop going easy on her!"

I frowned.

Glaring at me, as if somehow I was doing this wrong, Tehya swung her eyes toward the sky and back, trying to communicate something to me.

Whatever it was, she clearly didn't want to say it with the Vaade around us listening in.

I squinted at her. She wanted to fight in the sky? No… It was almost like… My eyes widened as it hit me. She wanted me to shift into a bird and fly away like I had the day before. That couldn't be right…

I tried to tamp down my reaction as we circled each other warily, looking for an opening. She made the

THE SECRET CURSE

gesture a second time. I hadn't imagined it, then.

All at once this strange fight made sense: she wanted me gone. If I wasn't here anymore, the Vaade would lose their negotiating power with the Jinn. Shem would refuse the marriage that *she* didn't want to happen in the first place.

She wanted me to escape.

Subtly, I shook my head at her, gazing around the circle of Vaade and then down at my injured arm to send her a silent message in return: *not like this*. Not surrounded by enemies, while hurt.

That wasn't a quick getaway, it was a death sentence.

Maybe she knew that and hoped I'd take the chance anyway? I couldn't say for sure, but in my irritation, I went on the offensive.

This time when I traveled, I landed in front of her, eye to eye, and whispered, "Back up."

Her sharp eyes dulled.

With the added eye contact, my Gift was taking effect!

She stepped out of the circle obediently.

The Vaade fell silent.

I should've been worried, but instead I grinned.

Someone clapped, and others joined in with cheers. Tehya's trance broke at the sound. She shook her head to clear the cobwebs.

Angry shouts broke through the conversation, as a handful of Vaade glared in my direction, while others stormed off as if they couldn't be in my presence another moment.

I waited for the punishment. It was my own fault for giving in to my frustration. No one liked their free will being taken.

It didn't come.

Shaking her head at me, Tehya gave me a reluctant nod and held out her hand to shake. "I should've been more prepared. I'll admit, I'm impressed."

A few more Vaade spat on the ground at her admission and stormed off as well. But most of them stayed, and there was more than one nod of agreement at Tehya's statement. I caught myself smiling. It was only because my plan to get them to trust me was working.

"Come," Tehya said, not bothering to hold my arm as we took the path back to camp. "Let's get something for that shoulder."

The throbbing intensified when she brought my attention to it. Between the injury, my exhaustion, and the number of Vaade still fairly close by, even if I'd wanted to run, I wouldn't have made it far. That didn't stop me from giving the sky one last longing glance before turning to follow her.

For all I knew, Shem might have a rescue planned. It could happen any minute now. Better to accept their food and medicine, and be fully rested when the time came.

She left me at the big outdoor bonfire, where I sank down among the other Vaade without a second thought because I'd pushed too hard again. I didn't even realize Tehya had left me alone with strange Vaade until she was

THE SECRET CURSE

halfway back from the longhouse.

When she crouched beside me, I tensed. As she reached for my arm, I unconsciously leaned away.

"If I had your magic, I'd tell you to sit still," she grumbled, pulling me back toward her. "Don't move, or it'll hurt more." She rubbed a salve that looked and smelled like the one Koda had used into my arm, but instead of wrapping it again, she left it exposed to the air. "It'll heal faster this way," she said without further explanation.

She left me unguarded for a second time as she returned the medicine to wherever it was kept.

Colorful eyes around the fire watched me closely. Unguarded wasn't the right word; I was far from alone.

Her mouth twisted almost like disappointment when she returned to find me in the same place. She must have a severely low opinion of the Jinn if she thought I'd run in my condition—not only did my arm ache, which meant there was no way I'd be able to fly right now, but after both the fight and the shifting, I was also starving.

Someone passed around some smoked meat and a type of thick bread, similar to what we'd eaten that morning. I took a second helping.

"Time to put you to work," Tehya said around a mouthful, pulling up a stack of long, thick reeds. "I'll teach you."

I wrinkled my nose. Grass baskets wouldn't hold any secrets on the covenant. Glancing around for Koda, I sighed. Unless he reappeared out of thin air, it didn't look like I had a choice.

We spent the afternoon making baskets—or in my case, attempting to.

"Like this," she said with a grunt, when I mixed up the fourth and fifth weave yet again. "Like a little deer running around its mother's legs, and then beneath, coming out the other side. Then the dragon eats it."

I snorted at the image.

She demonstrated with the strands, but I couldn't picture these deer she described, much less the dragon weave. Rolling my eyes, I muttered under my breath, "If you wanted a fancy basket, you should've asked someone else."

"Who says I want a fancy basket?" she retorted. I'd forgotten about her impossible Vaade hearing. "Maybe I just want to torture you."

"With basket-weaving?" I laughed at the ridiculous idea. "By all means then, torture on. We'll see how effective it is."

Instead of stiffening from my comments like Milcah would've, Tehya burst out laughing. "Prisoners of war sent to a basket-weaving class spill all their secrets!" She threw her head back as she cackled. "Can you imagine?"

I laughed too, caught off guard.

Tehya shook her head as we returned to the baskets, almost as if surprised by our easy camaraderie.

That made two of us.

The sun was low in the sky now, and Tehya had started looking over her shoulder constantly by the time

Koda finally reappeared.

"Any luck?" she murmured to him, forgetting me completely.

He hadn't, however. Taking her arm, he led her a few paces away where I couldn't overhear, before whispering. The sun on the horizon turned them into silhouettes.

I considered shifting my hearing, but they were done before I had the chance.

Fists clenched and red-faced, Tehya stormed off toward the longhouse without so much as a goodbye.

Koda came to sit by me, also without a word.

Stiffening in his presence, I realized how much I'd let my guard down today. During my short time with the Vaade, Koda had usually been the one to give me a sense of safety, but not right now.

Every muscle along his large arms rippled as he reached for a log from the pile behind us and threw it in the fire with such force I wondered if he'd imagined it was a person. He gripped another log, squeezing it as if wringing someone's neck.

I focused on weaving the basket I'd started hours ago. Without Tehya to show me where I'd gone wrong, the whole thing was hopelessly tangled. I started to sigh, then caught myself.

Too late. I'd drawn his attention.

Koda straightened. His face grew blank as he visibly shut the door on whatever bothered him. He tossed the second log on the fire much more gently. "I trust you've behaved yourself, Jinni girl?"

"Jezebel," I reminded him casually, attempting a smile. If I could, I hoped to make him see me less as a hated Jinn and more as a person. That would increase my chances of getting information from him. "And yes…" I hesitated, wondering if I should skip telling him about the fight earlier.

"Why does your yes sound more like a no?"

If he'd asked with a scowl, I'd have protested, but his slight smirk was returning. The golden light danced across his face, giving him an otherworldly glow. With that strong nose, thick brows, and mesmerizing eyes, he could rival Shem's good looks. He was like the sun—warm, strong, full of life—I stopped myself before I had any other traitorous thoughts.

"It was Tehya's idea," I began, holding my hands up in the universal sign of helplessness. "She—"

"Wanted to fight," he finished with a sigh, shaking his head.

"How did you know?"

"Tehya's always wanted to fight a Jinni, but our father refuses to include her on the raids."

I read between the lines. Koda had been on the last two, and I assumed probably the ones before that as well. Tehya and her brother had seemed close, to the point that I'd felt a twinge of jealousy, wishing I'd had a sibling who could care about me like that—but this hinted at a jealousy between them. Koda had something she didn't.

Keeping my voice neutral, I shrugged. "She got what she wanted."

"Who won?"

The fact that he didn't automatically assume it was his sister sent warm tingles through my body. "Who do you think?" I taunted, genuinely wanting to know who he'd bet on. But I couldn't help a small smile that gave me away.

His brows rose in appreciation, but he pursed his lips and tilted his head, teasing back, "So, Tehya then?"

"Tehya was the rightful winner," one of the Vaade on the other side of the fire slurred. Angry gold eyes met mine over the flames, glittering with unadulterated rage. "The Jinni snake cheated."

Used to fighting my own battles, I expected Koda to let me handle it the way Shem would. My mouth was open, ready to tell him I'd broken no rules, but Koda spoke first.

"You've always been a sore loser, Ahriman," he growled with a cold look in his eyes. "I've been spoiling for a reason to hit someone all day." Slowly he leaned forward on his knees, as he added in a soft tone that somehow seemed even more dangerous, "Feel free to say something else you'll regret."

Ahriman eyed him, swaying slightly. I worried whatever he was drinking would impede his judgment, but he managed to hold his tongue. Glaring at me, he stood and stumbled away from the fire.

Now that the sun had set, twilight was turning everything gray, including the forest, where he entered the shadows and disappeared.

I shivered once he was gone, feeling exposed and anxious with an angry Vaade wandering out there in the dark somewhere behind me. Discreetly, I scooted my log closer to Koda when he stood to put another on the fire.

A few other Vaade stood to leave as well. Their faces were unreadable, but Koda didn't relax fully until they were gone, leaving us alone.

"Would you really have fought him?" I whispered, unable to help myself, though I stopped before I added *for me?*

A muscle twitched in his jaw. He kept his eyes on the fire as he shrugged, but didn't look at me.

It was growing steadily darker, lending an almost intimate feel to the moment. I considered asking Koda why he'd been gone the entire day, opening my mouth to do so, when a twig snapped.

It was so light that at first, I thought it came from the crackling fire.

Some instinct made me tense though, sensing an attack. *Is it Shem? Is he finally coming to rescue me?*

Koda had heard it too, swiveling to face the unknown sound.

In the split second that followed, I found myself worrying for him, hoping he'd run when he found himself outnumbered instead of trying to fight.

But it wasn't Shem.

It wasn't anyone from Jinn.

16

FOUR SNEERING VAADE MATERIALIZED in the dusk of the forest at our backs, hidden from the rest of the camp by the trees.

The inebriated Ahriman had come back with friends. "Stay out of this," he said when Koda stood, widening his stance in front of me. "Even the Dragon wants it gone. I put you down earlier today, and I'll do it again."

"Only because I let you," Koda said on a roar, lunging at the same time they did. He met Ahriman midair, crashing to the ground, rolling in a blur of fists.

I froze as the other three stalked toward me.

How could I face three?

Panicking, I circled the large fire, keeping it between us.

My mind raced.

I didn't know the woods beyond this spot and couldn't see far enough to travel. I could either shift and face them—three to one—or I could attempt to run…

They circled the fire after me.

Having seen how far Koda could leap, I knew they were toying with me. They could cross this fire in a heartbeat.

Growls came from behind them. A fist connected with flesh. *Oof,* the sound of air knocked out of lungs. Another groan, followed by a snarl. Koda's struggle didn't sound like it was ending anytime soon.

This was up to me.

Run first, I thought, backing toward the woods, not taking my eyes off the Vaade's sneering faces. *Duck behind a tree. Shift. Disappear.*

Would it work? Or would they be able to follow my trail of magic like Koda had?

The Vaade leading the group crouched to spring. I didn't have time for a better plan.

Without a second thought, I jumped over the bushes into the dark woods and ran, dodging dark silhouettes of trees as they rose before me.

A rough hand latched onto my wrist, throwing off my balance. I fell, taking the Vaade down with me.

Grappling wildly, I shrieked, "Let go!"

I felt it the moment my Gift took effect on him, even though I hadn't looked in his eyes, growing stronger in my terror. His hands and body pulled back, just long enough for me to scramble to my feet and run.

Sheer panic flooded my body.

I'd never been so out of control before.

THE SECRET CURSE

Trembling hands turned into full body shudders, as I heard heavy breathing behind me. They were playing with me again, deliberately letting me run though they had the clear advantage. I stumbled.

Rocks bit into my knee, but I barely felt it, picking myself up and running on.

The last bit of fading sunlight hardly reached the forest floor. I should shift my eyes, but I was too frantic to focus, feeling branches rake through my hair, scraping across my skin, and ripping at Tehya's dress as I ran even harder, heart pumping.

I didn't get far.

A body slammed into mine from behind, and another hit me from the side a second later, knocking the air out of me as we hit the ground hard.

Hands wrapped around my neck.

My lungs burned as I tried to breath, but I couldn't think to shift or fight as I choked for air.

The other Vaade ground his hand into my wounded shoulder.

I opened my mouth to scream in agony, but no sound came out.

Unable to shift through the pain, I struggled weakly as another set of hands fell on my legs, stifling movement. The third Vaade hissed, "Finish it."

Struggling to breathe as my vision darkened, I choked out an anguished sob.

Then, the heavy weight on my body was gone.

My feet were freed next.

A roar of fury came from above me as someone crashed into the Vaade with his hands around my neck. I flung myself back, gasping, gulping down air, crawling away from the sounds of scuffling in the dark.

The only light now was the moon, barely reaching us through the trees.

My eyes darted wildly around, searching for more shadows, terrified more Vaade were coming. I bumped into a tree as I backed up and covered my mouth to stifle a scream. *It's just a tree. Get a hold of yourself, you've been in worse situations*, I lied to myself.

Trembling, I tried to shift. It wouldn't come. My body shook with silent sobs.

This is not *how I'm going to die.* With shaking hands, I felt for a low-hanging branch, and forced myself to climb, despite the burning in my shoulder.

More thuds sounded below along with heavy breathing and unearthly growls.

Then, a sickly crunch that sounded like a tree meeting a body, followed by silence.

I covered my mouth with my hand, squeezing my eyes shut, trying to stifle the sound of my breathing.

It had been three to one. The odds that Koda had won that fight weren't good.

They were coming for me.

I was only a few branches up. With the dim moonlight, I'd gotten stuck, unable to find another handhold.

I tried to shift again into a mouse or bird or bear or

even adjust my eyes to have night vision—anything would've been better than nothing—but the ice in my veins had blocked my senses, leaving me completely vulnerable which only intensified my fear, creating an impossible cycle.

Below, a shadow in the shape of a large man moved along the ground, straight toward me. His footsteps were silent.

He was stalking me.

My head pounded from when the Vaade had pushed it into the ground, along with throbbing wounds all along the rest of my body.

When he stopped at the base of my tree, I held my breath.

"Come down, Jinni girl," an angry male voice growled.

I tried not to throw up.

A sigh came from below.

I pressed my face into the bark, not caring if it scratched me, as my arms circled the trunk. I refused to make killing me easier for him.

"Jezebel," the voice said, softer now.

My eyes flew open.

Shivering uncontrollably, I peeked down at the hulking shadow beneath me, trying to make out a face.

I couldn't, but with that one word, I *knew* who it was.

Koda.

"It's safe now," he added in a soothing tone. When his shape moved slightly, landing in a patch of moonlight,

I realized he held out a hand. "You can sleep there if you want, but they won't be feeling very rational when they wake up. I'd prefer to go back to the smokehouse before I have to give them a second beating."

That got me moving.

Hurrying from one branch to another, they seemed farther apart than when I'd climbed up. Since I still hadn't managed to shift my eyesight, I slipped.

With a yelp, I fell the last few feet.

He caught me.

I wrapped my arms around his neck without thinking, dragging in a shuddering breath. He smelled like a mixture of warm bonfire and something I could only describe as *safe*.

When he set me on my feet, my legs gave out, too weak to stand. I sagged against him, embarrassed.

He held me without complaint. Quietly, he pulled me closer, tucking my head under his chin, and gently pressed my head to his chest.

I stiffened, but the sound of his steady heartbeat beneath my ear was strangely soothing. Relaxing slightly, I let myself stay where I was until the shaking subsided.

He still didn't pull back.

I knew I should, but I didn't want to.

"Thank you," I whispered into his chest finally, voice breaking.

A little moonlight touched his arm and then his face as he leaned back. It was impossible to read his expression in the dark, but I could've sworn his eyes slid over my face, stopping briefly on my lips, before continuing on. He seemed to catalog the many different scrapes as well as the evidence of tears where they'd trailed through the dirt on my cheeks.

Embarrassed, I pulled away enough to scrub at the dirt—and tears—with rough hands.

He still didn't let go.

My hands lowered until they landed on his chest, making my heart race again in an entirely different way. I dared to lift my gaze from them to his face.

His fingers tightened along my back, drawing me closer to him again.

All thought escaped me as his head dipped lower.

I tilted my chin up, lips parting.

A groan came from one of the nearby Vaade.

We stepped back as if we'd been caught, and thoughts of Shem flooded my mind. *What just happened?*

"We should go," Koda murmured. "I'll deal with them in the morning when they're thinking more clearly. Right now isn't the best time." He took my hand, as if he could tell that my eyesight wasn't up to par, and led me back in the direction of the camp.

The bonfire was like a beacon. With every step closer, it whispered, *You're safe. You're safe. You're safe.*

But how long would that last?

Once we stepped into the light, the pain from my multiple injuries grew more intense as my adrenaline faded, changing from minor complaints to screaming protests. My ribs ached from a punch I'd barely registered and my arms and legs were covered in bloody cuts. Though my shoulder burned, the blistering ache around my neck where those hands had been was the worst, like a necklace of fire.

All of it left me feeling weak, fragile. Two things I *hated*.

My shifting had failed me—*I had failed*. I didn't want to think about it, but my confidence was severely shaken. I was no longer certain I could save myself if the Vaade decided to get rid of me. And, though I did my best to ignore the whisper in my mind, I was starting to wonder if Shem was going to save me after all.

17

I WALKED IN A daze until Koda stopped us at the longhouse, reaching for the door.

"What're you doing?" I hissed, pulling my hand out of his, sharply returning to the present.

"We need to dress your wounds," he replied calmly, opening the door. He held it for me, waiting.

"Can you go get what you need and come back?" my voice came out pleading. I didn't know how many Vaade were inside, I only knew that I did *not* want them to see me like this. Jinn did not show weakness. Not under any circumstances.

"No."

I glanced at the open door. Voices floated out from inside, talking, laughing, oblivious to our quiet debate. "It's just a few scratches," I told him, waving a hand through the air, trying not to wince when it pulled at my wounded shoulder, which I suspected might be bleeding again. "I don't need anything."

He grabbed the wrist of my uninjured arm as I tried to walk past him, tugging me back. "There's also food inside. You need to eat."

My stomach tried to betray me with a gurgle, but I cleared my throat loudly over it. "I'm not hungry."

"Inside." He didn't give me a chance to argue again or let go as he stepped through the door.

Dragging my feet, I kept my eyes on his back. The now-familiar fear pumped through my veins as dozens of eyes turned our way and the room fell silent.

I must've looked worse than I thought.

Koda moved through the bunks along the walls to the center of the room, where every single log was taken, and at least two dozen more Vaade stood around the fire as well, all of them eating. Or at least, they had been, before we came in. Now there was a mixture of expressions: glares, curiosity, and confusion.

I tried to stop, tugging at his hand, but he pushed through the crowd, pulling me along with him and stopping in the center next to his sister, who stopped chewing at the sight of me.

"Up," Koda said to her.

His back was to me, but whatever expression was on his face made her cut off any arguments and silently stand.

He turned to me. "Sit." Again with the one word demands. When I saw the fury in his face, my eyes widened. I could see why Tehya hadn't protested but I still cleared my throat and tried, voice rasping a little, "I don't need to—"

"Now."

I sat.

And then I stopped breathing as he walked away and started digging through a trunk along the wall, leaving me in front of dozens of Vaade eyes that pinned me in place.

I expected to hear murmurs or gossip of some sort, but no one spoke as eyes darted between Koda and I. In the loud silence, we all heard Koda murmur for someone to go "take care of" the Vaade in the woods. "Lock them up for the night," he added to the men striding toward the door. "They need to cool off."

Distracted by their exit, I didn't notice at first how the nearby Vaade at the fire were staring at the bloody scratches along my bare arms and legs, or how Tehya's borrowed dress was now dirt-streaked and shredded.

I wrapped my arms around my body, trying and failing to cover the damage.

A few of those judgmental looks were pinned to my neck, where I could only imagine a cluster of bruises was forming.

When Tehya came back into my line of sight, she held an empty wooden bowl. Using the ladle in the large pot over the fire, she scooped a large helping of stew and held it out to her brother as he stalked back through the crowd with a handful of bandages and salve.

Instead of taking it, he gestured for her to give it to me, saying, "Eat."

"I'm not hungry." It wasn't true, but I'd happily go

without a meal if it meant we could leave.

"*Eat*," he said again, in a tone that said he wouldn't take no for an answer.

I accepted the bowl from Tehya with a timid thank you, suddenly aware I was starving. Digging into the stew, I ignored the way it burned my tongue, eating as fast as possible.

This wasn't like the council or the castle or anywhere in Jinn, where I could pull on a cold mask of indifference and let them think nothing touched me. Here, I couldn't seem to hide anything.

Which meant they all saw me wince and gasp when Koda unexpectedly pulled a dangling piece of the dress away from my shoulder to see the wound.

"I'm fine," I forced out, willing him to let it go. *I don't want to look weak.*

"They need to see this," he said. But he wasn't really talking to me, I realized. His voice was raised, hard eyes scanning the room, landing on every single person there. "They need to see that you're human too."

"But I'm not." I whispered it without thinking, then cringed. I could see what he was trying to do, and I wasn't helping.

Koda met my eyes now. "You are in the way that counts."

I couldn't speak.

When he broke our gaze, I blinked, trying to orient myself. Warmth spread throughout my whole body. He was like no one I'd ever met before. I didn't want to think of Shem in this moment, but I couldn't help comparing the two.

I barely noticed when some of the Vaade quietly began returning to conversations, though eyes still drifted to us frequently.

"The shoulder needs stitches." Koda wasn't speaking to me, but to Tehya, who nodded.

I paled. "I'd rather not." Back home, we'd go to a Jinni healer for something like this. I'd never had someone put a needle through my skin before and didn't want to start now.

"It won't heal right without it," he answered simply, as he started to wash the wound in preparation.

Tehya brought him a needle and thread far too soon, and I started to tremble again at the sight. Pressing my lips together, I refused to shame myself in front of so many. I held in a squeak when he started, shutting my eyes tightly and breathing through the pain as he continued. Eyes watering, I tried to blink to stop the tears from escaping, but one trickled down my cheek. I kept my gaze on the floor, pressing my lips together, hoping no one would notice.

The stitches seemed to go on forever.

I was ready to break my vow to myself and beg Koda to stop when he finally tied a knot and cut the thread with his teeth.

When he went over the cuts along my arms and legs, first washing them, then covering them with yellow ointment from a jar, I barely felt any of it through the sledgehammer slamming into my shoulder with every heartbeat.

I held the empty bowl in my lap, eyelids drooping.

Hands slipped the bowl from mine.

I stiffened, sitting upright, wincing at the way that pulled the stitches in my shoulder.

A Vaade woman with warm green eyes and golden-brown hair met my gaze without malice. "More?"

I hesitated.

Koda was kneeling by my knees, carefully pulling out little bits of rocks that'd been embedded in my skin from one of my many falls. He nodded subtle encouragement.

Clearing my throat, I nodded too and murmured, "Please."

She filled the bowl to the brim and handed it back to me.

I ate it like it was my first, finally starting to feel full. Chewing my lip, I dared to look up from the food and Koda to find the woman in the crowd.

I tried not to shrink back when I found at least a dozen eyes still on me, quickly darting from one to the next until I found the green-eyed woman and made myself speak, though it came out quieter than I'd wanted it to. "Thank you."

She gave me a solemn nod, eyes lingering on me until I looked away.

"She's tougher than she looks," a Vaade man next to her said. His voice was a normal tone, but it felt like he

THE SECRET CURSE

was shouting after everyone else had stuck to whispers.

Wide-eyed, I could only stare at him. He was the first Vaade besides Koda and his sister who hadn't referred to me as an "it." That felt significant.

"You just can't handle pain, Yona," another man teased him with a laugh, causing a round of good-natured ribbing that finally took the attention off me. I drew in a deep breath for the first time in what felt like hours.

"Told you," Koda murmured as he finished wrapping my knee, giving me a meaningful look. He didn't elaborate, but he didn't need to.

They needed to see I wasn't the embodiment of evil.

But what if I was?

I couldn't hold Koda's gaze, looking down at my hands instead. I was still planning to end this so-called covenant and escape, one way or another. I just felt a bit more guilty about it now.

The lighter mood around the fire was infectious. Someone began a story about the first man's hunt as a boy and how he'd somehow shot himself in the foot. They mimicked how he'd carried on, though even I could tell it was exaggerated, prompting a lot of laughter and more teasing at his expense. Koda even joined in a few times as he got a bowl for himself and finally ate his dinner. When a man offered to let him take the seat beside me, Koda shook his head, settling himself cross-legged on the floor between us instead.

I didn't realize I was staring at the back of his head until Tehya quietly cleared her throat behind me.

Flushing, I looked away, eyes catching on one laughing Vaade after another.

"Let's get you another dress," she said, bringing me back to the same bed and giving me a chance to change yet again. The new dress fell a little past my knees, with sleeves this time, and fancier needlework. Gripping the discarded dress and lifting one of the ripped pieces from the shoulder, Tehya's face darkened dangerously. "I'm going to kick their next child out of them," she growled to herself. But she tossed the ruined dress onto the bed without another thought, leading us back to the fire.

I met Koda's eyes as we returned.

His outline grew blurry.

I blinked, hoping he hadn't noticed the tears.

Koda didn't realize—or maybe he was smarter than I gave him credit for, and he knew *exactly* what he was doing—but having me here had not only caused the Vaade to see me differently.

It'd also changed the way I saw *them.*

My throat was tight. A mother tickled her little son who giggled, and the father tucked both of them into his lap with a smile. It would sound ridiculous if I said it aloud, because of course, it was obvious, but it still felt like a fresh revelation that meant something new: *They're people too.*

18

"COME," KODA SAID AFTER we'd sat by the fire for another hour or so. It wasn't that late, but my body swayed as I sat on the log, begging for sleep. I didn't argue with him.

We wove through the Vaade as we left, and I got a lump in my throat each time one of them gave me a respectful nod. Five Vaade men joined us without Koda saying a word. Cool air hit my face as we stepped out of the longhouse, making me more alert. But there was no sign of the Vaade who'd attacked us earlier. Only thousands of cheerful stars winking down at us, lighting our way. The moon had risen high in the sky, making the smokehouse visible as we approached.

The Vaade man who'd first spoken to me, Yona, held a hand up when we reached it. "I'll go first." Stepping inside, he shuffled around briefly before he popped back out. "It's empty."

Koda nodded, waving me inside.

"We'll make sure Ahriman doesn't bother you tonight," he said, clapping a hand on Koda's back as he passed.

Koda clasped the man's shoulder, murmuring, "Thank you, Yona."

And then he closed the door behind him, leaving us alone for the first time since the attack.

My lips tingled as my traitorous body remembered our almost kiss. We were close enough now that he would only need to reach out an arm to pull me to him again. We stood there for a long moment. *What's wrong with me?* I turned to sit on the furs stretched out along the floor from the night before, hoping that putting my back to him would dissolve the intensity of the moment. I tried to sort through the multitude of feelings I hardly recognized. *Why do I still want him to kiss me?*

Clearing my throat, I faced him, planning to say a formal thank you and cut off anything further.

He'd already lain down. It felt odd to talk to him from above, so after hesitating, I stretched out too, pillowing my hands under my head with a yawn.

Exhaustion stole over me. When I blinked my eyes open again, I found his face a few feet from mine, staring openly. It felt intimate to be laying here next to him. But also, if I were willing to admit it to myself, it felt safe. My body ached but not in the sharp, unbearable way it had earlier. Every scratch and bruise now reminded me of him and the gentle way he'd taken care of me.

THE SECRET CURSE

Koda cleared his throat. "If you ever find yourself in a situation like that again, aim for the throat." He gestured toward his chin, and his throat bobbed as he swallowed. "That's the one place our skin is vulnerable."

I nodded.

He was trusting me.

That was information I could use against *him*, but he shared it anyway.

Why did that upset me more?

I cleared my throat, which seemed loud in the silence, trying to find the nerve to speak. "You didn't have to do that," I whispered.

His voice was low as well, but he had a slight smile. "Do what?"

I frowned, not wanting him to make light of it. If I said *feed me*, I already knew him well enough to know he'd brush it off with "everyone needs to eat," and if I mentioned my wounds, he'd have an excuse for that kindness as well.

So instead, I just said one word: "Care."

His smile faded as he grew serious.

For a minute he didn't seem like he was going to respond. Flipping onto his back, he put his hands behind his head, making the powerful muscles in his arms grow even more defined. "I've never liked bullies," he said finally.

"Me either." Rolling onto my back as well, I stared at the wooden ceiling in the lantern light. I was fairly confident he was talking about his father, which made me think of my own. I should've left it alone. But part of me resonated with his words so much that I was speaking before I fully realized it. "I hate that bullies force you to either be the victim or become one of them. There's no other choice." I'd turned my father into a lizard and left him alone and defenseless for predators to find… But he would've done the same to me.

"You sound like you have experience."

Wrapped up in the memories, I'd almost forgotten Koda was there.

"Is that really the only option?" he added lightly when I didn't say anything else. "I hope you're not talking about me."

My lips twitched, wanting to smile. "If there's a third option," I said, still looking at the ceiling. "Then that person isn't really a bully at all, are they?"

We let the silence stretch comfortably.

But Koda must've been contemplating my words, because just as I was about to drift off, he murmured, "I still think there's a third option."

Yawning, I turned on my side to face him, waiting.

"I don't abuse my power the way he does." He spoke more to himself than to me, still laying on his back. "But I *did* learn to fight back."

I nodded, unsure how to answer.

He seemed to be waiting for my thoughts, twisting his head to stare at me, capturing my gaze.

"I… learned that as well," I replied softly, knowing that wasn't fully true. I hadn't chosen the third option, to become better than my father. I'd simply become him.

Not wanting to think about past mistakes I couldn't change, even if I wanted to, I thought of Koda's father instead. "What did he say to you today that made Tehya so upset?" *And you?* I added silently.

He turned back to the ceiling again. Maybe I'd pushed him too far.

Closing my eyes, I tried to settle in for another long night when he unexpectedly answered. "My father refuses to reconsider the covenant."

I snuck a glance at him from beneath my eyelashes. That was hardly a revelation. There had to be more to it.

Waiting, I was rewarded for my patience when he let out a long sigh. "I tried to fight back today, but I failed."

"How so?"

"I told him I'd take Tehya and leave. He said he'd lead a hunting party and find us before we reached the mountains."

Thinking back to when Koda had tracked me, I could only imagine they'd be extremely effective. Nodding, I held back from answering, sensing there was more.

Koda hesitated, still not meeting my gaze. "Then I told him I'd fight him for leadership of our people."

Though I tried to hold in a gasp, his sharp hearing still caught the catch in my breath. Meeting my wide eyes, he smiled, though it lacked any humor. "It was one of those times where your Jinni secrecy would've been the smarter choice."

I couldn't help myself. "What did he do?"

"His men detained me until sundown. It was his way of showing me I didn't have a chance. That they'll follow him over me, no matter what."

Suddenly his absence the entire day made a lot more sense. Still, I frowned. "I don't understand. I *saw* how everyone responded to you at dinner. They adore you. How can your father's control compare to that?"

"Is that a compliment from a Jinni?" he teased.

I flushed. "It was an obvious criticism of your father. That's all."

When he continued smirking, I tried to change the subject. "What made you decide to stand up to your father today anyway, when you haven't before?"

His expression closed. "Nothing."

The way he was hiding something from me for what might be the first time made me shiver, despite the heat of the smokehouse at my back. "There's something you're not telling me."

Koda's lips pressed together firmly. He crossed his arms and closed his eyes, drawing a clear end to our conversation.

Sitting up on one elbow, I stared down at him, growing more concerned, trying to puzzle it out. "When the Dragon first introduced the idea of the covenant, you were upset, but not enough to fight him."

Eyes closed, Koda grunted. "Go to sleep."

Undeterred, I continued thinking out loud, watching his face closely for a reaction. "The covenant is supposed to create a truce between our people, right?" I didn't need him to answer that. "I barely know your kind, but I've already seen enough of your father to know that he would never want to be mere equals with the Jinn."

Though the wrinkles in Koda's forehead were already there and he didn't move a muscle, an icy chill spread over me. I somehow *knew* I was right—the Dragon had a hidden agenda. Once again, I remembered Koda's words from when we'd met. *We don't want peace.*

In a hushed tone, I demanded, "What's he going to do?"

Koda refused to acknowledge me. His eyes remained closed.

Taking a deep breath, I did something I couldn't believe I dared to do: I poked him.

Technically, I poked his arm, and a small part of me noted how firm his muscles were underneath my touch, like poking a rock.

He sat up lightning fast, making me flinch back from a lifetime of habit.

Though he scowled at me, something flickered across his face, and he didn't move closer. "You're intentionally provoking me in your position?" he growled. "Do you think that's wise?"

It wasn't.

Not at all. And yet, I couldn't bring myself to feel worried. "You wouldn't hurt me," I murmured.

Those sunset eyes narrowed, pinning me in place. He didn't agree. But he didn't disagree either.

"Tell me," I asked again, softer.

Rubbing his forehead, he shook his head. "You're my sworn enemy."

I waved a hand at the tiny wooden shack we were in. "Who am I going to tell?" I made my tone incredulous, as if I'd completely given up hope of escaping. "I'm your prisoner until the covenant is completed, remember?" At least, I sincerely hoped they'd let me go if it came to that. "By then, it'll be too late for me to do anything."

When Koda still hesitated, I leaned forward, daring to touch his arm again, waiting until he looked up. I made sure to pull my hand away before I spoke so he'd know I wasn't trying to use my Gift this time. "We both want to stop this covenant, Koda." As I said his name for the first time, something shifted between us, at least for me. I wasn't acting anymore. I meant what I said.

In the softest whisper, in case any nearby Vaade were trying to listen in, I added, "Remember, we're on the same side."

Slowly, he faced me, imitating my posture, one hand cradling his head and the other resting on the furs between us, only a few fingers away from mine.

"What was it you'd said before about keeping secrets?" I tapped my lip as if trying to remember. "Oh yes, it was something about how you get in your own way?"

His lips curved into a wry smile. "You're very persistent, Jinni girl."

"Jezebel," I reminded him absently. "And I'm only just beginning."

THE SECRET CURSE

He sighed, already worn down. "It's a complicated story."

"I'm listening." I propped both hands under my chin.

"My father has a secondary spell that he plans to add to the covenant," he said hesitantly. "It will come after the weakening begins."

I sat up abruptly, with a rising sense of dread. "What kind of spell?"

"It's a forbidden forgetting spell."

A rush of anxiety made my heart pump faster. Spells in Jinn were rarely forbidden unless they affected hundreds—or more often thousands—of lives. "How does it work?"

"It was described as a mixture between ignorance and withering… It erases memories from existence and somehow fills in the hole left behind until the absence is no longer noticeable."

With each word, icy fear stole over me.

"You're saying the covenant—which is binding for both the leaders and their entire people—would take away all Jinni Gifts and Vaade strengths… And then we'd just *forget* that it happened?"

Koda raised himself to a sitting position as well, crossing his legs. He dipped his head in a slow nod.

My heart sank. This was far worse than I'd imagined. Every Jinni under Shem's reign would lose their Gifts *and* their memories of them.

Including me.

Koda couldn't meet my eyes.

"That's not just any spell," I whispered, lifting a trembling hand to my mouth and shaking my head. "That's a *curse*."

19

"IT DOESN'T MAKE ANY sense," I murmured, mostly to myself. "The Dragon wouldn't do that to his own people—" Raising my eyes back to Koda, I narrowed them. "Is it temporary?" Maybe his father planned to ambush Shem and the Jinn, attacking the marriage party while they were weakened? But that didn't make sense either, because the Vaade would be weakened as well…

"In this case, the curse would be anchored to the covenant, meaning it would remain in place until the covenant is completed." He fidgeted, touching the dragon tooth around his neck with one hand and flexing the fingers of the other, his eyes darting around the room, never settling in one place.

It put a pit in my stomach.

"You're a bad liar," I said in a low voice.

"It's not a lie," he insisted, forcing his body into stillness. But his eyes still flitted around us.

Staring at him as he glanced at me then away for the third time, I shook my head. "Fine, maybe you're not lying. But you *are* keeping a secret."

When he didn't argue, I pressed my back into the wall, needing the support, eyes closing briefly as I tilted my head back. "Tell me," I whispered, afraid to hear the answer.

He pressed his lips together, still refusing, but it didn't matter. My mind had already begun to puzzle it out. "The Dragon doesn't plan to *complete* the covenant, does he?"

Somehow, he wanted to leave the Jinn cursed.

A breath whooshed out of Koda, almost as if he were relieved I'd figured it out. He nodded, confirming it.

We'd be at their mercy.

Completely vulnerable.

Shock washed over me. The Vaade weren't trying to make *peace* with the Jinn. They were trying to permanently weaken our entire race, making us easy prey for them so they could violently conquer our world. Without a completed covenant, there'd be no magical truce protecting both sides. The Vaade could attack the weak and confused Jinn with nothing to stop them.

My people would never see it coming. *Shem would be ambushed.*

Another realization hit me. "Your father added the forgetting spell so that we'd never figure out what happened," I whispered, lifting a trembling hand to my mouth as I shook my head. "Koda, you have to stop this.

THE SECRET CURSE

He'll kill everyone."

Koda's face was grim as he ground out. "Not kill them."

Though he still held back the details, he made it easy to read between the lines. They'd make us their slaves. We'd be crushed underneath their heel and too weak to stop them.

"We have to stop it," I repeated, clasping my hands in front of me, pleading. "We *have* to!"

Rubbing his face with both hands before dropping them, Koda stared at me with an unreadable expression. "We can't. My father never backs down. And he never loses."

He'd already fought with his father over this.

"There's always a first time."

"No. There isn't." I could tell he fully believed that. "The Dragon always gets his way."

I sighed. "At least help me understand how the spell works?" The wooden walls scratched my bare arms as I scooted away from it toward him. "If it can be temporary, then memories and abilities aren't lost forever, right? They're just…" I tried to remember the word he'd used. "Suppressed somehow?"

Nervous energy made me want to pace. I almost stood, but I'd barely be able to take two steps in this space before hitting the opposite wall. Instead, I fidgeted with the furs, stroking them thoughtfully. "How fast does it take effect?"

"It's a bit slower than the weakening, but not by

much."

It felt like Koda was still trying to hold something back with these short answers. But I could infer what he meant. "There won't be time for Shem or anyone else to react before it's too late."

He hesitated, then nodded.

I leaned forward on my knees and asked the most important question. "How is your father going to sneak it into the covenant spell without Shem and the council noticing?"

"It doesn't matter." He waved that away as if the complete incapacitation of my people was a minor inconvenience. "The curse is just one small change to the covenant rituals. The only way to stop it would be to stop the covenant itself."

"But if we can't, how would the curse be added?" I pressed. *And how can I warn the prince before it is?*

Koda clearly didn't see this secondary spell as a priority the way I did, but if Shem somehow ended up going through with the covenant in the end, I needed to be absolutely certain this curse wouldn't be placed on *me*.

Somehow, I had to convince Koda to let his guard down and tell me. "If your father couldn't weave in the curse, he'd be less inclined to do the covenant, right?"

Rubbing the stubble along his chin, Koda tilted his head, dragging out, "Right."

"Then that's our answer," I declared. We'd finally found a solution. "We'll find a way to prevent the curse. Tell me how he's planning to include it."

THE SECRET CURSE

"Why should I trust a Jinni to help?" he asked in a flat voice, crossing his arms. "Everyone knows the Jinn are born liars."

I scowled, but couldn't argue with the generalization. My entire life confirmed it.

Before I could come up with an answer, he leaned closer, adding in a low growl, "Don't think you've fooled me for a second. I know you're still planning to escape." With a smirk, he added, "At least, you'll *try*."

I paled but held his gaze. "It didn't work out very well for me the first time, did it?" But of course, he was right, and he knew it.

"Besides," I added more truthfully, "I'm not going anywhere until I learn how to stop this covenant."

"No," he argued. "You're not leaving unless we let you." Leaning against the closed door, he casually draped one arm over a bent knee and stretched out his other leg right beside me, as if to remind me of our positions. Of the fact that he could do whatever he wanted.

I glanced at it pointedly, raising one brow. "Is that so?" This wasn't helping my cause. I sighed. "If you're so certain you'd catch me, then you have nothing to worry about, do you?" I didn't give him time to answer, because we were focusing on the wrong thing. "The truth is, whether I'm here or not doesn't matter. *If* I tried to leave, it wouldn't be to go home."

It was hard to hold his gaze. I didn't like lying to him.

"Think about it," I added as sincerely as possible. "The prince has abandoned me, along with the royal family. Why would I go back to them after that?" A little pinch in my chest made me wince at the words because there was some unfortunate truth to them. But Shem hadn't truly abandoned me, I reminded myself. He was protecting his people while looking for a solution to our problem. He would rescue me before the day of the covenant came. Hopefully sooner.

Though I hid my hurt quickly, wishing Koda hadn't seen it, he tilted his head, as if reconsidering.

"You don't have to tell me everything," I said, hoping to tip him over the edge into finally sharing. "Just what's relevant for us to find a way to stop it. Think about it." My gestures grew wilder along with my excitement. "If the curse is taken out of play, your father won't want the covenant anymore. If he doesn't want it, he'll find a reason to back out. And if he backs out, your sister doesn't have to marry the prince of Jinn. Everyone wins."

Koda gave me an appraising look. "You're good at making your case, Jinni girl. Is this how you convinced the prince to marry you?"

I flushed angrily, pulling my shoulders back and lifting my chin. "You think whatever you want—"

"I meant no offense," he interrupted, holding up both hands, giving me a crooked smile. "I just meant you make a good argument."

"There are better ways to say it," I mumbled, crossing my arms and avoiding his eyes. The insinuation bothered me more than usual, maybe because he knew about the rumors.

THE SECRET CURSE

"Fine." He changed the subject. "I'll tell you what I know about the curse, but it's not much."

He reached across the space between us and took my hand.

I tensed.

All of my senses fixated on my tingling fingers.

"The Vaade marriages are very similar to human marriages," he began, face solemn. "The two parties each bring a ring for the other." He made a circle in my palm almost unconsciously. "And in the covenant, as you know, these rings are imbued with magic. When placed on a finger, the enchantment begins. But"—he spread out my fingers, placing them across his palm—"the reaction is different depending on which finger they're placed on."

I swallowed, trying to focus on his words instead of his warm hand beneath mine.

Koda touched my pointer finger. "Mind." He moved to my middle finger. "Body." And finally, he stroked my ring finger. "Soul." He cleared his throat after a moment and pulled back, letting my hand fall to my knee. "When placed on a specific finger, the rings will pull those elements out. In weddings, we place rings on the soul finger because it draws out the souls and binds them together."

I tried to breathe normally.

My hand still tingled.

"The covenant is designed to make a soul connection," I whispered, recognizing bits and pieces of the spell's design.

He hesitated, then softly touched my ring finger again. "A typical human marriage would only involve this one element. But the covenant requires vulnerability as proof before the rings will accept the spell."

"Vulnerability?" I repeated stupidly.

"This finger," he said, pointing to my middle finger. "Is connected to the body. It pulls out a different connection. In this case, our physical strengths and your Gifts."

I glanced down at my fingers. "Where does the curse come into play?"

Koda's hand moved to my first finger, barely grazing it. "This finger is connected to the mind."

Mind, body, soul.

"The first finger triggers the curse?" I was afraid to hear his answer. It was so simple. Jinn didn't wear wedding rings and had little to no understanding of human—or Vaade—customs. If they placed the ring on the first finger instead of the third, Shem would never see it coming.

Koda nodded.

As he sat back, head bowed, he murmured, "It acts slower. There are thousands upon thousands more memories to erase than there are abilities. But after a day... maybe two, everything surrounding Jinni magic—including any knowledge of it—will be erased."

"Everything?" I imagined forgetting I was a Jinni... What I could do... My entire world would be turned upside down. Again.

"Like I told you," Koda said finally, sounding resigned. "We can't stop this 'curse' as you call it, because the spell is built into the rings. My father will present it as a necessary part of the covenant."

I didn't know how to argue.

He was right.

We'd lose our Gifts and never know what we were missing. The Vaade would overpower the Jinn without a fight.

Silence fell over us.

I laid down eventually, hoping fresh ideas would come to me after some rest.

Koda blew out the lantern.

His breaths evened out almost immediately.

But I couldn't sleep.

I couldn't stop thinking about what he'd said.

Stopping the curse was impossible.

Rolling over for the thousandth time, half-dreaming about the Dragon shackling Shem with this curse, my body tensed as if the curse was already happening and settling onto my own body.

A heavy arm landed across my upper body, startling me fully awake.

Koda mumbled behind me, "Go to sleep."

"I *was* asleep," I complained, trying to roll out from under his grip.

He held me tighter, which naturally dragged our bodies closer.

I froze.

Warm breath blew softly on my neck.

Shivering, I felt more awake than ever.

"Go… to… sleep…" he slurred again, as if he could feel my tension.

Despite our conversation, the weight of his arm across mine and the rise and fall of his chest behind me was oddly soothing. I wanted to both push him away and scoot closer, which drew out confusing feelings. Having this new all-consuming focus helped me finally stop thinking about all my other concerns, which then lulled me slowly and unexpectedly to sleep.

The last thought I had was that when I escaped—hopefully soon now that I'd finally unraveled the secrets of the covenant curse—I had perfect evidence to stop Shem from agreeing to the false truce. On top of that, we could use my knowledge of Koda and his father being on the edge of a potential civil war to our advantage. I drifted off with a confusing sense of regret at the thought of betraying Koda.

20

TEHYA'S GROUCHY MUTTERING IN the open door of the smokehouse woke me. Beside me was an empty fur blanket. Koda must've slipped out while I slept.

My disappointment irritated me. I scowled at Tehya as I exited the smokehouse.

"Sit," she said without bothering to greet me, gesturing toward a nearby log. "Koda wants me to check your bandages."

"They're fine." I brushed off her concern. Most of my scrapes were healing well, and the wound on my shoulder only throbbed dully. Honestly, the yellowroot seemed to speed the healing. I could ignore the occasional aches.

She smacked the back of my head.

"Ow!" I yelped. "What was that for?"

"It's like you don't even know how to be a prisoner," she mocked me, rolling her eyes and giving me a push toward the log. "Go. You're not a princess here."

"I'm not a princess anywhere," I muttered, but I did what I was told. "You're going to be the new princess, remember?"

Tehya glanced around, making sure no one was nearby. "That could still change." Her tone was flat and uninterested but her eyes latched onto mine, saying more. *She's desperate enough to come to me for help.*

"I don't know how," I replied as she slowly unraveled the bandage around my shoulder. But my eyes said, *Tell me how?* Turning away, I focused on the forest, as if I couldn't care less about this conversation.

Just as casually, Tehya replied, "Our spies say the prince hasn't officially broken off his engagement with you."

"What?" I forgot about staring aimlessly at the woods, spinning to face her. Was she trying to secretly give me hope or antagonize me? Whatever her intentions, it accomplished a little of both.

She unwrapped my shoulder with a firm grip, and I hissed in pain. She wasn't as gentle as Koda. "They haven't even revealed that you're gone," she continued. "Probably to avoid humiliation."

I winced at both the description and the way she rubbed that familiar yellow paste into the wound.

"My father thinks the prince is still hoping to get out of the covenant. It looks like the Jinn are keeping it hushed until they can't anymore."

"Oh, he's definitely hoping to get out of it," I replied

THE SECRET CURSE

scornfully, the way any Vaade would expect me to. Inwardly, though, I didn't know how to process the news. Was it as straightforward as Tehya said? Or was there more to it?

While Tehya finished working on my arm and wrapped a new, clean bandage around it, I closed my eyes and tried to imagine the scene.

Shem's parents seated on the throne, looking down on their son as they demanded that he think of his people first and marry the Vaade girl for the sake of the truce. But Shem yelled back that he was already engaged to a girl he loved and wouldn't abandon her.

"Done," Tehya said, breaking me out of my trance. I sighed.

I'd never seen Shem yell at his parents. Or do something for himself over his people, come to think of it.

My plans hadn't changed. Now that I finally understood the covenant, it was time to escape. And I no longer had the option to quietly bide my time, expecting Shem to swoop in and rescue me. Though I couldn't fully shake that hope, a growing part of me wondered if he was trying to save me at all.

I brushed off my borrowed skirt as I stood, trying to brush away the painful thoughts. I'd saved myself before and I could do it again—I still had time. How many days had I been here? Three? Four? I was losing track. But Shem had negotiated for two weeks.

"How long before the wound will be healed enough

to move it without pain?" I asked Tehya as she led the way toward the outdoor bonfire where we'd spent most of the previous day.

Narrowing her eyes at me, Tehya shook her head. "Not before the covenant, if that's what you're asking."

I tried not to react, which ended up being a reaction of its own. These blunt discussions with the Vaade continued to throw me off balance.

"A little more than two weeks then?" I managed to say after a slightly too long pause.

"At least."

I hoped she was exaggerating. I'd give it a few more days and then it'd have to be good enough. In the meantime, I'd prepare.

Groaning at my expression, though I could've sworn my face was blank, she veered sharply toward the longhouse closest to the fire. "Here." She waved for me to join her, putting her arm above her head as she leaned into the wall. "If you're determined to use it sooner, here are some stretches that will help."

I winced as I imitated her, but held the stretch, memorizing it and all the others she showed me after that.

At meals I could start to slip food into the deep pockets of my borrowed dress—nothing too perishable at first. Dried meat mostly, though I planned to start supplementing with bread and fruit. Though the bread might dry out and fruit could go bad, hopefully they both might still be edible if it took me a few days of searching to find the daleth on the other side of the mountains.

THE SECRET CURSE

When we entered the longhouse for breakfast and I spotted Koda by the fire, I flushed, focusing on other Vaade to avoid thinking about how I'd accidentally ended up nestling into him while sleeping.

He could've teased me, but he didn't. After we ate, he offered to take me hunting. As we left camp for the first time in days, taking a beaten path to the stream to fill the waterskins, I caught a flash of something almost white through the trees. It was too high to be a deer, too dark to be a cloud. "What's that?"

"Nothing important." Koda didn't stop moving.

I veered off the path, heading directly toward the movement. It was definitely fur... multiple furs even? In the air?

Voices came from the clearing ahead, drawing me on.

"What're you doing?" Koda hissed in my ear, as he caught up to me.

"You're hiding something." I slowed a bit as we drew close, lowering my voice as I challenged him, "I thought you said only the foolish Jinni kept secrets?"

"It's... not a secret," he ground out, but pulled me back before I could step into the clearing. Obviously, it was. The Vaade were calling loudly to each other as they set up... tents?

A dozen or so Vaade were constructing three tents out of furs sewn together, one much larger than the others. "Are more Vaade coming?" I whispered. Thankfully the Vaade were too loud to notice us. "Why aren't you setting them up in camp?"

"It's for your people," Koda said on a long sigh, rubbing a hand over his face.

I raised a brow.

"For the covenant," he added reluctantly.

That immediately ruined my mood. "They're planning to come here?"

"They don't want to, but my father is making it a requirement."

"They're still in negotiations?" I supposed that was good, but it was an uncomfortable reminder that I needed to make my escape, sooner rather than later.

"They are." Koda shrugged. "But the Dragon always gets what he wants."

I snorted.

When he tugged at my arm again, I let him pull me away, thankful for the distraction of the hunt.

We returned to the stream and continued along the path until Koda deemed us a suitable distance from the camp.

He shushed me for the tenth time not much later. "Your stomping around is scaring away the game."

Rolling my eyes, I shifted into a cat, padding along on soft, silent footpads.

He grinned and shook his head.

A soft purr of contentment rumbled through me at the sense of freedom. Back home, even if Shem and I had been alone, I'd never have used my Gifts so casually.

Each day, though I kept an eye out for the Vaade

THE SECRET CURSE

who'd attacked me, they didn't show their faces. Between Tehya and the broad daylight, I wasn't terribly worried, but I paid attention just in case. When I asked Koda about it, he told me the Dragon kept them busy from sunup to sundown working on the tents and other preparations for the wedding.

I didn't ask anything further.

After what felt like weeks working on my first basket—though, in reality, it'd only been a few days—I finally finished. The weave was loose in some places and tight in others, twisting the smooth sides into lumps, but I still admired it proudly.

"Can I try making a bag like yours?" I asked Tehya after I'd shown her my basket.

Sighing as if I'd asked for something unreasonable like being allowed to go home, she sat down to teach me nonetheless.

I'd use it to hold all the food I'd been saving.

One afternoon, someone left an empty waterskin unattended, and I pocketed it when Tehya wasn't looking.

That night, I added it to my stash of food beneath the furs once Koda blew out the candle in the smokehouse and his breathing evened out.

The small knife was my best addition, though.

Late in the afternoon, the day before I planned to leave, Koda brought me inside the longhouse to get more yellowroot for my wound, but someone followed us in, calling his name. "Message for you," the Vaade said, eyes darting between Koda and I. "Not for Jinni ears."

I didn't recognize him, but this had happened on and off all week.

Though I was curious, I rolled my eyes as if I couldn't care less, moving toward the empty circle in the center of the room where the cookfire was banked.

"I'll be right back," Koda called to me, following the other man toward the door. Over his shoulder he added, "*Don't* go anywhere."

I heard the insinuation. If I tried to repeat my last escape, he'd be ready.

As if I'd be foolish enough to run when he was expecting it.

That didn't stop me from snooping through the Vaade's things while he was outside, however.

Some bunks only had blankets, while others held random items like clothing or furs. A knife caught my eye. Glancing around to make sure the longhouse was still empty, I snatched the small knife off the bed and stuffed it in my pocket.

"I saw that," a high-pitched voice spoke from one of the beds.

I whirled around.

A little boy sat up in a bed, one row down.

"Saw what?" I said with a smile, peeking past him at the door. Koda would be back any second. Slowly, I strolled toward the boy.

He jumped up into a crouch on the bed.

He was going to run.

"It's okay," I attempted to soothe him with the full

THE SECRET CURSE

weight of my Gift, holding his gaze.

Hesitating, he was still just long enough for me to reach him and touch his arm.

"Don't be afraid." I held my smile and imagined my Gift pouring off me in waves, hoping his young mind was malleable enough to bend to my will. "You didn't see anything, did you?"

His little forehead wrinkled. "I—" He blinked, then shook his head, blinking again.

The voices outside grew louder. Koda was about to come back.

"Tell me you saw nothing," I pushed, hoping it was the right choice.

The familiar blank look spread across his face. "I saw nothing," he repeated.

"Good," I said as the door swung open, giving him another relieved smile. Softly, I added, "Go back to sleep."

As he collected the yellowroot, Koda had me sit by the light of the cookfire to help me with my bandages. He nodded toward the little boy. "Making friends?"

I felt the weight of the knife in my pocket. "Something like that."

When he pulled my bandages back, I distracted him by pretending it hurt.

I didn't get a chance to hide the knife throughout the rest of the afternoon.

Sitting by the cozy evening cookfire inside the longhouse that night, with Vaade all around, I tried to ignore the hidden weapon in my pocket as they laughed and told stories, allowing me to be a part of it.

I joined in laughing in all the right places, but Koda gave me an odd look that told me he'd noticed my mood.

I shook my head when he raised a brow.

He wouldn't understand.

It'd hit me, as I sat beside the fire soaking in the warmth and company, that *this* was the sense of home and family that I should've had growing up. What I'd always been missing, even if I'd never had a name for it before.

I thought of my chilly room back at the castle where I spent most nights alone.

Uncomfortable, I shook my head, trying to rid myself of the comparison.

I stood, silently gesturing to Tehya and Koda that I needed to stretch. Since Tehya had shown me the exercises to speed healing in my arm, I'd done them faithfully every morning, noon, and night.

They nodded, not bothering to follow.

I moved to the back wall alone. Pressing my whole arm against the wood, I gently turned the rest of my body back toward the fire, feeling the gentle pull in the muscles.

Glancing at Koda and Tehya, I bit my lip. Neither watched me. I'd spent the last week being the ideal prisoner, doing everything they asked, staying in sight, always announcing before I did anything too startling.

They'd let their guard down.

It was exactly what I'd hoped for.

Turning my back on the room, I squeezed my eyes

shut, tipping my head forward, trying to force my rebellious heart into submission.

Tomorrow, I'd escape.

As I did the stretch a second time for good measure, my free hand lightly brushed along the pocket where the knife lay.

The young Vaade boy hadn't said a word about it.

My other pocket held an apple and some extra cornbread I'd slipped in a few minutes ago when no one was looking.

Lifting my arm straight above my head, I leaned into the wall, completing the final stretch.

My shoulder barely pinched anymore. The skin beneath the stitches had changed from a raw wound with inflamed redness all around it to a mellow pink line.

Yawning, I glanced over the fire at Koda. At the sight, he stood, bidding everyone goodnight, heading toward me. A few of the Vaade waved at me as well, and I shyly nodded back. I wished for the thousandth time that I didn't have to deceive them. Or Koda.

Pushing through the door, I led the way outside, breathing in the fresh, cool night air. I kept my eyes on our feet as we walked. It wasn't just the deception that bothered me. After experiencing the warmth of the Vaade for a full week now, I finally admitted it to myself.

I wanted to stay.

Koda and I didn't speak on the way to the smokehouse.

There was an odd tension between us.

Maybe I was imagining it. Or maybe it was all on my end.

But I couldn't think of anything to say that wouldn't sound like a goodbye.

As we stepped inside, he didn't say anything either.

It didn't matter if I wanted to stay here. It wasn't an option. Steeling myself against the conflicting desires, I reminded myself of the reasons I needed to leave:

I'm a Jinni among Vaade.

I don't belong here and never will.

They might be kind to me, but that doesn't mean I have a home here.

The castle is my home.

More importantly, Shem is my betrothed—I love him.

I barely know Koda.

I didn't know why I felt the need to add that last part, but it irritated me enough that I lay down without another word, putting my back to Koda.

He blew out the candle, and the room settled into darkness and quiet breaths. Crickets chirped outside.

I listened to soft scuffling as he laid down and got comfortable. I counted to a hundred, and then did so a second time before I slowly lifted the furs next to me, revealing the soft bag I'd woven with Tehya's help. It was long and skinny, with a rough flap over the top, and tomorrow I hoped to learn how to weave a thin handle which would allow me to turn it into a bag I could throw over my shoulder.

Quietly, I slipped the apple, cornbread, and my new

knife into the makeshift storage space and replaced the furs over it.

With that done, I tried to slow my rapid heartbeat so Koda wouldn't hear the anxiety in my breathing.

Eyes closed, I listened for his usual soft snore.

I didn't hear it.

Tensing, I tried to keep my breathing even, but in the silence, the hitch was audible.

"Don't let me stop you," Koda's deep voice rumbled in the dark, sending my pulse racing. "We can turn the light back on if that'd make it easier."

"What?" My voice came out breathless, and I cursed inwardly.

A flicker of flame returned as he lit the candle.

I forced myself to meet Koda's gaze. If only I could get my traitorous heartbeat to slow. It thundered in my ears, and I knew he heard it too.

"Are we pretending I can't smell the food supply you're keeping here?" he murmured. "For when you plan to leave?"

I coughed. "I don't know what you mean. Sometimes I keep extra food for when I get hungry at night, but that's hardly a supply."

"Is that what it would look like if I took out the bag you've been working on?" he asked, pointing directly at the corner where I'd hidden it.

My stomach sank. If he knew what and where it was, he'd already seen it. He must've come in here while I was with Tehya and found it.

He waited, but I was out of excuses, and we both knew it.

Another long silence passed as we stared at each other.

Koda spoke first. "What if you stayed?"

"You mean... after the covenant?"

He nodded.

I didn't know what to say. When I opened my mouth, the word came out in a croak. "Why?"

Another heated moment passed. I licked my lips, wanting to hear him say... I don't know, something *more*. Something that might indicate how he felt.

His eyes tracked the gesture, but he shrugged. "You're not going back, right? You said so yourself. So you don't have anywhere else to go."

Disappointment made me hesitate, but I nodded. That's what I'd told him.

"Well, there you go," he said. "If you don't have anywhere else to go, you might as well stay here."

"You make a compelling case," I said dryly, though my mind raced, imagining it. What if...

I couldn't deny anymore that I was attracted to him. We fit well together. But *together* wasn't really what he was offering, was it?

I waited, hoping he might say more.

He only chuckled at my words.

Gritting my teeth, I remembered my goal: to escape. And now that he knew about my supplies, I needed to convince him I wasn't planning on using them anytime soon.

I tapped one finger to my chin. "I'll consider it."

The relief crossing his face was unmistakable. I tried to smile convincingly, nodding when he moved to blow out the light again.

When his quiet voice spoke up again in the dark, I found myself turning toward him.

"Whatever you decide to do, no one will hurt you. Whether you choose to leave in a week… or if you choose to stay. No one will touch you either way." My heart squeezed as he added in a rough tone, "I'll make sure of it."

My throat closed. A single tear managed to escape and trickle down my cheek, landing in my ear, followed quickly by another before I pinched my eyes shut. I couldn't speak for a long moment. "Thank you," I whispered, choking on the words. "That means more than you know."

And it did.

But his promise didn't change anything.

Except to make me wish even harder that it could.

21

DUST MOTES DANCED ABOVE my head in a thin ray of sunlight that peeked through a crack in the wooden walls. At some point in the last hour, I'd given up on sleeping, waiting for Koda to wake up and trying to figure out how to take my food stores with me today without tipping him off.

I couldn't.

I'd tossed and turned all night with this problem weighing on me, but I kept coming back to one answer: leave it behind.

He wouldn't expect that, which would give me more time before he realized I was gone.

Hopefully it won't take more than a few days to find a portal anyway. If it took longer than that, it wouldn't really matter, would it? Koda had already proven how good he was at tracking. While I'd spent hours considering this as well, I couldn't guarantee that wading through streams and avoiding use of my Gifts would prevent him from finding me. It was a chance I had to take.

A creak sounded. It was the only warning we had before the door swung open, yet Koda was already on his feet before the early morning light touched my face.

It was Tehya.

"You need to talk to him," she said to Koda, glancing at me briefly, but focused on him. "It's urgent."

I knew without asking that she meant the Dragon.

Koda didn't ask for an explanation either. Nodding to his sister, he paused halfway through the door to look at me. "I'll be back when I can." Holding my gaze, I could tell he was thinking of our conversation last night. Probably trying to figure out where I stood today.

Intentionally relaxing my shoulders, I yawned and nodded back. "Take your time. I'll be here." I smiled through the lie, refusing to let myself feel the sadness creeping over me as I looked at him for the last time.

Goodbye, Koda, I added silently once he'd turned his back, allowing myself one moment to grieve. *I'll miss you.*

Tehya chewed on her nail, watching him leave as well.

I took the opportunity to grab the handbag I'd woven and hidden in the corner, holding it up as she turned back. "Could you show me how to make a strap for this today?" I asked innocently.

"Sure," Tehya replied absently, waving for me to

hurry up, distracted by whatever was going on between Koda and her father. "Let's go."

She seemed preoccupied as we sat by the fire until I reminded her to teach me how to weave the strap again. Fortunately, it turned out to be simple. While I wove the long grass together, attaching the long handle to the bag I'd made, Tehya hunched over a log and stared into the fire.

"What's going on?" I finally asked, as I slung the bag over my shoulder and tested the strap. It was perfect.

Tehya and the other Vaade at the fire exchanged meaningful glances. "Nothing. Don't worry about it."

I frowned, fiddling with the remaining long grass that I hadn't used. If it was really nothing, she'd have told me without thinking twice about it. The fact that she kept it from me was worrying. Was it about the negotiations? They couldn't be failing, or she'd be happier. Did that mean they were improving? My mood soured at the thought.

"Come," I said, standing. "You can't sit here brooding all day. Let's go for a walk and get some distance from… whatever's going on."

Though my tone was casual, my plan depended on her agreement. This was the perfect excuse to get her away from the others. I couldn't take on all the Vaade, but I could take on Tehya alone—especially if she didn't see it coming.

Tehya hesitated, glancing toward the woods.

"Unless you want to wallow." I gave an exaggerated

THE SECRET CURSE

shrug, moving back toward my log.

"No." She stood, brushing off her hands. "A walk will be good for me."

Good for me, too.

I let her lead. It didn't really matter where we went, so long as we were out of earshot.

We strode through the forest, along one side of a meandering creek toward the training grounds where Tehya had challenged me days ago.

She set a brisk pace.

Breathing hard, I didn't argue. Part of me didn't want her to stop at all.

Because once she did, I'd have to move to the next stage of my plan.

I was dreading it.

Guilt over betraying both her and Koda consumed me, and I hadn't even done it yet.

I barely noticed where we were going, until we reached the clearing where we'd had our brawl.

Swinging around to face me, she held up her hands invitingly, the way she had during that first fight. "Want to go another round?" It was obvious now that she'd been aiming for this spot for that exact reason.

I wished she hadn't asked.

It made the next stage of my plan all too easy.

To escape, I needed to incapacitate her, and while she was expecting a fair fight, I'd come prepared.

She'd never see it coming.

Koda had unknowingly solved the last piece of the

puzzle for me when he'd told me where the Vaade could be hurt. *Go for the neck.*

I resisted the urge to touch the small jar of paste around my neck. The Vaade had never smelled the paralytic on me or even noticed the dark paste inside.

Regret settled onto my shoulders like a familiar mantle, as I accepted what I had to do.

Waiting would only make it worse.

Slowly, I started to pull my bag over my head to set it on the ground. Halfway through, I dropped it, shifting my fingers into claws, and lunged.

Laughing, Tehya jumped back, barely noticing the light scrapes across her shoulder. Then she paused, touching a finger to the side of her neck, brows rising.

One tiny cut.

Blood trickled down the side of her tan skin, even after she wiped it away.

"I'm impressed." She laughed again, crouching to continue the fight. "Maybe the Jinn have some strength after all."

While she'd been looking at the small drop of blood on her finger, I'd twisted off the lid of the tiny jar and scooped out a bit of the paste.

I hesitated.

Once this was done, there was no going back.

But I'd never planned to stay here, had I? It had to be done.

Another unexpected leap toward her, followed by a scuffle where we rolled in the dirt.

A little paste was smeared over the cut.

Tehya slammed me to the ground making me wince as my still healing shoulder pulsed with pain.

"Sorry," she said with a grin, not at all apologetic. Then her grin fell sideways. "That's strange," she muttered to herself.

That was all the time it'd needed.

The paralytic acted fast.

With a gentle push, I easily shoved her off me, rolling her to one side so I could sit up.

Tehya's eyes widened as her fingers twitched, barely responsive now. "What did you do? What's happening?"

She tried to wrap her fingers around my wrist.

I gently pried them off.

"I'm sorry," I whispered. "Truly, I am. I didn't have any other choice."

I wanted to say more—to tell her how she'd become my friend and how much it'd meant to me, but I knew it'd only infuriate her more.

Helping her lay down as her body grew stiff and immovable, I stared into her eyes as she fumed, turning red in the face.

"You're a fool," she snapped as she tried and failed to move. "It's too late to change anything. All you've done is make things worse for yourself when I become queen of Jinn."

Ignoring her threat, despite the way my stomach clenched, I murmured, "You might feel a bit dizzy when you wake up."

Her head twitched slightly, as if she'd tried to shake it.

I reached for her hand. "You'll have to trust me, it's for the best."

Her whole body jerked in an attempt to get away.

I let my hand drop into my lap. "You don't want to marry Shem, anymore than I want you to. You'll thank me for this once I find a way to end the covenant."

She'd lost the ability to speak, but it didn't stop her from glaring at me.

What did she mean, "too late"?

Though she tried to fight the paralytic, it slowly stole over her mind as well as her body, and her eyes fell shut as it took effect.

I couldn't stop thinking about what she'd said.

Too late.

Her frantic appearance that morning came back to me. Koda hadn't returned from meeting with his father. Tehya staring into the fire, more despondent than I'd ever seen her.

Fear took root in my stomach as my imagination conjured up the worst possibilities.

What were Koda and his father doing back at camp?

Carefully, I pulled Tehya up and propped her against a tree, turning to pick up my bag from where I'd dropped it. I slung it back over my shoulder. "You'll be safe here until you wake in a few hours." Give or take. All that mattered was it'd be long enough to give me a head start.

Out of sight, a little creek gurgled cheerfully, calling

for me to follow it onward toward the mountains—to the daleth on the other side. Best case scenario it could take days for me to find it. *I have a week*, I reminded myself. But did I?

Tehya might've been livid, but that didn't mean she'd been lying.

Making my way back to the stream, I started toward the cliffs, but a tug pulled at me from the opposite direction—from the Vaade camp.

We hadn't walked far.

I could go back, just for a minute, and see what I could overhear…

My feet were moving before I'd consciously made my decision.

Returning to Tehya, I crouched in front of her still form.

It was easier to shift and imitate someone exactly if I could look at them, notice every freckle, the exact way the cheek curved, the color of dark hair when the sunlight softly stroked it.

When I stood, it was done.

I was Tehya.

22

IF I RAN INTO any Vaade between here and the camp, this disguise should keep me from being captured a third time. I shouldn't take the risk, but my instincts wouldn't let me continue without discovering what Tehya had meant. *Too late.*

Too late for what?

I'd already begun my escape when she'd said it, so she couldn't be referring to that. *Too late to warn Shem?* I couldn't think of anything else she might mean, but I hoped I was wrong. I didn't fully understand it. Had they hurt him? Or had he found a way out of the covenant without my help? But if so, why hadn't he come for me?

With each new worry, my feet moved faster, until I was sprinting back to camp. Tehya's Vaade form gave me increased speed and heightened senses. It was exhilarating. If this was even half of Koda's strength, no wonder he'd pursued me so easily. I wished I'd

THE SECRET CURSE

experimented shifting into a Vaade sooner.

As I drew closer to camp, I passed the place where the Vaade had set up those tents.

I paused.

If the Vaade were hiding something, it wouldn't be in the camp where no one could keep anything private—no, whatever Tehya meant, my gut told me it had something to do with those tents and the imminent arrival of the Jinn.

Turning on my heel, I slipped through the woods toward the clearing.

Once I'd left the path behind, I knelt briefly to tuck my bag between the roots of some trees where no one would find it. If Koda saw me with the poorly made bag stuffed with food, it'd be a dead giveaway that I wasn't his sister.

Hesitating, I chewed on my lip and decided to remove the little jar around my neck with the paste, putting it inside the bag as well. If the Vaade *could* smell it, they might associate the smell with me, which would also give me away.

Underestimating them had been my biggest mistake.

This time, I wouldn't take the risk.

Slowing as I drew close enough to see the tents, I used everything I'd learned from Koda to steal through the woods as soundlessly as possible.

Thankfully, the cloth tents were thin. Deep voices drifted along the wind toward me.

Tiptoeing closer, still hidden within the trees, I

stopped a few dozen paces from the closest tent. With Tehya's sensitive ears, I could eavesdrop from here without their ridiculous hearing picking up my breathing.

"This conversation is over," a deep voice growled. The Dragon.

"It's *not*." I recognized Koda's voice. "I don't care if the prince officially agreed to the covenant taking place today," he growled. "It's *not happening.*"

I gasped.

The voices stopped.

Panicking, I jumped to my feet. These Vaade and their unfair supernatural hearing—

One of them yanked the tent pole from the ground on one side while the other ripped through the cloth at the back of the tent with a hiss.

I froze.

Narrowing his eyes, the Dragon shook scraps of tent cloth from his hands and scowled at me. "Get her ready," he said to Koda who held the tent pole, turning his back on me.

He thinks I'm Tehya. I wanted to laugh in relief that my disguise had worked, but Koda was still looking at me, brows pinched together.

"The ceremony begins at sunset," the Dragon added, before he flung open the entrance and disappeared.

Koda appeared more worried than I'd ever seen him as he dropped the tent pole behind him, not caring that half the tent sagged when it landed. Taking my arm, he pulled me through the trees. He didn't stop or speak until we'd put a good distance between us and the tents.

I wanted to stop him, to ask a thousand questions, but I couldn't. I had Tehya's body, but not her voice. Shifting my voice was something I hadn't done in ages. It took practice and testing to get the vocal chords right, to sound exactly like someone else. If I spoke, he'd know it was me.

So I didn't.

Part of me didn't even care if he discovered me, though, because of what I'd overheard. Shem was going through with the marriage. He was *here*. It was happening *tonight*.

Koda stopped finally after a glance over his shoulder, letting go. "What're you doing? Where's Jezebel?"

I shook my head at him. Tears rose in my eyes, unbidden, as I gestured back toward camp.

He misunderstood. Grabbing my shoulders, he gave me a little shake. "You don't have to marry him, Tehya." He yanked me in for a crushing hug.

It knocked the air out of me.

My heart was splintering in my chest a little more with every second that passed.

Shem hadn't come for me and he never would.

I lifted my arms to hug Koda back, needing it as badly as Tehya would have. Gripping his tunic and trying not to sob, I let him hold me, wishing he didn't think I was his sister.

When he stepped back, I reluctantly let go.

"Stop eavesdropping," he chided. "It's time for you to run like we talked about, do you understand?" When he paused, I nodded, though I had no idea what he was talking about. "It won't stop him forever," Koda said more softly, almost to himself. "He always gets what he wants. But maybe it'll buy us a little more time." Raising his head, he added with a note of resignation, "Take Jezebel with you. She'll be more than happy to go."

I nodded again, hoping he'd accept that as an answer.

Wrapping my arms around my body, I watched him go.

He turned, walking backward as he added, "Don't tell Jezebel about her prince yet." He paused, sighing. "She doesn't need to know he abandoned her. It would break her heart."

It already had.

Tears filled my eyes again, but he was staring at the ground and didn't notice.

"We'll find a way out of this, little sister," he said firmly. "I'm not done looking for another way." He started moving backward again. "Get supplies and leave as soon as you can. And whatever you do, stay away from the tents. The Jinn are already here." With that, he turned on his heel and jogged back toward camp.

My jaw dropped.

The Jinn were already here.

If that was true, Shem was in one of those tents.

23

I HAD TO SEE him.

At the very least, if he was truly forsaking me, I needed to hear it from him, or I'd always wonder.

Determined to hear the truth, I snuck back toward the tents, still in Tehya's form, without a plan or anything even resembling one. I only knew I couldn't leave without talking to him.

The tent where I'd listened in on the Dragon and Koda's conversation sat lopsided where they'd yanked out a stake, leaving it half-caved in. There were two others. The one in the center was large, big enough for witnesses to gather, and likely intended for the ceremony. I gave that one a wide berth, heading for the smaller tent that looked like it might hold a dozen or less.

It was oddly quiet.

Too quiet.

My hopes rose—it was spelled!

Someone in the Jinni Guard would be capable of making a sound barrier to prevent the nosy Vaade from listening in on them.

If Shem was here, this was where he would be.

I didn't hesitate.

Striding around the tent, I aimed for the front flap, still in Tehya's form. I hurried, hoping no one would enter the clearing and see me.

Since I could hardly knock on fabric, I had to risk calling out. "Excuse me. I'm here to see the prince." I was counting on the fact that none of them knew Tehya well enough to notice her voice was different.

I peeked over my shoulder. Someone was coming through the trees. When he stepped into the clearing, my pulse skipped a beat. It was the Vaade who'd chased me through the woods days ago, Ahriman. He must've come back when the Dragon did. With a respectful nod in my direction, he moved toward the broken tent pole and began working to fix it without a word.

He sees Tehya, I reminded myself, trying to calm my pounding heart.

The flaps pulled back.

Two Jinni guards I didn't recognize stepped out. "The prince will see you."

I hurried inside, letting out a soft breath of relief when they dropped the flaps behind me.

Shem had stood as I entered. He gave me a formal nod when I met his eyes. It was hard not to rush toward him, but he was clearly uncomfortable standing before someone he believed to be the daughter of his enemy.

That sparked the tiniest hope that maybe he still had some unknown plan to get out of this. I needed to speak with him as *me*. "Can we have privacy?" I tried to keep my tone neutral, non-threatening but firm.

Captain Uriel stepped into view then. I'd been too flustered to survey the tent after seeing Shem, but a quick glance showed he'd brought half a dozen Jinni Guards and just as many council members. I found myself wanting to greet the familiar faces. Even Milcah's presence in the back of the group with that condescending expression on her face was welcome right now.

"I'd strongly recommend caution," Captain Uriel was murmuring in Shem's ear, before stepping back again.

That was the Jinni way of saying, *Don't you dare risk being alone with her.*

They didn't trust the Vaade, despite coming here in a supposed truce. That was encouraging. It added to my hope that Shem wasn't going through with this. Once I told him about the second spell intended to give the Vaade the full advantage, he'd implement his plans immediately.

"Please," I said to Shem, ignoring the captain and all the guards. "Your Highness," I added with a respectful bow of my head.

He squinted at me. I hoped that meant he recognized my voice, even if he didn't know why.

Fortunately, he'd always been a bit of a risk taker—at least when he thought he had the upper hand. "I'll speak with her."

Without waiting for anyone to argue, I moved toward the slit in the curtain that divided the two sides of the tent, lifting it. Entering, I held it open from the other side in invitation.

"Your Highness," Captain Uriel murmured again, anxiety written all over his face, even if it wasn't in his voice.

"I'll be fine, Captain," Shem reassured him, stepping through the divider.

I let it fall shut.

Aware of our keen audience on the other side, I met his eyes and held a finger to my lips.

I shifted.

His eyes widened. To his credit, though, he didn't make a sound. "Jezebel?" he mouthed, shaking his head a bit. In a nearly silent whisper, he added, "How?"

"It's a long story." I tilted my head toward the divider, picturing every single Jinni with their ear to the curtain.

Nodding, he returned to it and poked his head through. "Step outside, please. All of you."

"Your Highness?" Captain Uriel repeated the title for the third time, as if he was too incredulous to think of anything else to say.

"Prince Shem," Milcah spoke up now in a haughty tone. "As your advisor on the council, I'd suggest—"

"You as well, Milcah," Shem cut her off.

He waited for everyone to shuffle out before letting

THE SECRET CURSE

the curtain fall back in place.

This time when he turned back to me, he held his arms wide. I stepped into his embrace, closing my eyes and breathing him in. He stood a bit stiff as he held me and pulled back after only a few seconds.

Sniffing, I opened my mouth to tell him all about the tricks the Dragon planned to play with the covenant, but he spoke first. "I'm so sorry it has to be this way, Jezebel." He rubbed a hand on my arm, then let go completely, running a hand through his hair. "I'm actually thankful I have a chance to speak with you before the ceremony. When I arrived and they still wouldn't let me see you, I started to fear you were dead."

Before the ceremony. Dead.

The words bounced around my head but wouldn't land. "You… thought I was dead? Is that why you didn't come for me?"

He groaned. "It was the hardest decision I've ever made."

"That isn't really an answer," I said softly. Koda's straightforward manner had rubbed off on me more than I'd realized. In the past, I never would've challenged Shem. My fingers trembled. I tucked them underneath my arms.

"My council told me the chances that you'd survive if I refused the covenant were highly unlikely…" he paused. It was another non-answer, but if I was honest with myself, it told me all I needed to know.

"You're going through with it." My voice was flat.

"I don't want to," he said fervently, reaching for my hands. "Jezebel, I will always wish we could've had a chance. If there was any other way to protect my people—to protect you—I would take it. But there isn't. I must do this."

All the air rushed out of my lungs as the truth hit me with the speed and force of a Vaade attack, leaving me breathless. I couldn't deny it anymore. He was truly going through with this wedding. Our engagement was dissolved in a breath, as if it'd never been.

Shaking my head, I took an involuntary step back and then another as spots danced in my vision.

He doesn't love me. Not if he's willing to marry someone else.

That was the first thought that registered, and the second was even more painful.

Maybe he never did.

My mind ran in circles, desperate to explain this the way I had everything else Shem had done over the past week.

But the heartbreak still found me, crushing my poor heart like a fly under a fist.

Shem had let me go. As if I'd never even existed.

I couldn't be more off-balance if I'd stepped off the side of an island into thin air.

Just like that, I was no one once again.

I'd been a fool to think it could've been any different.

24

"JEZEBEL," SHEM WAS SAYING as I stumbled back.

I shook my head.

I couldn't.

If I let him say another word, I'd burst into tears. And I refused to let that happen.

Shifting into fly form, I leapt toward the ceiling as I did, aiming for a hole near the top of the tent and flying hard, thinking he'd reach for me the way Koda had in the past.

He just watched me go.

It was lucky for me that my fly form couldn't weep.

I flew above the trees, heading unconsciously back toward the Vaade camp. In this tiny form, the short distance felt like miles, but I embraced the physical effort, pushing myself until I could hardly breathe.

When I couldn't go any further, I flitted down to a

tree branch to catch my breath and corral my wild thoughts. *What now?*

I couldn't go home—I didn't *have* a home anymore.

In one fell swoop, I'd lost my home, my betrothed, and my future.

I had nowhere to go.

"Dragon," a voice drifted up to me from below. The bonfire was closer than I'd realized. Below, Ahriman had returned from fixing the tent to sit by the fire. The Dragon sat on the opposite side. "Why are you allowing these Jinni scum to roam our world without consequences?"

I contemplated shifting into something large with sharp teeth to show him exactly what *this* Jinni thought of that. What did I have to lose? It's not like it mattered anymore.

"Would you rather go to Jinn?" the Dragon scoffed.

"They're too close to camp," Ahriman persisted with clenched fists. He bared his teeth. "We'll have to move on to a new one. Again."

"It doesn't matter, Ahriman," the Dragon's voice rasped. A tree blocked my view of him. "After sunset, they won't remember a thing."

"Why do we have to wait until sunset?" Ahriman whined. "The rings are ready. The Jinn brought theirs with them. Why not strike now?"

"We can't give them any reason for suspicion, you fool," the Dragon snapped, losing patience. "The prince brought his strongest guard with him. They won't lose their so-called 'Gifts' until the ceremony begins."

THE SECRET CURSE

One of the other Vaade chimed in. "That's what I've been telling him. If we attack now, they'll fight back and use their own daleth to escape. If we wait until the curse takes effect, they'll only have their flimsy spears. We'll use their own portal to go after the rest of their kind."

My wings fluttered. That sounded less like they planned to conquer the Jinn, and more like a massacre. Did Koda know about his father's full plans? He might, if he knew about the curse...

I never had a chance to tell Shem about the curse!

"I don't need your help," the Dragon spat, stepping into view as he loomed over the man. "And those spears are an offense to our treaty," he added as a sly grin replaced his usual frown. "They'll have to give those up if they want to move forward with our covenant."

He strode away from the fire without another word.

Those spears would be their only defense when the Vaade's curse fell into place.

I had to tell Shem about the curse before it was too late.

The idea of returning to Shem's tent was utterly humiliating. But if I didn't warn him, they'd use his desire for peace to remove his Gifts and memories, along with every other Jinni's under his rule—myself included.

The Dragon would attack our world in full force. And he wasn't the merciful type.

I couldn't let that happen.

Taking off, I flew back toward the tent. Fuzzy shapes stepped out of it, walking toward the larger tent. In fly form, my vision was short-distance, but it looked like the Dragon was already at the entrance with a few other Vaade behind him. They stepped inside.

Now what?

I couldn't exactly walk in after him and demand an audience with Shem.

If I didn't think of something soon, it'd be too late.

Wings beating the air, I flitted around the camp in circles, not knowing what to do. I couldn't think in this form. Below, in the shadow of a longhouse, a lone Vaade stood with arms crossed.

Flapping my little wings, I drew closer.

It was Koda.

The muscles in his arms bunched up as he held himself in place, glaring in the direction of the tents, though he couldn't possibly see them.

With some satisfaction, I thought of Tehya, asleep in the woods. Soon they'd start looking for her. I wanted to reassure Koda that the sunset ceremony wouldn't be happening. The poison shouldn't wear off before then.

But eventually they'd find her. Even if she didn't wake in time, it was only a temporary delay.

There had to be another way to stop the covenant. Not for Shem's sake, but for mine.

It was what I should've been doing all along—looking out for myself.

Fueled by anger, I flew with a purpose now. Koda would want to stop this as much as I did.

Landing behind the longhouse, I shifted into my true

form again, leaning around the corner to whisper, "We need to talk."

Startled, he straightened to face me. "What're you doing here? Where's Tehya?"

"She's… away from camp," I said vaguely in case anyone was listening, knowing he'd assume she was fleeing and that I was covering for her. I felt a twinge of guilt at lying to him, but we had more important things to worry about right now.

"Why aren't you with her?" he pressed, coming around to stand in front of me with an anxious glance over his shoulder at the path to the tents. "You shouldn't be here."

"If you mean because Shem is here, don't worry. I already know."

"Tehya told you," he said flatly.

I didn't bother to correct him. Instead, I moved away from camp, gesturing for him to follow so we could talk without worrying someone was listening in.

We climbed through the woods to a steep hill, stopping when we reached a clearing that looked down on the camp, revealing a tiny glimpse of the tents beyond as well.

"Did you know about your father's plans for what happens after the ceremony?" I demanded once we'd put enough distance between us and camp.

He looked at me blankly. "After the ceremony?"

"To murder my people. You really didn't know?" I'd meant to sound challenging, but my voice cracked on the second half.

"He wouldn't," Koda declared, shaking his head. "He only wants to subdue them so that we hold the power."

"I heard him say it myself."

Frowning, Koda repeated, "He wouldn't." This time, though, he had less conviction.

"He would," I said back softly. "But there's still time to stop it. We need to steal those rings."

Grunting, he shook his head. "Trust me, I already considered that. My father has them carefully guarded, from me in particular. But it doesn't matter. It wouldn't stop them for long."

"How long would it give us?"

"Maybe…" He paused, considering. "Two or three days at most?"

"At least it'd buy us time to think of something else." But we both knew that wasn't enough.

We stared down at the tents.

What if we didn't just steal the rings… but used them too?

I held my breath.

It was an insane idea but… what if it could work?

Could Koda and I make the covenant with each other instead? *Without* the curse? If we did—and completed it—it'd render the Dragon's schemes useless. As a magical truce, it'd force the Vaade and the Jinn to get along by making it impossible for us to attack each other. It'd also prevent us from losing our abilities, which was

THE SECRET CURSE

almost enough reason on its own.

The covenant was permanent though.

Binding.

It was a true marriage.

I'd be joined with Koda forever.

Subtly, I snuck a glance at his profile. He was certainly not hard to look at. *Fine. He's extremely attractive,* I admitted to myself, tracing the lines of his face. He noticed me looking and returned my gaze, raising his brows in silent question. Shyly, I ducked my head, looking back at camp, not quite ready to suggest it.

What would forever with Koda be like?

I thought back to the nights by the warm fire, the stories and laughter, eating and working on different projects each day that contributed to the community. Being by Koda's side as he eventually became leader of the Vaade—maybe sooner rather than later. Being by his side at night as well. I shivered. It might be wonderful.

It might be *home*.

I'd never had to hide my abilities from the Vaade. I hadn't had to hide at all.

More importantly, no one would be able to dismiss me ever again. As Koda's wife, I'd be respected. Valued. The way I *should've* been with Shem.

I'd been trying not to think about it, but the rejection was still so fresh. Seething, I imagined Shem's face when he learned the covenant was completed by me instead. It'd make me irrevocably tied to the crown, impossible to ignore ever again.

The icy rage soothed the heartache, sealing my decision.

Now I just needed to convince Koda.

"I have an idea," I told him without looking away from camp. "But you might not like it."

25

THINKING THE WORDS AND saying them out loud were two *very* different things. I forgot about Shem as I stared into Koda's dragon-eyes. He didn't rush me.

I forced myself to say it in a rush. "You and I should complete the covenant instead."

Watching his face, I held my breath.

Would he consider it?

I found myself hoping he would. Maybe I wasn't the only one who could picture a future together…

"You… and me…" he repeated, taken aback.

A blush bloomed on my cheeks. I'd just proposed marriage to a man I'd only met a week ago. Not only that, I was still technically his prisoner… his enemy. If he said no, I wouldn't be surprised. I regretted asking at all. When he dismissed the idea, it'd be almost worse than Shem's rebuff.

Koda had made me feel like I *mattered*. In one short week, he'd done more to make a place for me with his people than Shem had done in months. He'd treated me like an equal. It dawned on me that my feelings for Shem had been far more superficial than I'd realized, and if Koda were to give us a chance, I might actually grow to love him.

All of these thoughts flashed through my mind in the span of a few heartbeats.

"Nevermind," I mumbled when the silence stretched longer, and Koda's stunned expression hadn't changed. "It was a stupid idea."

"No, it's not. I just… need to think," Koda said finally, shaking his head as if to clear it.

Humiliated for the second time in a single hour, I shook my head as well. "Don't bother. I don't know what I was thinking."

I tried to hide the tears in my eyes by looking down and fiddling with a loose thread on my dress.

Koda's big hand appeared beneath my blurry vision, covering my own. "Is this what you want?" he asked softly.

"It doesn't matter what I want." I shrugged, unwilling to reveal my feelings any further. But I couldn't bring myself to pull my hand away. "This will save your sister and my people, and it's the only plan we have."

He reached out and tilted my chin up, forcing me to meet his eyes, and murmured, "It does matter."

I swallowed, trying to shove the hope back down

before it could betray me.

"Is it what *you* want?" he repeated, holding my gaze.

Blinking away tears, I was terrified to answer and expose myself to him. It took all my courage to nod.

He let go of my chin with a small smile. "Good."

"Good?"

His smile grew teasing. "I think I like this plan of yours."

"You do?" Hope rose against my will.

Growing serious, he took my hand again, weaving his fingers through mine. "It would be an honor to have you as my wife."

I bit my lip, unable to stop a smile of my own. "What now?"

"We'll need to steal the rings," Koda said, but his frown returned as he faced camp again. "They're imbued with the power to make the covenant on both sides. Without them, we would only be making the agreement between the two of us." He squeezed my fingers. "But my father will expect me to try that to help Tehya."

"Then, *I'll* have to steal them." I grinned at him, feeling lighter than I could ever remember, despite the circumstances. "And you can be our distraction."

26

WE PIECED TOGETHER A rough plan.

"You're sure you can do this?" Koda asked. He wasn't questioning my confidence the way a Jinni would have, though. He was merely confirming that I had the ability.

I nodded, keeping my reservations to myself. "I have to. We don't have a choice."

"Meet at the smokehouse?" he asked.

I shook my head. "Too risky. We need to meet somewhere they can't easily find us once the ceremony begins." I couldn't seem to stop blushing whenever I thought about it. Nothing about this wedding was the way I'd imagined it for myself, but I was surprised to find I was looking forward to it.

"I know a place." Koda gave me instructions on how to find a path to a lake at the foot of the nearby cliffs. He described a peninsula to use as a landmark to find each other. "It's only a few hours on foot. Wait for me there."

"I'll probably fly." I enjoyed the ease of saying those words. There was freedom in not needing to hide any part of myself.

"Always trying to show me up," he teased.

My cheeks filled with heat. I shook my head, shooting him a smile.

With the details settled, we began the descent back to camp. "I wish Tehya was here," Koda said quietly, more to himself than to me.

I cringed. I'd have to tell him what I'd done to Tehya at some point, now that I wasn't leaving. Maybe I should tell him now. I could pretend I'd done it for her own good, to help her get out of the wedding, though I doubted she'd see it that way.

In the end, though, afraid it might change things between Koda and I, I didn't risk it. "It's good she's not here," I said instead, trying not to let my shame show. "Once they realize she's gone, they'll be so busy looking for her they won't know we've started the ceremony until it's too late."

"True," he agreed.

We circled the camp until we reached the path, stealthily making our way toward the tents. Koda rolled his eyes whenever I crunched a twig underfoot, but didn't say anything, frowning as we drew closer.

When we stepped off the path toward the clearing, while the tents were still out of sight, he grabbed my hand and drew us to a stop. "A kiss for luck?" he murmured, lifting a hand to my cheek.

My heartbeat doubled. I managed a nod, eyes fluttering closed as he leaned in.

His lips brushed mine.

It was nothing like kissing Shem. With the prince, a kiss felt about the same as a handshake: pleasant and warm, but not unexpected. Koda's kiss felt like shapeshifting—affecting every single part of me. Sparks danced behind my closed eyes and heat spread from my chest to the rest of my body. Even my bones felt soft.

He pulled back too soon.

I opened my eyes with a soft sigh.

Stroking a thumb across my cheek, he stepped back slowly, a promise of more in his eyes. "See you soon."

Lifting my fingers to my lips, I watched him go, wishing the moment had lasted longer.

With a shaky breath, I crept around behind the tents and waited for the signal.

Loud voices erupted from the other side, one of them Koda's, arguing with his father.

Shifting into lizard form, I slipped beneath the edge of the tent easily.

From this height, it looked like a forest of logs, where they'd been placed as seating inside the tent. There was a table near me where a lone Vaade stood on one side and a Jinni Guard stood on the other, both standing an equal distance from a large, intricately-carved box that sat in the center of the table, right where Koda had said it would be.

The Vaade and the Jinni eyed each other as the

commotion grew louder, moving as if by silent consent toward the tent entrance. Their backs were to the table.

I didn't know how long they'd be distracted. I'd have to move quickly.

Slithering up onto the table, I moved as silently as possible, though I doubted the Vaade would hear me over the chaos outside.

I tried to lift the lid.

It wouldn't budge.

In this form, I was too weak.

Glancing at the Jinni and Vaade guarding the box, I worried one of them would look back, but Koda wouldn't be able to hold their attention forever.

If I shifted, would the Vaade notice the use of magic? Just in case, I hid behind the box first...

I shifted into a badger.

A second later, the Vaade in the tent shouted, "What did you do?"

"Nothing!" the Jinni Guard yelled back, but the Vaade was already hauling him by the back of his uniform toward the tent entrance—the Jinni vanished in retaliation, taking the Vaade with him.

Well, that was a happy accident.

I scurried around the box. They could be back any second.

My newly formed claws and larger size should've made it easier to open the ceremonial ring box, but without thumbs, I still struggled.

If anyone came through the entrance right now, I'd

be caught instantly.

Frantic energy made me claw harder at the box as the shouting increased.

The two guards must've reappeared outside.

Finally, one claw managed to hook the lid, and I yanked it open.

Two rings nestled inside on a soft velvet pillow, which stood out amongst the Vaade logs and patch-work fur tent. That had to be a Jinni addition.

The first ring was crafted of white gold with a perfect ruby set beside a pure diamond—it clearly belonged to the Jinn. The second ring was thicker and far less delicate. It was meant to be given to Shem by Tehya, so it represented the Vaade with a dragon head curving over a shield, mouth open wide in a roar. A magical energy came from both rings, similar to what I felt around the enchanted artifacts back in the royal Jinni vault.

I scooped them up and shut the lid, pinching them cautiously between my claws as I leapt off the table.

When I reached the tent wall, I shifted back into a lizard, though the extra shifting drained my energy, to slip out beneath the furs, dragging the now-heavy rings behind me.

With one last shift, I returned to my own form, and then I was sprinting away from the tent.

Heart racing, I cheered inwardly.

Then stopped.

My bag!

All the food and water I'd gathered was in it, not to

THE SECRET CURSE

mention the knife—we'd likely need those supplies while Koda and I hid from the Vaade for a while.

Turning back, I tried to remember which tree I'd hidden it by. They all looked the same. I walked in a few circles before I spotted those overgrown roots and dug out the bag.

Unfortunately, the shouting had drawn unwanted attention from camp.

Vaade ran down the path toward the noise.

If I hadn't stopped to find my bag, they'd have run right into me.

I ducked behind a tree.

More Vaade followed.

If I traveled right now, they'd sense it, so instead I waited for them to pass by, followed by a few more, then carefully picked my way through the trees.

Only when I crossed the path and reached the stream, leaving the tents far behind, did I finally draw a full breath.

From here, I could barely hear Koda and the other's angry voices carrying on, but he was still stalling.

Good.

The longer it took them to realize the rings were gone, the better.

Time to go to our meeting place.

Though I'd boasted that I'd fly there, I couldn't carry my bag that way. Not to mention, after changing shape so many times in a row, I didn't want to exhaust myself further by shifting again.

I considered traveling, but only briefly.

It'd be agonizingly slow in these thick woods, but more importantly, it'd leave a magical trail that any Vaade could follow.

Walking would be easiest. According to Koda, it was only a short hike. And this way, he could catch up to me.

With a racing heart, I began the trek, constantly glancing over my shoulder. After at least a quarter hour passed, and then another, I began to worry.

Where was Koda?

He should've caught up to me by now.

Had the Dragon detained him? Would he put his son in confinement a second time? That would ruin everything.

My anxiety surprised me. For a plan we'd only just created, I couldn't remember the last time I'd wanted something more. Even my engagement to Shem hadn't been this exciting.

Nervous energy made me move faster, and I reached the edge of the mountain sooner than expected.

It was exactly like Koda had described. A clear, quiet lake rested at the foot of the mountain surrounded by a field of prairie grass and flowers. In the water, the mountain peaks were reflected back, creating a beautiful duplicate.

I stood waiting on the peninsula where it stretched out into the lake, feeling exposed.

If the Vaade came after me instead, they'd spot me easily. I wished Koda's meeting place could've been a bit more private.

Moving to sit on a large rock, I gazed down at the water. If the worst happened, I'd throw the rings as far into the water as I could, before turning into a fish and swimming away.

Feeling slightly better, I was still staring at my reflection in the water when another face appeared over my shoulder.

27

I SCREAMED.

"It's just me!" Koda hurried to say, catching my wrist when I swung at him.

"What took you so long?" I demanded, embarrassed, pulling away. "Did they discover the rings were taken?"

He grinned. "If they haven't yet, they will soon."

"That's not very reassuring."

"You don't seem like a woman who needs to be reassured," he countered, still radiating excitement.

I couldn't keep my frown, turning to stare at the mountains as I hid a smile. "What now?"

When he didn't answer, I turned back to find him suddenly serious. He slowly took my hand again, tracing a thumb over my skin. "Now, we begin."

A shiver swept over me.

We were really doing this.

Pulling the rings from my bag, I held them in my

palm for him to see. The larger dragon one was obviously meant for a man. I picked up the delicate Jinni one that had been intended for Tehya. I put it down and picked up the dragon ring. "I don't think this one will fit me…"

"It shouldn't make a difference which one you wear," Koda said, taking the gold dragon ring from me to inspect it himself. "My father explained the covenant spell to me multiple times. We prepared our ring and instructed the Jinn on how to prepare theirs—both rings are enchanted to speak for their people, but they won't begin pulling on our power or our promises until the covenant begins."

"How will we know if it works?" I met his eyes through the circle of the gold ring.

"There will be a weakening as the spell begins to slowly pull out our strength."

A weakening. The word reminded me of how he'd described the covenant when we'd first met. I still remembered my response: *Why would anyone willingly be vulnerable? I would never trust someone enough to consider that.*

Yet here I was.

I swallowed audibly, staring at the ring now instead of Koda as he lowered it.

With a finger under my chin, he brought my gaze back to his, as if he'd remembered our conversation as well. "I have full trust in you," he murmured. "Can you say the same of me?"

Afraid to speak, I managed to nod.

He ran a thumb softly over my bottom lip.

I shivered.

This time, the kiss wasn't rushed. I drew in a ragged breath, closing my eyes. His fingers slipped through my hair. Pulling me closer, he lifted me suddenly, and I broke off laughing as my feet dangled in the air. He spun us around, and with one lingering kiss, he finally pulled back, but only enough to kiss my forehead.

I lowered my eyes to hide the sudden emotion. "I haven't been to any weddings in the human world, Vaade or otherwise," I murmured. *Or any weddings at all, for that matter.* "But I believe the kiss comes at the *end* of the ceremony?"

Wryly, Koda laughed, stepping back. "Then let's hurry up and start so we can get to the end."

I bit my lip, holding back a laugh too. "I'll follow your lead. How do we begin?"

Like before, Koda pointed to my three middle fingers one at a time. "Mind, body, soul."

Had it sounded this romantic the first time he'd explained? I stared into his eyes, memorizing the amber sunset colors, and the way they warmed as he looked down on me.

"A typical human marriage places the rings on the soul finger," he repeated the words he'd said the first time. "But the covenant requires vulnerability as proof before the rings will accept the spell."

This time a different word caught my attention. "Proof of what?"

THE SECRET CURSE

"Trust."

The one word that had haunted me since before I could remember, causing me pain at every turn. Could I accept it now? Koda waited patiently, as my inner battle manifested itself in pulling back with tense shoulders.

He reached across the growing space, fingers softly touching my cheek, tucking a loose hair behind my ear gently. "Can you trust me, Jezebel?"

Hearing him speak my name instead of *Jinni Girl* made my lips twitch.

He didn't know what he asked of me.

But in all my time here, he'd never broken a promise. He'd been the one to rescue me from the Vaade who'd attacked me. He'd tended my wounds, told me the truth about the Dragon's plans. He'd even tried to protect me from the pain of discovering Shem's betrayal. As his prisoner, I'd been obligated to rely on him, but still, he'd never let me down.

"Okay," I whispered finally, taking the hand he held out. "Time for you to make me weak and defenseless."

He chuckled. "As long as you'll make me the same."

I still held the delicate Jinni ring, so he moved to take it, holding it in front of my middle finger, clearing his throat. "The ceremony begins when we each place the other's ring on the middle finger and speak the words of the enchantment. Once this is done, the weakening starts. Our abilities will fade gradually." He paused, gazing down at our hands intertwined in front of us. "We'll say our vows, before completing the ceremony by moving the rings to the last finger with a final oath."

Wordlessly, I nodded. I couldn't have spoken past the tightness in my chest if I'd tried.

"Say this after me," he began, intoning in a deep voice, "To prepare the soul, I surrender the body."

I cleared my throat, which was suddenly dry, and rasped, "To prepare the soul, I surrender the body."

As I finished, he slid the ring onto my middle finger.

Immediately, a tingling sensation flooded through me like a cool inner wind running through my veins. When I grasped for one of my Gifts, they seemed distant, as if they were housed in my body, but had moved to another "room" of sorts. Shifting felt just out of reach, and the distance I could normally travel felt like it was decreasing steadily, shrinking away like the water lapping at the shoreline beside us.

Koda was speaking, and I made myself focus, as he repeated the vow for himself. At his nod, I slid the dragon ring onto his middle finger.

He flinched a little, clearly not liking the weakening any more than I did.

When he blinked back at me, his sunset-colored eyes were a little less vibrant. If I hadn't spent a full minute staring into them moments ago, I might not have noticed. Subtly, they continued to change, dark pupils growing less narrow and more round by the second, visibly proving that the covenant had begun.

Back in the Vaade camp—and all of Jinn—our people would be feeling the covenant start to take effect, slowly leeching away their Gifts and strengths as well.

If they hadn't noticed the missing rings before, they certainly knew now.

An image of Shem panicking caused a confusing mixture of satisfaction and guilt all at once.

"Now the vows," Koda murmured, staring at our hands shyly, cheeks growing red. "There aren't any required words for this part. It's usually just the standard wedding promises... We can make up our own."

As his words sank in, I felt a full-body flush as well. He meant we needed to say how we felt. That might be even more vulnerable than the temporary loss of our abilities. "You first," I managed to squeak.

He cleared his throat. Staring out at the water, he thought for a minute, then turned back to me. "When I came to Jinn that day, I didn't expect that I'd be kidnapping my future wife," he began with an ironic grin.

I scoffed, shaking my head, but gave him a small smile.

"I promise to protect you," he continued. "Even when you might not see it that way." I frowned at his choice of words. That was an odd way to make that vow. Perhaps it was a Vaade saying? "To provide for you," he went on, distracting me from asking. "And to prove myself worthy of being a husband. I look forward to learning to love you."

He leaned in, whispering, "Based on my experience so far, I don't think it will be hard."

His breath tickled my ear.

I shivered. Warmth stole over my body as I dared to meet his eyes. I could admit now, in this moment, if only to myself, that I *wanted* this.

It was my turn.

Gathering my courage, I drew a deep breath and let it out slowly. "I vow…"

My mind went blank.

What was I willing to promise him? Nothing felt safe. But that was the point, wasn't it?

"I vow to tell you the truth," I began in the softest whisper, growing more confident as I spoke. "To always try to love you back, and to… trust you."

Simple words.

Not nearly so simple to put into action.

His eyes softened, and he squeezed my fingers gently. When he didn't continue, I blinked away the emotions and cleared my throat. "Now what?"

He hesitated.

An odd emotion I didn't recognize flickered across his face, too fast to read.

"Now," he said in a slower voice, "We say the final words to complete the covenant as we place the rings on… the next finger."

Slowly, he drew the delicate white gold ring off my finger, staring down at the ruby and diamond for a long moment before he lifted my hand.

There was that strange expression again. It was gone before I could name it.

With his hand and the ring poised in front of mine,

he dipped his head lower, until there was only a breath of space between us. "With this ring, I take you, Jezebel, to be my wife in every way, until death takes us."

As he slid the ring onto my finger, he closed the distance between us and captured my mouth with his. The kiss flooded my senses as strongly as the magic had the first time. My entire body trembled.

When he pulled away, my mind felt almost fuzzy from the kiss, as if a fog had come over me.

Eyes closed, I laughed on a shaky breath as he finally pulled back. "That wasn't technically the end," I reminded him in a teasing tone. "We still have to do your ring."

"I know." His smile was close-lipped, almost tight at the corners. One hand absently touched the dragon tooth necklace. He didn't usually fidget. Our covenant must be making him more nervous than he'd let on. "I just couldn't hold back."

Pulling his own ring off his middle finger, he held it out to me and stretched the fingers of his left hand out so I could place the ring on his ring finger.

As I reached out to take his hand, a flash of white and red on my own finger caught my eye.

It struck me as strange.

My thoughts felt uncharacteristically out of reach, like I was forgetting something important.

"What am I supposed to say again?" I asked Koda to cover my hesitation, staring down at the ring on my first finger.

"With this ring, I take you, Koda, to be my husband," he chanted the rest, but I slowly stopped listening.

The ring.

It was on my *first* finger.

What had Koda said before we'd started? It was a struggle to remember his words. Straining, I found them one at a time. *Mind... body... soul.* The ring finger was for the soul—for the marriage *and* the covenant to be completed.

But he'd put it on…

The first finger.

Mind.

Something teased my memory… Something to do with forgetting?

My heart stalled as it finally came to me.

The curse.

Drawing in a slow, careful breath, I managed through years of practice to keep a calm mask on my face as I met his eyes. They were shifting from sunset orange and yellow to a darker hazel. Was the weakening completed? If so, I was entirely defenseless… and I might've made the biggest mistake of my entire life.

"What's wrong?"

All kinds of alarm bells were ringing in my head.

He wasn't stupid. He wouldn't put the ring on the wrong finger by mistake.

I hoped I was wrong.

On instinct, I kept my suspicions to myself as I repeated the vow carefully, watching his face the entire

THE SECRET CURSE

time. There was a tightness in his eyes even as he smiled. It added to my growing tension.

"... until death takes us," I finished, staring into his eyes the way he had mine.

I slid the dragon ring onto his *first* finger.

Just like he'd done for mine.

When panic flickered in his eyes, my heart sank.

The emotion was gone so fast though, I almost thought I'd imagined it.

He cleared his throat. "Good," he said as he pulled the ring off again, though I got the distinct impression he did *not* think it was good.

He placed the thick dragon ring in my palm. Stretching out his hand toward me for the third time, palm toward the ground, he said, "Now move it to the final finger, to connect the soul, and the covenant will be completed."

I took it.

Then, I slipped my own ring off as well.

Holding both of them in shaking hands, I held mine out to him, wanting despite everything to trust him. Desperately hoping he'd prove me wrong. I whispered, "You first."

Stricken, he didn't take it. "I... can't."

28

SLOWLY MY HANDS FELL to my sides, still holding both rings as my lungs constricted.

I couldn't breathe.

I couldn't think.

Everything hurt.

"You can't," I repeated.

He might as well have taken a knife and stabbed me in the chest. It hurt the same. Maybe more.

His betrayal was worse than Shem's… because I'd chosen to trust him fully. I'd been all in.

Koda looked anguished as he finally spoke. "I'm sorry. I can't explain."

Every word slammed the knife in deeper. My heart shattered into little pieces and then each of those pieces broke again a thousand times more. I wrapped my cold fingers around the dragon ring in my palm as the same ice stole over my heart, trying to mend the fragments, piecing them together in a jagged new shape that didn't resemble what it used to be.

It never would.

"You were never going to complete the covenant for me, were you?" My tone was deceptively soft, hiding my growing fury. I didn't need his explanation. "You did exactly what your father wanted. You used me."

But he shook his head. "The covenant and the curse would've happened one way or the other. My father would've made sure of it."

I shook my head as a tear slipped out.

He reached out to wipe it, but I leaned away, and he let his hand drop. "This was the only way I could—" he broke off briefly, shaking his head as if frustrated. "The only way I could protect Tehya," he pleaded, hazel eyes tightening around the corners. "She wants to marry Akeena, not your prince."

My prince? For a split second, I felt a gap in my memory like a gaping hole, then the hole was gone. He meant the Jinni prince.

"There *had* to be a marriage to use the covenant spell," he was saying. "And I know it doesn't seem like it, but this solution saves you as well as Tehya. You would've been a target along with the rest of Jinn, but now, as my wife, I can keep you safe."

I scoffed. "Safe, while the rest of my people are enslaved or worse?"

Forehead wrinkling, Koda pressed a hand to it as if

searching for something. "I… I don't think that's what my father plans. He only needs the curse in place for a short time. A few months or a year at most."

"A year?" I gasped, shaking my head. "There will be nothing left of us."

"I can't explain," Koda repeated. "It *has* to be this way. But with you as my wife, I'll have the power to end the curse as soon as we—" he cut off, almost like he'd choked on something, then growled softly. "As soon as we conquer Jinn," he said instead of whatever he'd been about to say. "Your Gifts won't be gone forever."

I couldn't hold his gaze anymore. My eyes shuttered as I squeezed the rings in my hands tight enough to hurt. "You really believe that, don't you?"

"I swear it," Koda vowed passionately, trying to touch my cheek again, but I opened my eyes in time to dodge his hand. He let it fall. "I'll keep you safe in the meantime. I promise."

Your promises mean nothing.

I didn't say it aloud, though. My mind raced, tripping through the holes that kept springing up, confusing me as I tried to think. How could I stop the curse?

"I have to do this, Jezebel." Koda's voice broke a little, as if he was somehow hurting too. "For my people."

He'd always wanted to help his people conquer mine—the truth had always been there, yet somehow, I'd forgotten it, despite the fact that *he* was the one who'd kidnapped me in the first place.

"Don't talk to me about your people," I spat, taking

a step back. It was the exact reasoning Shem had given me. Did I matter so little? "*I* was supposed to be your people. Your *wife*. You lied to me."

Our wedding vows weren't even fully finished, and they'd already been broken.

"No," he swore. "I meant every word. I'll protect you from all of it. You *are* my wife now, which means my father can't touch you. No one can."

Who was his father? I somehow couldn't quite remember.

His fingers continued to twitch like he was desperate to reach for me and forcing himself to hold back. "Your people will forget. It has to be this way. But I can remind you of the truth"—he squinted, as if he either didn't know or maybe couldn't recall how it worked—"every day if need be. And when the time is right, I'll make sure we complete the covenant to bring your abilities back."

"When the time is right," I repeated dully.

"It's not like you care about your people anyway." He threw up his hands as if he was truly surprised by my reaction. "What do you care if we take power away from Jinn? The Gifts are an unfair advantage."

"That's how you see me?" I stood frozen in place, fracturing further with every new revelation. I thought he'd been the first person to respect my Gifts, that he didn't resent them. But he'd wanted them to be removed all along.

"No, of course not," he was protesting, but I barely heard him.

A numbness stole over me.

I didn't know what to do.

Maybe we could find a way to backtrack this covenant somehow before it was completed.

I could go my own way, and he'd go his. I'd never have to see his backstabbing face again.

Turning away, I moved to pace.

Koda grabbed my wrist, stopping me. "What're you doing?"

I'd meant to put a little space between us, just temporarily, to figure out how to talk this through with him.

"You can't leave."

I looked from his hand on mine to his now fully-human hazel eyes, barely recognizing him anymore. "Let go."

"I can't do that," he growled. Though his Vaade strength had faded, he was still stronger than me. When I tried to tug away, he only gripped tighter.

I reached my free hand into my bag for the knife. If he wanted to bully me, I could threaten him right back.

My hand brushed against the little jar with the paralytic that I'd used on... someone... I couldn't remember who... before my fingers curled around the knife.

I yanked it out, pointing it at Koda's face. "Let. Me. Go."

Something in my expression must've told him I was serious. He finally loosened his grip, holding his hands up

THE SECRET CURSE

in surrender. "This is going all wrong." He gripped his head, shaking it slightly as if to clear his thoughts. "We're on the same side, remember? You have to finish the covenant by putting the ring on my finger."

When I took a step back, he followed. "I will if you go first."

"I already told you, I can't." He matched me stride for stride as I backed up, speeding up when I did, ignoring the knife. "Not yet. For our plans to work, we need the Jinn to be completely cut off from magic. Nothing else will be enough."

"Why? What do the Vaade plan to do?"

"I can't say."

"Why?"

"I—I don't remember," he admitted, rubbing his brow with a frustrated hand, then shaking his head again. "You have to trust me."

I scoffed.

That was the one thing I never should've done in the first place.

On instinct, I tried to travel away. But of course, I couldn't. A spike of fear raced up my spine when I realized I couldn't even remember how.

"Listen to me, Jezebel," he continued as he stalked me along the water's edge. "I swear on the dragons themselves that I will make sure the covenant is completed for you by placing a ring on your finger eventually. It will only be a few years at most. I'll protect you the entire time."

"What an offer," I snapped. "You'll only betray me temporarily."

He had the good sense to look ashamed, but it didn't stop his progression toward me.

I'd never wished for my Gifts more than I did right then. If I could've, I'd have traveled away to the mountains and out of reach. Or maybe shifted into a Lacklore and attacked him. Could I do that? It seemed more like a dream when I thought about it.

Glaring at him, I shook my head.

How could I have ever trusted him?

As he prowled closer, I spun on my heel and ran through the meadow. Behind me, long grass crunched under our heels as Koda gave chase. The steep slope of rocks at the base of the mountain rose up on all sides, quickly blocking my path.

Koda was driving me into a corner.

His betrayal became secondary to finding a way out of this. It was either him or me. He was making all kinds of promises, but I knew better now. I was the only one I could trust.

Hands held out in a gesture of peace, Koda cornered me as I backed up against the rock wall. "I don't want to hurt you, Jezebel."

"Too late," I said bitterly, clutching the rings against my stomach. "You should've thought of that sooner."

He pounced.

Swiping at him clumsily with my knife, I aimed to skewer him, but instead I only managed to slash a shallow cut along his arm.

When he hissed in pain and fell back, staring at the wound with a surprised expression, I ducked around him, trying to run back through the meadow.

He crashed into me from behind.

His weight knocked me to the ground with a painful *thump* as the knife tore out of my hand and soared through the air, landing far out of reach.

We wrestled wildly. The rings went flying, disappearing into the tall grass along with the knife.

Grunting, Koda grew less gentle in his frustration, yanking my arms down and pinning them to my sides as he used the weight of his body to hold me down.

I squirmed, refusing to give up.

"You shouldn't have thrown the rings," he grumbled, searching for some sight of them in the long grass that rose above our heads. "You're only prolonging the inevitable."

"Are you saying you'd force me to put the ring on your finger?" I asked, breathless from the struggle but also from his heavy weight on my chest, hampering my lungs. "Because that's the only way it will happen."

Though his brows drew down unhappily and he wouldn't meet my eyes, Koda nodded. "I will if I have to."

That decided it then.

As he leaned to one side, feeling around with one hand through the grass while still pinning me to the ground, he unwittingly freed one of my arms. My bag was slightly under my hip, but I managed to wriggle it out and slip my fingers inside, gripping the wooden cork at the top and easing it off.

There was a tiny bit of paste left.

I scooped it out on one finger.

The shallow cut on his arm oozed blood, dripping down onto my dress and shoulder. It was the perfect opportunity.

Still, even after everything Koda had done, I hesitated.

This wasn't the same as what I'd done to Asher, my first crush, or to Shem when I chose to marry Koda. If I did what I was imagining, it would affect an entire race.

But that's what the Vaade had planned to do to us.

"Found it," Koda declared triumphantly.

I made my decision.

This wasn't just Koda's plan, it was... another Vaade whose name escaped me. It was what all of them had wanted. If it was backfiring on them, then that was their fault too. They had only themselves to blame.

I struggled again, straining under his weight and grabbing his arm as part of my feigned attempt to break free.

Koda held me down easily.

The paste smeared across his wound.

He was too busy grappling with my other hand to notice anything strange, trying to force me to hold his ring and place it on his finger.

I made a fist. Tightening my fingers against his

THE SECRET CURSE

attempts, I gasped as he wrenched them open one by one. Though I tried to fight back, he was overpowering me.

Just a few more seconds!

I didn't know if I could hold out much longer.

He'd pressed the ring between my stubborn fingers, and his own finger was poised to put it on, when his grip began to loosen.

Gasping, I ripped my hand free.

His body started to sag as the paralytic took effect.

Finally.

I rolled him off me.

That was the Vaade weakness: they didn't think they had any.

"What did you do?" he gasped, just like his sister had, whatever her name was.

The dragon ring fell to the ground as he lost his ability to hold it.

I left it there.

As he lay gasping in the long grass, I stood, ignoring his continued stream of complaints and demands as I searched for the other ring. Koda tried to sit up and follow, but his body continued to weaken and betray him.

The Jinni ring took forever to find.

"Please, Jezebel," Koda begged as he fell back in the grass, unable to hold himself up any longer. "Please."

I refused to respond until I found the ring, struggling to focus as different gaps in my memories continued popping up, confusing me—I couldn't think straight with this second spell clouding my mind.

There.

It'd landed near my knife, which I made sure to pick up as well. Then I lifted the thin white-gold ring with its diamond and ruby from where it'd been half buried in the dirt.

Wordlessly, I drew a deep breath and faced Koda. Since he'd tried to force me to put the Vaade ring on his finger to complete the spell, I'd do the same with my own ring.

I approached carefully, making sure he'd lost all feeling in his arms and wouldn't fight me further. "Please, Jezebel," he repeated in a whisper now, as if he couldn't find anything better to say. "I care about you more than I'd like to admit. I wasn't just marrying you for the covenant."

I lifted his limp hand in mine. My fingers pinched his together so that he held the ring, and though he groaned, he couldn't move as I used his own hand to slip the ring on my ring finger.

Where it should've been all along.

I feared it wouldn't work without the vow, but we *had* both said them. The rings should be the very last step...

The cool metal circled my finger like an embrace.

Instantly, my missing memories began flooding back, making me feel like I was waking from a deep sleep. Were my abilities returned as well? I tested them out by traveling from one side of the meadow and back in the span of two heartbeats.

THE SECRET CURSE

Covering my face, I let out a huge breath of relief, shoulders relaxing.

"Finish the covenant," Koda's voice rasped. The paralytic was working fast, but he fought it. "Your prince doesn't want you anymore," he growled, going for the jugular. I winced, remembering exactly who he was talking about now. "This is your only option."

Was it? I stared down at him, mourning everything I'd thought we had.

The return of my memories made it hurt more.

I shook my head. "It stopped being an option the moment you betrayed me."

"Please," he used his last bit of strength to beg. His whole body strained toward the ring that lay beside him, but he couldn't even lift his arm to pick it up. "I swear I would've reversed the curse."

I knelt next to him.

Reaching down, I gently lifted the ring, staring at it. "I don't believe you." But part of me still wanted to. It brought tears to my eyes against my will. I could use my manipulation Gift to get honesty from him, but I wasn't sure I wanted to know the truth. Instead, I forced the tears back with a ripping sensation, burying them deep.

I put the ring in my pocket.

"You can't do this!" Panic mixed with anger flashed across his face. "If you don't finish the covenant, you'll condemn us to live like humans… without any memories of who we really are," he managed to say, as his eyes started to drift shut. "We'll never end…" he trailed off.

"If you could do it, then so can I."

He blinked rapidly, forcing his eyes open. "We were only going to… use the weakness temporarily. It's completely… different."

"I disagree," I murmured.

"We keep written records," Koda slurred, fighting a losing battle. "You can't make us forget forever…" As he lost consciousness, his eyes fluttered closed and didn't open again.

"Thank you for letting me know," I said quietly, though he couldn't hear me anymore. "I'll make sure to send someone to destroy them."

Leaning down, I lowered my head and let my lips brush across his one last time. "I could've loved you more than anyone," I whispered, allowing the tears to fall. They dripped onto his cheeks before trailing into the grass. "If you hadn't broken my trust, I would've been yours forever."

29

I STOOD.

The cheerful setting of the prairie grass in front of the lake and majestic mountains hadn't changed much—except for the places where we'd trampled the grass—but I felt darker.

"I imagine you'll forget what happened today," I told him softly, hoping he could hear me though he slept. "And the story of the covenant will no doubt get twisted and erased over time. But just know…" I paused, throat tightening. "I won't forget you."

Now he had nothing, and I had even less.

No home.

No one to trust.

As much as I'd grown to like the Vaade, I'd never again be allowed to sit at their fire. That dream was over.

Could I somehow go back to the castle?

The Jinni prince had rejected me, while Koda, the

prince of the dragons, had betrayed me, leaving me without a place on either side.

Your prince doesn't want you anymore.

Koda's words played over and over on a loop in my mind.

Doesn't want you.

Wallowing in the loss, I looked down at Koda and thought darkly. *At least I still have my Gifts.*

I sucked in a breath. My Gifts of travel, shifting, and... manipulation.

I could *make* Shem want me.

Unlike Koda, whose strong mind had been immune to my Gifts, Shem's wasn't. Before I'd grown aware of my newest ability, I'd accidentally used it on him more than once.

That would solve everything.

If I forced him to take me back, I would have a home, a husband, and a future.

If I did this, I'd be queen.

I closed my eyes so I didn't have to look at Koda, clutching the ring as I searched for any of the old guilt over using my Gift of manipulation on others.

I couldn't find it.

Instead, my resolve only hardened. Shem had been manipulating *me* by making me think he truly loved me, that he would fight for me, when in reality, he'd thrown me aside as easily as Koda had when the opportunity came.

When I imagined using my Gift on him to

manipulate him into marrying me—the way he'd promised to already—I had no reservations.

Shem had already proved he would've overrun my own desires just as easily.

What did I have to lose?

The answer came to me as soon as I asked the question: *nothing.*

I stood and left Koda lying in the grass without a backward glance.

Traveling to the camp used very little energy and cut the time down from an hour to a few short minutes. The camp was oddly quiet. As if most of the Vaade were gone.

Probably looking for the rings, I thought, creeping closer.

Four large Vaade men stood near the tent arguing with each other. One of them was Ahriman, the Vaade who'd attacked me. He sported a bruised and swollen eye.

Jaw clenching, I lifted my chin.

Too easy.

Though they were no match for me now, with the curse weakening them more with each passing minute, I was spoiling for a fight.

I strode out into the clearing directly toward them. "Where is everyone?" I mocked them. "Did those 'feeble' Jinn somehow get the best of you?"

"Jinn?" Ahriman squinted at me, then his eyes widened in fear. "You're a Jinni!" To the others he added, "I told you I could smell something off!"

They'd forgotten so much already, Ahriman didn't

even know who I was anymore. It was oddly disappointing. "Are you the only ones here?"

They had the good sense to raise their weapons.

"No," Ahriman scoffed. But I didn't really need an answer. If there had been other Vaade here, they'd have appeared by now. The Dragon must've sent all the Vaade to hunt us down when he first felt the covenant begin.

Nodding as I reached them, I simply said, "Good. That should give me a little time."

I clapped my hands on the shoulders of Ahriman and the Vaade closest to him.

We traveled.

I chose the farthest place I could think of, besides the lake where I'd left Koda: the place where the Dragon had first held negotiations.

When we reappeared, I let go.

And traveled again.

"Filthy Jinni sna—" another Vaade was saying as I flashed into the camp directly behind him.

Beside him, the other Vaade whirled with his fist out.

But I was prepared, and he was not.

Without his extra senses, the second Vaade didn't realize I was crouching by his feet instead of standing, and he missed, setting him off-balance.

I grabbed both guard's ankles and traveled again.

We landed on the other side of the clearing this time, across from their fellow guards who were snarling and tearing through the woods toward us as soon as we appeared.

THE SECRET CURSE

I caught Ahriman eyes.

Giving him a dark smile, I traveled back to the tents once more, leaving them there.

It was probably only an hour or two from camp, but with the memory loss they were experiencing, they might never find their way back. I didn't care.

I hesitated at the entrance to the tent.

Throwing the flap open, I froze on the threshold.

Shem and every single member of his retinue sat tied up on the floor. Only Milcah was free.

Did they not realize their Gifts were back yet?

Wide-eyed, they all stared at me. Milcah had been bent over Shem's ropes behind his back, painstakingly sawing at them with a small pocketknife. She lifted a finger to her lips.

I scowled. "Don't shush me, Milcah," I said loudly, enjoying the way they all flinched as they waited for the Vaade to storm in and find me. "Did you not notice that I used the front entrance?" I mocked her, enjoying this more than I should've. "The guards are gone."

She straightened, looking at the other Jinn. "The king and queen must've sent—"

The audacity.

"*I* took care of them," I interrupted, striding up to her and yanking the knife from my bag. With one sharp cut, Shem's ropes dropped to the floor.

Shem brought his hands around in front of him, rubbing his wrists. He, at least, looked happy to see me. "Someone stole the rings," he told me, as I made my way around the room slashing ropes, freeing the rest of the council members and the guards. "And started the covenant on their own—"

"Again, that was me," I muttered.

Captain Uriel tensed, eyeing me more closely.

Gritting my teeth, I threw up my hands. "I had to. They added a curse to the covenant, and when I tried to warn you, you didn't give me a chance." That wasn't the full truth, but they didn't need to know that. "I'm sure you felt it? After your Gifts began to weaken, when your memories began to disappear?"

"That was part of the covenant?"

"No," I repeated. "It was a secret curse the Vaade added to the covenant."

Shem ran a hand through his hair. "How did you stop it?"

The thought of telling Shem about Koda was too painful. "I'll explain later. The Vaade could come back at any time," I said, grateful that it was true, as I cut the last rope for the remaining guard. "We need to go. Now."

"Maybe this is our opportunity to get the better of them," Shem said to Captain Uriel instead, as if already forgetting me. "If they're still weak, we could call for more members of the Guard—"

"The Vaade threat is over," I interrupted, blood boiling. "I took care of it. They won't be bothering us anymore."

"You don't know that, Jezebel," Shem said with a sigh. Had he always been this condescending?

THE SECRET CURSE

"I *do* know," I insisted through clenched teeth. "It's time to go home."

"I completely understand your desire to go home." Shem patted me awkwardly on the shoulder. "I'll have Milcah take you to the daleth on the way to call for more guards."

"Where is the portal?" I said flatly.

"Just a mile or so to the east—"

"Good." I took his hand and traveled, knowing the others would follow.

"What're you doing?" Shem protested when we reappeared.

Looking him in the eyes, I used the full force of my Gift of manipulation. "We're going home. Right now. You're taking me to your parents."

As expected, the rest of Shem's retinue quickly followed my trail, arriving in a chaotic shouting mass.

"Join hands," I shouted back at Captain Uriel as he seized my arm.

Under the influence of my Gift, his eyes grew blank, and he obeyed.

"Now," I snapped at the others.

Though I wasn't touching the rest of them, they looked from Shem to the captain, both of whom calmly held onto me, and grudgingly followed suit.

Without my previous reservations about my Gifts, I was fueled by my fury, feeling all of them expand in ways I hadn't thought possible before.

I traveled.

Shocking them all, I easily carried the entire group of twelve. Maybe it was the adrenaline or the absolute rage driving me, or both, but I barely felt tired by it. Following Shem's directions, I traveled one final time and arrived a few dozen paces from the daleth.

"To the king and queen," I repeated for everyone else's sake, watching Shem closely for signs that my Gift was fading. He remained obedient, leading the way through the portal.

We landed directly in front of the castle gates, which was as close to the castle as we could get with the enchantments surrounding it. We'd need to physically cross them, as well as one of the castle's grand entrances, before we could travel within the castle itself.

Cold fury poured out of me as Shem stepped up to politely ask the guards to open the gates.

Not waiting for him, I made my voice heavy with the full weight of my Gift, though they were too far to touch, and stared into their eyes as I snapped, "Take us to the king and queen immediately."

I couldn't be sure if it was the size of the group already obeying me, my tone, or the Gift itself growing, but something made them jump to obey.

We strode through the castle toward the throne room.

"The king and queen are currently holding court," the guard told us nervously over his shoulder, as we reached the grand doors. "They're going to share an announcement of some sort." *Probably about to tell everyone their son is marrying a Vaade.* "You can slip

THE SECRET CURSE

into the back here and speak with them after."

"No," I said in the same flat, hard tone, slamming my Gift into him with all my strength. "We'll join them on the stage. Bring us to the side door." Before he could argue, I hooked my arm through Shem's, daring him to speak back to both of us and added sharply, "Now."

30

WE WERE LED TO a side door that opened onto the stage.

King Jubal and Queen Samaria both turned at the sound, cutting off whatever they'd been about to say. "Shem?" The queen rose, hand to her lips. "What happened?"

Her gaze seemed to sweep right over me. King Jubal didn't even spare me a glance. They focused on their son, drawing him forward.

I didn't let go of Shem's arm.

With a pointed glance at my fingers, Queen Samaria finally turned her attention to me.

I stared coldly back.

This was the family who'd left me to the Vaade without a second thought. Just like their son.

"Mother," Shem was saying, bowing his head respectfully. "Father."

THE SECRET CURSE

I kept my chin high.

Turning to the crowd, I took in the throne room, full to the brim with Jinn, waiting to learn about a marriage to the Vaade that was no longer happening. Their judgmental eyes should've made me step back—in the past they would have. Today they didn't affect me. I hardly cared what they thought anymore.

By now, King Jubal was coming to the conclusion that the marriage covenant clearly hadn't happened. He looked between his wife and son, considering.

They'd want to hear the full story privately and discuss it before revealing anything to the public.

Too bad.

I raised my voice as I spoke to them, making sure everyone gathered would hear, all the way to the back. "Good, you've gathered everyone. That's exactly what Shem and I were hoping for."

King Jubal narrowed his eyes at me. "Thank you, Jezebel." His tone was polite, but he gripped my shoulder firmly, trying to intimidate me. "That will be all."

I ignored him, speaking louder. "The Vaade threat has been extinguished. By me."

He'd lifted a hand to call for a guard, but this made him pause. Queen Samaria gave Shem a wide-eyed look in question, and he confirmed it with a slightly dazed nod.

Now, finally, I designed to give them a small bow along with a tight-lipped smile. "You're welcome."

King Jubal caught Captain Uriel's eye, subtly summoning him.

I stepped between them, capturing the king's eyes with my own, sensing my Gift rise at the ready the more I used it. "Shem and I knew you would want the kingdom to hear the news immediately. I'm sure you'd like me to explain."

I'd never addressed the prince so informally in a public venue before, and I knew the onlookers didn't miss it.

Neither did King Jubal.

I couldn't tell if my Gift overpowered him or if he simply didn't want to lose the image of a united front, but he grudgingly nodded for me to continue.

Turning my back on him, the queen, and Shem, I spoke directly to the people. "You may have felt your Gifts weakening in the last hour or so." Though I didn't wait for anyone to nod, I took some satisfaction in the widening eyes throughout the room. Had everyone tried to hide it from their peers? Koda was right, we concealed everything. In this case, it worked to my benefit.

"The Vaade attempted to steal our Gifts." I let my voice carry, let the pause after my words grow heavy before I continued. "I personally turned this curse back on them, stripped the Khaanevaade of their strength and other abilities with a spell that will last a thousand years."

To sound more powerful, I left out a few key details, such as the fact that I had no idea if the curse would last that long. I didn't know if it would *ever* end if Koda didn't receive a ring.

"Without their magic, all currently living Vaade

should be dead within a century or two at most." I paused for emphasis, lowering my voice slightly so that they had to strain to hear, which naturally added emphasis to my words. "They'll never be a threat to Jinn again."

Shock swept across the room.

The Jinn weren't usually the cheering sort, but a murmur of excitement swept across the room, and slowly, they began to applaud.

Glancing back at the royals, I held back a satisfied grin at the astonishment on their faces.

When Queen Samaria stepped forward to take my shoulders, subtly preparing to edge me away from the stage yet again. "No." I stood up to her for the first time. "You will let me speak." I'd use my Gift on her without a second thought if she didn't listen.

Stunned into submission, she loosened her grip and let go.

Turning, I caught her hands in mine, causing another surge of murmuring in the crowd at my boldness. This time I did use my Gift, leaning heavily on it as I glanced between her and King Jubal evenly. "Thank you for sending your son to come for me when the Vaade took me hostage." *I'm giving you false credit for what you should have done,* I thought bitterly. Speaking far louder than necessary, I made sure this story would be spread far and wide today. "I know how much thought you put into my rescue and how worried you were." *In other words, not at all.*

Both their faces grew blank under the influence of

my Gift, and they nodded slowly. "We were terribly concerned," Queen Samaria murmured, almost to herself, agreeing with me fully now. King Jubal looked slightly confused, as if he were fighting my Gift, but losing.

Continuing loudly, I guided them on, "That's why Shem and I both knew you'd agree to the wedding taking place today." They startled, but the reaction was dimmed by my Gift and their own desire to show confidence in front of our audience.

The buzz from the crowd was growing louder. It covered the queen's quiet question, "You're... getting married?"

"Shem and I have decided to wed as soon as possible," I told her and the king, lowering my voice so no one else would overhear. "To prevent anyone else from trying to take advantage of our people again." She nodded slowly, though King Jubal still seemed to be resisting my Gift. In a harsh whisper, I added, "Your son was already going to be married at sunset. It's very fortunate for you that it will now be to his original bride."

That finally seemed to sway him. "Yes," he murmured. "...very fortunate indeed."

I waved an arm grandly toward the crowd. "And here you are, prepared for it with witnesses already gathered. It was meant to be."

My Gift made them bob their heads in agreement.

It was what they *should* have done all along.

To Shem, I added, "You'll want to share the full story of the Vaade's breach of the agreement to pass the

THE SECRET CURSE

time. I'll be back in a quarter hour." His confused expression smoothed out as he nodded in agreement.

Before I left, I made sure to raise my voice for the audience, "We look forward to celebrating this glorious turn of events with you. The wedding will begin shortly."

Though it obviously struck the onlookers as strange that I spoke on behalf of the royal family, they didn't dare question it while the king, queen, and their son stood beside me in direct support.

I strode out in a hurry.

Without experimentation, it was impossible to know how long my Gift would hold power over the royals if someone tried to talk them out of it.

Either way, after the speech I'd just made, it was highly unlikely they would find an excuse to change their minds and still save face before I returned.

Just to be safe, though, I wouldn't dawdle.

"You and you," I pointed to two of the queen's council members lurking outside the throne room doors, waiting for her. "Go get Milcah, Jerusha, and Dorcas, and tell them the *princess* needs them immediately in her rooms. Make sure they don't delay."

I allowed myself a satisfied smile as they hurried off. I'd chosen those three to help me into my dress, knowing how much they'd hate being forced to serve me. Knowing that if I had to, I would *make* them obey.

The more I used my Gift of manipulation, the more I wondered why I hadn't let myself use it before. It was untraceable. As long as I took care not to stretch someone outside of their will too much, no one around them would question it. In some ways, this Gift could be more invisible than Shem himself.

And, if anyone *did* catch on to what I was doing, it'd only take a few words to make them forget.

Traveling directly to the residential hallway where Shem's council members lived, I opened the door to my room and entered.

It was exactly the way I'd left it.

Not a single person had left a note or other sign of their presence, because no one had cared that I'd been gone.

That was about to change.

I was done living in the shadows of what other people wanted.

From now on, I would *make* them value me.

My dress hung along the side of the wardrobe.

White and pure.

As I shucked my ripped and dirty dress to the floor, I wished there was time to bathe before the ceremony. It wasn't worth the risk. But first thing when it was over.

Once this wedding was done, there'd be time to do whatever I wanted. No one would order me around ever again, least of all Shem.

That was the benefit of marrying him instead of Koda. He would do whatever I said.

As I stepped into the wedding gown, pulling the delicate lace over my shoulders and staring into the mirror, I began a shift without thinking.

THE SECRET CURSE

The fabric darkened.

Black lace.

It was the color of mourning.

Fitting.

When Milcah, Jerusha, and Dorcas arrived a few minutes later, I'd already run a brush through my hair and taken a few minutes to shift my features in the mirror—adding a soft blush to my cheeks, removing the bags from under my eyes, and reddening my lips.

"You called?" Milcah asked dryly when I answered the door.

I didn't invite them in. Meeting her eyes with a saccharine smile, I infused my words with my Gift. "I need jewelry fitting for a wedding ceremony. You have some jewels in your room, don't you? Bring me your favorite?"

Her eyes grew blank in response.

When she obeyed, traveling out of the hallway to another part of the castle, Dorcas gave Jerusha a startled glance and shrugged.

"Dorcas, help me with the buttons." I gestured to my back, swinging the door to my room open finally and turning. I didn't use my Gift, wanting to see if she'd cave in simply because Milcah had done so first.

Dorcas stepped forward, starting at the bottom. The little pearlescent buttons led all the way from my lower back to the base of my neck, drawing the dress in to fit my curves.

Jerusha wasn't willing to stand idle in the hall, so she

reluctantly stepped inside as well, closing my door softly. Between the two of them, they were finished by the time Milcah returned.

They brushed out my dark hair so that it lay along my shoulders in waves, while Milcah placed a gold headpiece with a pale blue gem the same color as my eyes around my brow.

As she carefully fit matching gold earrings into my ear, she muttered to herself, "I don't know why I'm letting you borrow these. They're my favorites."

I turned from the mirror to grab her arm, smiling innocently for the other ladies' benefit as I let my Gift flow over her. "It's because you're secretly happy for me to marry the prince." It came so naturally now, I hardly had to think about it. Her face softened in response as my words sank in.

Facing the mirror again, I touched the pretty blue gem in the center of one of the earrings. The gold pieces dangled all the way to my shoulder, making me smile for real this time. "They make a wonderful wedding present."

When Milcah didn't argue, Dorcas and Jerusha glanced at each other again. Over my shoulder, I caught a glimpse of Jerusha studying Milcah in the mirror.

"Jerusha, will you take us to the throne room?" I said to distract her, using my Gift on her this time, just because I could. Taking her arm, I moved us toward the door. "I have a wedding to get to."

Smiling sweetly, I waved for the other ladies to follow, and they did with a nervous chuckle.

THE SECRET CURSE

"To the main entrance," I told Jerusha as we stepped into the hallway, and she nodded. I could've traveled on my own. The request was strategic. Now was the time to assert my authority. When we reappeared at the great hall, I wanted everyone to see their deference to me, not rolled eyes behind my back. And, I admitted to myself, it felt *good*.

We landed in the grand hallway outside the double doors leading to the throne room. Two Jinni Guards stood outside, giving us stern looks as Dorcas and Milcah appeared behind me. Ignoring the guards, I told all three ladies. "Follow me in and lead everyone in a bow when we reach the front." Blank obedient looks passed over their faces.

Turning to the guards, I captured their gazes and demanded, "Open the doors with a bang. Let's make a grand entrance."

Slowly, they followed orders, moving stiffly like puppets with their strings being pulled.

Lips curving in satisfaction, I stepped back as the doors swung wide.

They hit the outer walls with a loud crash, as the guards gave me the striking appearance I'd asked for.

Inside, the room grew hushed as all eyes turned toward me.

Not waiting for permission, I strode forward.

An orchestra hastily put together near the front of the room lurched into song.

I didn't bother to check if Milcah, Jerusha, and

Dorcas trailed after me. They didn't matter. Nothing mattered except saying our vows before the people and completing this marriage.

Jinn parted, making an aisle for me to walk toward Shem. I didn't hurry. With long, slow steps that fit the music, I made them wait, savoring the control I held over the whole room.

When I met Shem's eyes, I forced a smile for appearance's sake.

It was only a week ago that I'd looked across a crowded room seeking his face, but it couldn't have felt more different. No longer was I hopeful or naïve. Now, when I looked at him, I saw things plainly. Shem had fallen for a simple Jinni girl who didn't mind that he prioritized his crown over her. But that girl didn't exist and never had. He couldn't possibly love me when he'd never truly known me. And maybe that was for the best.

Koda's face replaced Shem's in my mind, unbidden.

A twinge of regret struck me.

He wouldn't have let me walk all over him the way Shem was now. That was one of the many things I'd found myself liking about him. He wasn't soft, but he didn't try to make me soft either.

With a slight shake of my head, I forced myself back to the present.

A malleable husband was exactly what I needed in this relationship.

It would be *me* who ordered the Jinni Guard to subtly search for the records Koda had mentioned, removing all traces of the Vaade's history permanently, while they were still vulnerable. I'd make sure they believed they were human. Shem hadn't been capable of facing them, so I'd do what had to be done. Once we became king and queen, he'd step back, one way or the other.

In the meantime, I'd make it my personal mission to find and close as many daleths to the human world as possible. King Jubal and Queen Samaria had left far too many open. I'd also appoint someone to find the spell the Vaade had used to open portals. Not that they'd remember creating them anymore. But better to be safe and remove any chance of them rediscovering it.

Though, perhaps I'd keep one open.

Then I could still check in on Koda now and then.

I bit my lip, unsure if I wanted to when he had no memory of me.

As long as the Vaade never received a sacrificial ring with the intention of marriage, Koda would never recognize me—or my Gifts—ever again. None of the Vaade would. And I'd make sure Shem was under compulsion to never speak a word of them either. All my secrets were safe—both my Gifts *and* what'd really taken place in the human world.

And if the covenant wasn't completed, neither was the magical truce. We would put the Vaade in their place.

Reaching the stage, I solemnly took the stairs, holding Shem's gaze the entire time—not to search for a sign of love in his eyes, since I wouldn't believe it even if I saw it—but because I wouldn't deign to give his parents or the onlookers a single glance.

Reaching him, I accepted the hand he held out. Remembering how so many daughters of Jinn hated to see affection between us, I leaned closer.

Over time, I was sure the tale of what'd happened today would become twisted.

But I'd know what'd really happened.

Despite my best intentions, I pictured Koda, lying alone in that field, and my vision blurred.

I blinked away the tears, smiling like the blushing bride I was supposed to be.

I'd never forget.

It wasn't until King Jubal stepped forward to begin the ceremony that it occurred to me—the ring.

Though the large dragon ring was somewhere back in my room in the pocket of my dress, the delicate Jinni ring was still on my finger.

I slipped it off, tucking it into my palm and out of sight, hoping no one had noticed.

King Jubal raised a hand to the orchestra, and they fell silent. "We gather for an unexpected reason today," he began, as he took my hand and Shem's, leading us toward the thrones where we would sit during the ceremony. Royal weddings were long and full of rituals. Queen Samaria moved to a seat on one side to settle in for the long haul.

As we approached the thrones, while my back was to the audience, I tucked the Jinni ring with its ruby and diamond inside the bodice of my dress, safely out of sight.

THE SECRET CURSE

When I turned to Shem, he took my hands in his own. They were cold. Squeezing my fingers, he probably intended to be reassuring, but I felt nothing.

We stopped before the thrones where we would wait silently until we were allowed to sit in a later part of the ceremony. Though we stared into each other's eyes per tradition, I focused on his father striding around the stage out of the corner of my eye.

King Jubal expounded on the values of a strong marriage and the importance of a wife who would represent the people. It was a slight, meant to remind everyone listening that I was no one of importance and Shem was stooping below his station to marry me. It seemed my Gift had convinced him to let the marriage happen, but that didn't make him happy about it.

I let the insult roll off my shoulders.

It didn't matter what anyone thought of me, when I could change their opinion with a word.

As the king began the first call and response with the people, the orchestra played an undertone beneath it all, and Shem took advantage of the moment to lean closer to me. "I never wanted to go through with it, Jezebel. I always wanted to marry you."

I forced a smile that I didn't feel to keep up the ruse for those watching and whispered, "I don't feel the same. But you'll think that I do, and that's all that matters."

A flicker of disbelief crossed his face, leaving as fast as it came with my final words. It felt good to speak the truth, even if he wouldn't remember.

"I'll always care for you," I told him, using my Gift to soothe his confusion.

But I will never trust you again.

EPILOGUE

ONE YEAR LATER

SEATED ON THE THRONES, the prince and I were mid-ceremony yet again. This time, however, I casually held his hand—a habit of mine that'd formed over the past year. It made it much easier to guide him in the directions I preferred.

My other hand rested on my belly.

As a patch of warm, colorful light from the stained-glass windows danced over us, I felt a little kick.

This was my biggest victory yet.

When it'd become clear that I couldn't manipulate the king and queen day in and day out, not to mention their subjects, I'd considered other ways I might change their loyalties.

The answer had been obvious: a baby.

Though it was incredibly rare for a Jinni to get

pregnant so effortlessly, with my shapeshifting Gift and a careful study of anatomy during pregnancy, it was easily done.

Somehow, though I'd barely begun to show, I already guessed it was a little girl.

I'd name her Hanna.

The corner of my mouth tilted up at the memory of Queen Samaria's face when I'd told her I'd become pregnant in less than a year's time.

It was unheard of.

King Jubal lifted the crown from his head, drawing my attention back to the present briefly. "The ancients crafted a spell called the B'har," he intoned, projecting his voice for the entire throne room to hear. "Every fifty years, this spell allows the crown *itself* to choose who rules our land."

Though King Jubal's current speech wasn't funny or uplifting in any way, I allowed my smile to grow wider. If I liked this little one well enough, I might even consider having a second child—now *that* would really set Jinni tongues wagging! Maybe I'd wait a century or two, though. I didn't want to disrupt my new life here too much.

Shem's hand squeezed mine when I glanced over at him, still beaming, though his return smile was slightly off. There was a glazed look to his eyes most days. I'd considered easing back on my Gift, but I couldn't risk losing his support right now. He'd settled into the role of doting husband agreeing with his wife easily enough.

That had to mean my demands didn't bother him too much, didn't it?

"As I step down," King Jubal proclaimed in a monotone voice. "The crown will choose our next ruler based on their worthiness and the desires of the people themselves."

He raised the crown into the air.

A crackle of energy filled the room, lifting the crown from the king's hands and bringing it up toward the stained glass of the vaulted ceiling.

The crown dangled in midair.

The audience waited with bated breath.

King Jubal stared up at it reverently, while his wife followed suit from the front row. Shem and I remained seated.

I wasn't worried.

The people loved Shem.

I had no doubt in my mind they'd accept him as the next king, despite any lingering feelings about his wife.

A spell like this just needed time. There were thousands of Jinn spread across dozens of islands, but the people would choose Shem.

Eventually our patience was rewarded.

The crown slowly sank from the high vaulted ceiling toward the thrones, toward Shem.

It landed softly on his head.

King Jubal and Queen Samaria immediately bowed, followed by the people, until everyone knelt before us—before Shem technically.

King Jubal raised his voice. "Long may he live, long may he reign."

"Long may he live," the people repeated his words, their voices blending together in a powerful chorus. "Long may he reign."

"Long may I be a good ruler," Shem replied. His words resounded across the large space as he bowed his head in respect for their choice.

After a long pause filled with weighty silence, he let his gaze sweep across the solemn Jinn around the room. "Please rise."

Shuffling filled the room as everyone returned to their feet, except us.

Shem lifted my hand to his lips to press a chaste kiss to my fingers. We sat on the thrones while the orchestra played and a slow progression began to cross the stage one at a time, bringing offerings for the new king.

Thanks to Jubal and Samaria's encouragement, the rest of the kingdom was in full support of this shift in leadership. Especially now that a babe was on the way.

Though the true Jinni taking King Jubal's place would be me.

I'd already decided Shem would begin to take on more assignments in the human world, searching for any last trace of Vaade history.

Assignments that would leave me behind to rule in his place.

If something happened to him in the future on one of these missions, I'd mourn his loss… But in many ways,

THE SECRET CURSE

I'd already done that the day of our marriage.

I didn't love him anymore.

When I looked back and compared what I'd first felt for him to what Koda had made me feel, I wasn't sure I'd *ever* loved Shem.

Absently, I squeezed his hand.

In truth, I didn't feel much of anything for him at this point.

Quiet applause from the audience followed each supplication. Perfumes, gold, resin, and even the occasional cow or goat, though the animals were of course left to the side of the stage instead of paraded before us.

My serene expression never shifted, but I sighed to myself, wishing this whole unnecessary performance was over already.

My mind was already on the meeting I'd set with Milcah after this, in the vault filled with enchanted objects above the royal family's suites.

The next few hours were full of formal rites and traditions, offering artificial smiles to each new well-wisher. Thinking about what Milcah was bringing to our meeting was all that got me through the dull repetition. Finally, after the ceremony ended, we stood beside the grand double doors of the throne room as a slow trickle of guests exited, all of whom stopped to congratulate Shem, and myself by association, on their way out.

"You seem a little ambivalent for a new queen," Shem's father jibed from one side during a quiet moment. He still didn't like me much. Though he yielded to my

Gift whenever I asked something of him, his will remained otherwise strong. While I could've forced him to change his mind about me, I'd come to enjoy sparring with him. On any other day, I'd have relished coming up with a sharp retort. Putting him in his place reminded me how far I'd come.

Today, however, I'd had enough of the false niceties.

Placing a hand on his shoulder, I smiled. "Make your excuses for me, would you? You know how important it is for a pregnant woman to rest."

Not waiting for his reply, I traveled across the castle, landing in the east wing, directly outside the royal family's vault.

The room where they kept their collection of enchanted objects.

Milcah was waiting in the hall outside the vault looking the other way, arms crossed, unable to get in. *Without me.*

My lips curved upward at the irony of her needing me. "Did you find it?"

She startled.

Whirling to face me, she glanced between the Jinni Guards standing at both ends of the hallway. "Perhaps we should talk inside?" she murmured, trying to shame me for talking about enchanted objects in front of them.

As if I'd ever intentionally give away my own secrets.

"Why?" I stage-whispered. "Are you worried they'll figure out we're putting something in the vault?" I glanced meaningfully at both guards. "Give them a little credit, Milcah. I think they're intelligent enough to put the pieces together themselves."

Flushing, she stiffened.

Before she could find another barbed retort, I placed my hand on the swirling iron snakes that formed a lock across the blue vault door, still chuckling. The snake heads uncoiled and struck, wrapping around my wrist. I waited patiently. The locks clicked open as the iron snakes released me with metallic scrapes, allowing me through.

"After you." I waved Milcah inside as I opened the vault.

I rarely used my Gift of manipulation on her. It was far more entertaining when she was aware that she was being forced to obey.

Inside, soft lights flickered on in response to our presence, lighting on dozens of artifacts, from lamps to mirrors to dusty old books. Most of the items, besides the jewels of course, seemed unimportant at first glance. But everything besides the jewels—and possibly some of those as well—was enchanted in some way.

Milcah pulled a small object wrapped in soft wax paper from the travel bag slung over her shoulder.

She held it out to me.

An enchanted mirror that would allow the bearer to see anyone they loved.

My heart beat faster. "You actually found it," I whispered. "I was starting to think you never would."

She stiffened at the insult. "I've only been looking for six months." Her retort was restrained, since she was speaking to her queen now and knew better than to snap at me. As a result, she sounded like she was whining.

"You're right, I suppose," I said offhandedly, as I caressed the soft wax paper, feeling the solid shape beneath. "Anybody could've tracked it down in that amount of time."

A sharp hiss of breath let me know I'd won this round again, and I held back a grin. "You may go." The sooner she left, the sooner I could unwrap the item and discover if it truly worked the way rumors described.

Milcah moved to the door, but she wasn't ready to accept defeat quite yet. With her hand on the doorknob, she spoke. "May I ask whom exactly you hope the mirror will show you, when everyone you love is here in the castle?"

I arched a brow in her direction, finally deigning to look at her. "Oh?" I replied in a cool tone. "Is my mother in the castle? I was not aware."

She flushed for the second time in as many minutes and let herself out without another word, letting the vault door slam shut behind her.

Alone now, I allowed a small smile.

Turning back to the little parcel, I peeled away the wax paper, revealing the object inside.

It was a small hand-mirror.

Slightly larger than my fist, it had a thick frame of dark silver, etched with circular designs all around the mirror and along the handle.

Would it actually show me my mother?

I had no idea.

My mouth was dry as I held it up to my face and gazed at my reflection and spoke her name: "Sariah."

I waited.

Only my pale face with dark brows, pale blue eyes, and rosy lips stared back at me.

Nothing else.

I sighed, but truthfully, I wasn't surprised. After all, I barely knew my mother. How could I love someone that I didn't even know?

No, if I were honest, it wasn't her face I was craving a glimpse of at all. The true reason I'd begun my hunt for the mirror was an entirely different person.

Nervous energy flooded my veins, making me hesitate, shifting from one foot to the other.

Would it work? Would I finally see him again?

Though I'd kept close tabs on information regarding the Khaanevaade people as they adapted to being seemingly human, I hadn't allowed myself to visit the human world myself.

If I went to see Koda, I was afraid of what he might say—of what *I* might say.

If he remembered me, he'd call me a thief and a liar. And he'd be right.

The less exposure to Jinn, the better, if the Vaade were to remain skeptical of magic like the humans. After pressing King Jubal into action, I'd convinced him to send his guard, who'd destroyed all written records of the Vaade that they could find. Now and again, rumor reached us of a zealot urging the people to see that they were descended from dragons. But the majority of the Vaade scoffed and called them lunatics. The curse held firmly in place.

Wincing at the year-old memories that still felt like they'd happened yesterday, I decided not to torment myself any longer.

I whispered his name, "Koda."

The mirror flickered. A white mist spread across the glass, quickly replaced by a quiet scene of a man sitting at a small kitchen table.

A woman swept past along the side, and I flinched.

Though he'd never technically become my husband with our vows left unfinished, it sometimes felt like he was, even more so than Shem. I *hated* the idea of another woman taking that place in his life.

I blew out a sigh of relief when I saw the woman's face. *Tehya.*

She bumped his shoulder in their familiar version of rude affection as she left the room, while he sat staring down at the little wooden table, lost in thought. As he brought a cup to his lips, I caught a glimpse of his now ordinary-looking hazel eyes. They'd grown dull.

It broke my heart seeing him like this. I could almost forget the way he'd betrayed me and forgive him. If we'd been in the same room, I might have.

Carefully, I rewrapped the mirror in the wax paper,

hiding the painful images from sight.

I slipped it into one of the pockets in my voluminous navy dress and stepped out of the vault. The guards only saw me for a split second before I traveled to the royal suite of rooms that I shared with the prince. *No,* I caught myself, *the king now.*

That would take some getting used to.

Opening the door to our collective suites, I crossed the central sitting room with unseeing eyes, passing the door that led to Shem's room and entering my own private space, locking the door behind me.

I pulled out the little mirror again, setting it on my desk beside a small, but carefully detailed map of all the known daleths in both the human world and our own.

I'd made it a priority to study their locations so I'd never be caught unaware again. And while I'd had Shem give orders to close dozens of them already, I couldn't bring myself to close all of them.

They were my last link to Koda.

After that one glimpse, I'd fully expected to satisfy my curiosity. Clenching my fists, I admitted to myself that it wasn't nearly enough.

Contemplating the much larger mirror that hung on the wall beside my wardrobe, I considered my reflection, shifting my eyes, hair, and skin until I resembled the Vaade, enough to be mistaken for Tehya's sister or cousin.

It could work.

Touching the little hand-mirror again, I thought of

Koda's despondent expression and how seeing him had brought up a hundred more questions than it'd answered.

I might have to make a visit.

THE END.

COMING SOON...

Want an exclusive bonus scene from Jezebel and Koda? Check out the omnibus hardcover, THE QUEEN'S RISE, which contains all three stories plus bonus content—launching on Kickstarter here:

https://www.kickstarter.com/projects/bethanyatazadeh/the-queens-rise-series-deluxe-content

BETHANY ATAZADEH

THE QUEEN'S RISE

SHE WAS INNOCENT... UNTIL BETRAYED

SIGN UP FOR MY AUTHOR NEWSLETTER

Want more from this fantasy world? You can get a free short story with a sneak peek at Jezebel much later in her rule by signing up for my monthly newsletter, as well as exclusive bonus content, helpful tools for fellow writers, behind the scenes updates, sales alerts, and more!

WWW.BETHANYATAZADEH.COM/CONTACT

THANK YOU FOR SUPPORTING ME AND MY STORIES!

I hope you enjoyed this epic finale of Jezebel's story!

Before you close the book and move on to your next read, please consider **leaving a review on Goodreads or Amazon**!

This five minute task is EXTREMELY helpful for a book's success, so huuuuuge thank you in advance if you have time and feel comfortable doing so!

Either way, I sincerely hope you enjoyed Jezebel's story and can't wait to hear what you think!

<3 Bethany

READ MORE IN THIS
MAGICAL WORLD OF JINN

THE STOLEN KINGDOM

How can she protect her kingdom, if she can't protect herself?

Arie never expects to manifest a Jinni's Gift. When she begins to hear the thoughts of those around her, she hides it to the best of her ability. But to her dismay, the forbidden Gift is growing out of control.

When a neighboring king tries to force her hand in marriage and steal her kingdom, discovery becomes imminent. Just one slip could cost her throne. And her life.

A lamp, a heist, and a Jinni hunter's crew of thieves are her only hope for removing this Gift - and she must remove it before she's exposed. Or die trying.

THE STOLEN KINGDOM is a loose Aladdin retelling and the first book in a complete, four book series of fairytale retellings. Set in a world that humans share with Mermaids, Dragons, and the elusive Jinni, this isn't the fairytale you remember…

books2read.com/thestolenkingdom

ALSO BY
BETHANY ATAZADEH

THE STOLEN KINGDOM SERIES :

THE STOLEN KINGDOM

THE JINNI KEY

THE CURSED HUNTER

THE ENCHANTED CROWN

THE COLLECTOR'S EDITION

THE QUEEN'S RISE SERIES :

THE SECRET GIFT

THE SECRET SHADOW

THE SECRET CURSE

THE NUMBER SERIES :

EVALENE'S NUMBER

PEARL'S NUMBER

MARKETING FOR AUTHORS SERIES :

HOW YOUR BOOK SELLS ITSELF

GROW YOUR AUTHOR PLATFORM

BOOK SALES THAT MULTIPLY

SECRETS TO SELLING BOOKS ON SOCIAL MEDIA

PLAN A PROFITABLE BOOK LAUNCH

GLOSSARY

Council – each royal family members has a group of counselors that form a council, which they use for different political purposes.

Jezebel (JEZ-zuh-bell) – young Jinni shape-shifter

Jinn/Jinni (Gin/GIN-nee) – Jinn is the name of the country and the people of Jinn as a whole (i.e. *the Jinn, the land of Jinn*); Jinni is the singular, used to refer to an individual Jinni and also as a possessive (i.e. *a Jinni, a Jinni's Gift*)

Jinni Guard (GIN-nee Guard) – the dangerous and uniquely talented Jinn who guard the royal family

King Jubal (JOO-bull) – king of Jinn

Khaanevaade (Hah-nah-vah-DAY) – a people group even older than the Jinn, the supposed ancestors of dragons, often called Vaade for short

Lacklore – a beast in Jinn with the head of an ox and the body of a bear

THE SECRET CURSE

Prince Shem (Sheh-mm) – prince of Jinn

Queen Samaria (Saw-MARE-ree-uh) – queen of Jinn

Resh – capital city of Jinn

Severance – when a Jinni's Gift is severed from its owner

Traveling – a common Gift that allows Jinn to instantly cross an enormous distance in the span of a heartbeat

Three Unbreakable Laws of Jinn:

1) Never use a Gift to deceive
2) Never use a Gift to steal
3) Never use a Gift to harm another

ACKNOWLEDGMENTS

Another series is complete! What am I going to do now?

Originally Jezebel's story was just going to be a little novella. Somehow it transformed into three full novels. So my first shout out goes to the beta readers and reviewers of that initial story who said, "I think Jezebel has a lot more story to tell!" This series happened because of you.

A huge thank you to my critique partners Brittany Wang and Jessi Elliott—there's nobody I trust more with my stories and I'm so thankful for both of you. Thanks for being cool with me sending unexpected, sometimes nonsensical polos full of complex plot holes.

To my incredible beta readers: Alexia, Courtney Denelsbeck, Katherine Schober, Lesley Barklay, Lia Anderson, Makenna, and Rachel Sikorski. Your feedback was my absolute favorite! This particular beta reader group felt like being part of a bookclub because of all your sweet reactions, but you also took this story to the next level in a huge way with your thoughts and suggestions. Thank you!

To Bailee for offering her editing services, it was really cool to work with you and get your thoughts on the story.

Huge thanks to my amazing ARC reader team for being willing to read and review this story, it means so much to me!

And to my readers (yes, talking to you! ;) just wanted to say thanks for supporting this story. You're the best.

<3 Bethany

Bethany Atazadeh is best known for her young adult fantasy novels, The Stolen Kingdom series, which won the Best YA Author 2020 Minnesota Author Project award. She is a mama to a cute little boy and a corgi pup, and is obsessed with stories and chocolate.

Using her degree in English with a creative writing emphasis, Bethany enjoys helping other writers through her YouTube aka "AuthorTube" writing channel and Patreon page.

If you want to know more about when Bethany's next book will come out, visit her website below where you can sign up to receive monthly emails with exciting news, updates, and book releases.

CONNECT WITH BETHANY:
Website: **www.bethanyatazadeh.com**
Instagram: **@authorbethanyatazadeh**
YouTube: **www.youtube.com/bethanyatazadeh**
Patreon: **www.patreon.com/bethanyatazadeh**

www.ingramcontent.com/pod-product-compliance
Lightning Source LLC
LaVergne TN
LVHW041742060526
838201LV00046B/880